Taking Lottie Home

The Kidnapping of Aaron Greene

The Runaway

Shadow Song

To Whom the Angel Spoke

To Dance with the White Dog

Dark Thirty

After Eli

The Year the Lights Came On

Taking Lottie Home

A NOVEL

TERRY KAY

WILLIAM MORROW

An Imprint of HarperCollins*Publishers*

TAKING LOTTIE HOME. Copyright © 2000 by Terry Kay.
All rights reserved. Printed in the United States of America.
No part of this book may be used or reproduced in any
manner whatsoever without written permission except
in the case of brief quotations embodied in critical articles and reviews.
For information address HarperCollins Publishers Inc.,
10 East 53rd Street, New York, NY 10022.

HarperCollins books may be purchased for educational, business,
or sales promotional use. For information please write:
Special Markets Department, HarperCollins Publishers Inc.,
10 East 53rd Street, New York, NY 10022.

FIRST EDITION

Designed by Jo Anne Metsch

Printed on acid-free paper

Library of Congress Cataloging-in-Publication Data has been applied for.

ISBN 0-688-17646-1

00   01   02   03   04   RRD   10   9   8   7   6   5   4   3   2   1

For Tommie,
who has endured the moods that make the words

This advice to young writers: never trash, burn, or delete the words you have written. There could be a time when you will discover in them the story you always intended, but could not quite understand in the early writing.

Such was my experience in the writing of *Taking Lottie Home*.

In the mid-70s, I began a story that was inspired by living in the same hometown as the great baseball player Ty Cobb. I wanted it to be the story of a small town's reaction to celebrity. Four or five book-length versions later (so long ago, I don't remember details), I was advised by the publisher to stop punishing myself (and them), and to start a new book. I did. But I did not destroy what I had written.

Early in 1999, while struggling with a story that I passionately wanted to write, but found irritating and elusive, I browsed through my files one day and found the old book. (It was titled *The Memorial.*) Something compelled me to read it again. A few pages in, I found Lottie, a minor character. I knew immediately that I had failed her in that early writing. And in the mystic way that characters have of revealing themselves, she forgave my blindness and began to tell me who she was.

Still, I do not believe writers can crank a handle and have characters pop up like grinning faces from a jack-in-the-box. They exist ethereally in those fragments of experience that reside with everyone. I will not use names here, but Lottie, for me, was the newborn voice of a young girl I knew as a child. I heard her saying, *"I might have been, I might have been . . ."*

I hope the reader understands her journey.

Taking Lottie Home

O n e

———

I CANNOT SAY, as fact, this is what happened, or how it happened, yet it is, I believe, fairly close to the truth — truth being what it is, a piecemeal kind of thing best told with enough stretch in it to fit more than one certainty.

Some of it was revealed straight to me in the straight kind of way that you trust without the slightest thought of doubt. Some of it was hearsay from so many voices in so many tellings, it was like an echo that is far off and mystic. Some of it was taken from a journal written in the thin cursive strokes of a young woman who was in love, and from letters tied in a stack by a green ribbon, then tucked away in the corner of a trunk to become dry and brittle over dry and brittle years. Some of it — most of it, to be honest — is nothing more than my imagination playing fancy with could-have-beens.

I know this: it was important to put it all together, to discover the things — good and hurtful — that have had me on a search for much of my life, like an old and addled prospector following a bogus map in his hunt for gold, gold so pure that the touch of a pickax would cause it to seep from the earth like honey.

Some things sound so good it is impossible not believing in them.

Gold flowing like honey.

Home.

I HAVE CHOSEN to begin in 1904 with the dream-ending sorrow of two men who are as embedded in me as bone marrow, one through his blood, one by his presence. It is the most likely place I know to begin. In the odd way that life, or circumstance, bumps people around, sends them colliding into one another, they would find themselves in the company of a girl-woman named Lottie, and she would change them forever.

As she would change everyone who knew her.

———

TWO PLAYERS WOULD be cut from the team and Foster Lanier would be one of them.

Foster knew it.

He had known it for three weeks, in the same way animals could sense terror, and now it was the night before the cuts and he had taken a bottle of Kentucky bourbon and walked alone to the bridge that crossed the Savannah River, separating South Carolina and Georgia like a steel hyphen.

The night was black and hard, thick with unmoving heat and the urine smell of the river sliding through the back streets of Augusta. Foster did not like the river and the sour odor and the heat and the plague of bugs crawling at his face and neck to drink from the perspiration that oozed from him. He did not like Augusta. He could not breathe clean, sweet Kentucky air in Augusta. Augusta air lodged in his throat, leaving him choking and weak. But he would soon be on a train for Kentucky—tomorrow night or the day after—and there

would be a pickup game with a pickup team and he would hear
people in the stands muttering his name with surprise, telling their
children, "There's Foster Lanier. You never saw nobody as good as
Foster Lanier." The thought pleased him. He smiled and drank a
full swallow from the bottle. It was good bourbon. Kentucky on the
label and Kentucky in the taste. It was to be his last night in professional baseball. He deserved good bourbon.

He walked below the pilings of the bridge to the river shore, to a
weeping willow with dying limbs. He sat in the grass and stared
across the river at the row of tiny homes with eyedots of kerosene
lamps glowing in windows. River shanty homes. He was twenty-nine
years old. He had collapsed during wind sprints on the first day of
workouts. His legs ached. There was a sore on the shin of his right
leg where the blade of a spike had sliced to the bone. The sore had
not healed in two years. It stayed scabbed and bled on touch and
the skin around it had begun to crinkle like cigarette wrapping paper.
The sore leg had made him sick. He had lost weight and he could
hear sloshing sounds in his abdomen when he tried to run. There
were mornings when he struggled to pull himself from his bed.

He was twenty-nine years old and he had played professional baseball for a dozen years. Not with the big teams. Not with the New
Yorkers or for Boston or Detroit. But he had played against the best—
by God, the best—from Kentucky to Louisiana, including one season in New Jersey. He had seen the big leaguers come and go, had
played with them and against them, and, by God, he had been as
good as any of them on the best of his days.

The best of his days were over, he thought. Tomorrow he would
be cut. Cut from a team of boys who had played lately on sandfields
and in pastures. God-o-mighty. Boys who were not long weaned from
dragging at their mother's milk-swollen tits while he was turning
double plays for a team in Lexington, like a New York stage dancer
fancy-footing a tap dance that made hearts race with gladness.

He scrubbed the perspiration from his face with the forearm of his shirt, swallowed again from the bourbon, and the fire of the alcohol burned his throat and he sucked for air—open-mouthed, slow, deep, wheezing. The bourbon seeped into his brain and into the bloodless ash coloring of his face. He sat quietly, knees up, his wrists locked over his kneecaps, holding the bottle in the fingers of both hands, gazing at the sliding river, thinking of the games he had memorized.

No, not games. Moments of games. Fragments of rude, physical awakenings when the body moved faster than the mind, and the act, the feat—impossible to other men—was done.

Those moments called often to him, called to him from clear bell-voices of other years, and when he heard them he could feel an energy invade him like a parade of costumed marching bands.

He shuddered and ducked his head. His fingers played nervously along the neck of the bottle and he listened as the bell-voices of other years came out of the wind, came out of the waters of the Savannah, came out of the crying of cicadas, came out of the buzzing of flies and mosquitoes.

Their voices were mighty, telling stories that were legendary.

The great grand slam in Mobile on a September day blackened by rain-heavy clouds, and the curious timing of it, how the rain began to fall at the precise moment the ball he hit was falling beyond the desperate reach of a racing left fielder. The rain fell over the cheers of the great grand slam as he waved his god-wave to those who leaned out from the stands, leaned for him and for the moment.

The triple play in Dayton—the hated Daytons—when he leapt at the rifle-clap of the bat and the ball buried into the fat padding of his glove and he touched the dashing runner from first and then outraced the runner trying to get back to second, and the play was finished before the echo of the rifle-clap had ended.

Foster snuggled the bottle close to his chin and smiled pleasantly at the mind pictures, at the tuba beat and the singing trumpets of the gaudy, strutting parade of memory. The mind pictures were his eulogy to baseball, and his soul yearned—cried, shivered—for their return.

The river flowed in its jelly thickness before him, carrying bobbing wads of garbage which had been thrown in darkness from the tiny houses with kerosene eyedots lining the riverbank. He watched the river numbly, breathing in its acid gases. He tipped the bottle to his lips, swallowed. His throat began to deaden. He closed his eyes and was very still.

Arnold Toeman had announced that two men would be cut from the team tomorrow, and he knew that he would be one of them. He was twenty-nine years old, an ancient among boys, an ailing second baseman who could no longer bend and twist and run on a decaying right leg. He could no longer play the game, and he would be cut away from it, like a useless limb on a tree. It was the meanness of the game, but the game, in 1904, was mean. Only the quick and the strong survived. Foster was neither.

He swallowed again from the bourbon, a spilling swallow, and he said aloud, but not loudly, "They gone cut me." He nodded in agreement with himself. "Wonder who else they gone cut?" he said. His mind searched the faces of his teammates, like an inspection. He laughed warmly, shaking the bourbon in the bottle. "They all wondering the same thing," he said to the river. "Yeah. They all wondering."

He knew there would be a terrible pain when Arnold Toeman cut him from the team. He had heard older men—players long disappeared—speak of it, and none of them had ever been able to take the pain without crying out. "By God," they had said. "It comes down on you like a ax. Cuts the guts right out, before you know you been hit. You ever seen a cow killing, you seen what it's like."

And that is how it would happen, Foster thought. It would happen following the game with the Savannah Seagulls. Arnold Toeman would call out two names — Foster's and one other — and tell them to leave his team. Arnold Toeman would tell the two, "You're finished."

———

FOSTER AWOKE LATE from his drunk-sleep, breathing hard, aching, and he missed breakfast and the early-morning workout with the team. When he arrived in uniform for the afternoon game at Hornet Field, Arnold Toeman stared at him — in surprise, thought Foster — but said nothing, and Foster went to a bench in the corner of the open wood shelter occupied by the Hornets. He sat leaning against the back of the shelter and watched his teammates perform the rote exercises of small pregame dramas which were staged as sacrificial offerings to Arnold Toeman.

They were young. God-o-mighty, they were young, Foster thought. He knew how they had arrived — knew it by his own life: each with a letter in his hand, wrinkled from too much handling, recommending his skills to the dark-faced Arnold Toeman, who wore black suits and a black hat and managed the Hornets with an evil voice that spoke only imperatives. None of the boys had ever known such a man as Arnold Toeman. He stood over them like a thundercloud, an ugly, boiling person, watching them from the slits of small, dark eyes. He had one obsession as a manager: "Do it again." And again. And again. And again. His voice lashed leather whelps across boys who had never been away from their homes. His voice berated. His voice dehumanized. In the three weeks of spring tryouts, 1904, Arnold Toeman had not uttered a kind world to anyone. Ten boys had left the Hornets' camp voluntarily, at night, when Arnold Toeman slept. If he slept.

Foster knew all these things. And he knew the strong young men who had stayed were tense and frightened and confused and home-sick. He knew by their manners, by the impeccable courtesies of their voice, and by their posturing. They were abiding by promises they had made to their parents. Their parents had said, "Be nice and that's how you'll be treated, son."

Their advice was an acceptable code of conduct for civilized people, but it did not apply to Arnold Toeman's dominion.

At night, in the solitude of their beds, boys who believed their wrinkled letters were passports to dreams pulled covers over their heads and balled into a fetal knot of despair, praying prayers to God that were meant not for God but for the secure presence of their parents.

Foster knew what the strong young men felt, and how they would change, yet he also knew they were mesmerized by childish fantasies of Detroit or Boston or New York or one of the other far-off cities where the big leaguers played. Lord God-o-mighty. Jesus Christ, savior of man. They believed, all right. It was there for the taking, and they could do it. Their letters of recommendation were proof. Foster pitied the boys. One may make it, he reasoned as he watched his teammates. One. Maybe two. Maybe Milo Wade. There was something unique about Robert Milo Wade. He had skill. And he had anger. He would not easily be executed by the likes of Arnold Toeman.

Foster shifted on the bench, moved his back against the plank wall, crossed his left leg over his right knee to press down on the pain that burned in his shinbone. Milo Wade may make it, he thought. Maybe Nat Skinner. Foster liked Nat. He had arrived in Augusta from a small community in middle Georgia with the odd name of Fryingpan. Nat was a left-handed pitcher who threw with remarkable precision and speed, and he had become a favorite of his new teammates and the press. A newspaper reporter had written a story about Nat. The headline read: FROM FRYINGPAN INTO THE FIRE: WILL HE MAKE IT? It was a story about the young hopefuls of Arnold Toeman's 1904 team of strangers.

Maybe Milo Wade and Nat Skinner, Foster decided. Maybe they'd make it. No one else. God, he thought, somebody ought to tell them. They should be allowed to return to their homes with dignity. At home they could play in the town leagues and become heroes. "Why, he could've been playing with the big leaguers if he'd wanted to," the townspeople would declare. In the town leagues, they would be remembered. At Augusta, they would only be hurt, and Foster knew about hurt. It was in his leg, bleeding against his uniform. It was in his heart, and in his oldness at age twenty-nine.

He wanted to bellow out at them, wanted to say, "Look at me."

He sat in silence, knowing they would not have heard him. They were boys from sandfields and pastures, boys with wrinkled letters in their pockets.

———

THE GAME BEGAN. It moved before Foster's hurting eyes with the fury of a loner's cry for praise, with anguish and with pleading. It was his last game in professional baseball and Foster had not walked onto the field; had not wanted to. He did not care to play in his last game in professional baseball. He wanted to sit and watch and to hold for all time that memory of seeing himself as he might have played the game, but did not. His last game would be a game of luxury.

The time was very near. Two men would be cut from the team and he would be one of them, and then he would be free.

Tomorrow, he thought, the team would be different. The team would feel safe, reprieved.

Tomorrow, the team would gather and speak of the two missing faces and join in an unknowing ovation to survival. Foster had heard that ovation often, knew it by memory:

"*I thought I'd make it.*"

"*Didn't have no doubts, myself.*"

"*Can't have doubts and make it.*"

"*Shoot, we got us a team now.*"

"*Too bad they had to get the boot.*"

"*Way it is.*"

Foster could hear the words.

THE GAME PIVOTED from inning to inning, scoreless, like an artless fencing match between amateurs. To Foster, it was a listless game, clumsy and unbalanced, tactics spoiled by blunders. He listened to the harsh song of boy voices and thought of Kentucky and the sweet, clean air that would let him breathe again.

Still, he could not remove himself from the game that surrounded him with its panic for survival, and he sat in the asylum of the home team shelter and watched boys hiding their failures like scolded innocents, whining profanities, staring at their offending hands and feet as though the hand or the foot had violated a trust with the rest of their body. It was an exorcism Foster knew well. Damned leg, he thought. Damned leg that won't let me run. Won't run a lick, he thought. He wanted to show his leg to the boys who sat with him. Somebody ought to tell them. Somebody.

It was late in the game—the top of the eighth inning—and the Seagulls were at bat. Jordan Beasley, who played third base for the Hornets, misplayed a surprise bunt and Savannah had a player on first base. Nat Skinner struck out the next batsman, but Noble Winn, who was playing second base in Foster's place, fumbled a slow roller, too late for a play at second, and then he threw the ball away at first. Two Seagulls were on base, at second and third, and the cries for Nat Skinner grew to a wail.

"C'mon, Nat, you can do it!"

"Throw it by him, Nat! C'mon, boy!"

Nat responded by striking out the next batsman on three pitches. There were two outs and two runners still on base.

"One more, Nat!"

"You got 'em, Nat!"

The batter at the plate was tall and powerfully muscled and he had a cocky, daring smirk on his face. Nat wiped his fingers across the front of his jersey, took the ball from his glove, rolled it in his hand, then began his pump-arm windup. His body pivoted over his left foot and his arm snapped in a quick half-circle at his shoulder. The batter lashed at the pitch and a cracking sound, like a flesh slap, spit from his bat. The ball soared toward center field, then began sinking. Foster sat forward on the bench. He saw Ben Phelps moving, sprinting. He saw Ben diving, his left arm extended in front of him, his body off the ground and falling. And, suddenly, there was a shrill cry from the stands and a man yelled, "Great Goda'mighty!" — yelled it like a proclamation — and the Hornets' players spilled out of their shelter and rushed toward Ben, shouting.

"You got it, Ben! You got it!"

"Great God, Ben, I never saw nothing like that."

"You done it, Ben! You done it!"

And they were around Ben Phelps, embracing him, pounding him, slapping at him, celebrating him with their awe.

Foster sat and watched. He could feel a bloodrush in his chest. He had known such moments. The great grand slam in Mobile, the triple play in Dayton. God-o-mighty, they had loved him for those feats. They had lifted him over their heads like a trophy and marched him around the field. On the day of the triple play, a newspaper artist had drawn a likeness of him pointing three fingers in the air. And that was the worth of all game, the worth of everything.

Foster turned his face and looked at Arnold Toeman standing in the shade of the shelter in his dusty black suit, his arms crossed. Arnold Toeman's mouth was curled in a half-smile, but he was not smiling. He was laughing, laughing at something only he understood.

A chill seized Foster. He stood at the bench. The team was moving toward him, herding Ben from the field, and Ben was yelping excitedly, touching the hands that reached for him. My God, thought Foster. Ben. It was Ben who would be cut with him. Foster knew it. Knew it with certainty. And it did not matter that Ben Phelps had made an impossible play and was being celebrated. Arnold Toeman had decided: Ben Phelps would be cut from the team.

Foster knew he was right. He had watched too many executions to be wrong. He turned again to Arnold Toeman, and Arnold Toeman was staring at him with warning, with eyes that dared him. Foster sat slowly and laced his fingers over his legs. Son of a bitch, he thought. Ben. Ben would be the second cut. Should have realized it, he reasoned. Ben, who could run, but could not hit. And he had tried. By God, he had tried. But he could not overcome the sickening fear of being struck by the ball. At first, it had been comical, yet there was something about Ben's failure that was to be pitied, and his teammates had worked patiently with him, urging him. Still Ben could not hit. Still he fell away from the plate.

Ben would be cut, Foster thought again, and it would hurt. It would hurt because Ben and Milo Wade were from the same north Georgia hometown and had played baseball together for years. Yet Ben did not have the skills or the anger of Milo Wade. Ben had a child's awe, and even his grace in the outfield — the grace of an untamed, running animal — could not save him.

Ben entered the shelter quivering with gladness. He sat beside Foster and Foster mumbled, "Good play, Ben. Good play."

Ben answered with a slap to Foster's shoulder. "Didn't think I'd get to it, but it was there. Didn't even feel it hit." Ben was smiling and licking his dry lips with his tongue. He leaned toward Foster. "Maybe that done it for me, Foster," he confided. "I was telling Milo and Nat I didn't think I'd make it. Maybe that done it for me."

Foster nodded. He stared across the playing field and watched the Seagulls complete their warmups. He knew that Ben Phelps's heroics had inspired his teammates. There was a blood scent of victory in the restless chattering that swirled around him. To Foster, it was the music of operas, and it did not matter that the first two batters lifted weak fly balls to the infield. The music was strong, then grew louder when Jordan Beasley doubled to right field and Milo Wade approached home plate.

Milo Wade was only eighteen years old, yet he played baseball with the command of a man who demanded attention. In only three weeks, he had become the most feared and respected player on the Hornets' team. In Milo Wade, there was always a possibility, always the simmering hiss of an explosion.

"C'mon, Milo! Get him in!"

"Get a hit, Milo! Get a hit!"

"You can do it, Milo! You can do it!"

Foster listened to the eager young voices, still shrill from childhood. He saw Milo step to the plate. Milo was tall and thin and muscled like a swimmer. His face was intense, his eyes clear and hard, the color of blue under ice. He had a habit of curling his lower lip between the bite of his teeth. He stood at the plate, clawing the ground with his cleated shoes. He lifted the bat and pushed it before him, his hands spread apart on the handle. Foster had never seen anyone stand so far up in the batter's box, and he had asked Milo why he did it. "That's for curves," Milo had explained. "They throw me curves, I get a lick at it before it breaks. It's nothing but a fastball to me." Foster had tried it in batting practice, but he could not swing the bat fast enough, and he knew Milo Wade had a rare talent.

"C'mon, Milo, bust it!"

"You got 'im, Milo! You got 'im!"

Milo squeezed his hands on the bat. He looked at the infielders, playing him to hit the ball to right field as they had been taught to play against a left-handed hitter. There was a gap between third base and the third baseman. Milo moved his hands on the bat handle, making a calculation with his fingers.

The pitch was high and outside and Milo slapped it easily, almost casually, guiding the ball two feet inside third base. Jordan Beasley scored and Milo was standing on second base when the left fielder recovered the ball.

"Way to go, Milo!"

"We got it now! We got it now!"

Ben had been in the on-deck circle, still giddy from his catch and wildly waving Milo to second. Now he was walking toward the plate, swinging his bat.

Arnold Toeman spoke: "Phelps." His voice was deep, blunt. Ben turned. Arnold Toeman was standing beside the shelter, his arms crossed. His dark hat shadowed his dark face.

"Yes sir?" replied Ben.

"Come on in," commanded Arnold Toeman. He gazed down the bench at Foster. He smiled slightly. "Lanier," he said, "get a bat."

Foster knew that Arnold Toeman had ended Ben's career, that in his grandest moment, a moment that had lifted Ben higher than wings could carry him, he had also been executed. He moved slowly off the bench. And this, too, was his execution, he thought. But there was nothing grand about the moment for Foster. He walked to Ben, took Ben's bat from him. "You guess it's got a hit in it, Ben?" he said gently.

Ben's face trembled. He looked at Foster with a bewildered gaze, asking what Foster already understood.

"It's all right, Ben," Foster told him. "It's not what it's made out to be, nohow."

Ben turned to stare at his teammates, now silent in the shelter. They, too, understood. He walked slowly toward them, then stopped and looked across the field at Milo Wade. Milo dropped his head and kicked at the second base bag.

"Phelps, get off the field," snapped Arnold Toeman.

Foster moved to the plate. Ben and me, he thought. Now they know. Well, goddamn them, they ought to stand up and give us a bow, then they could hang us out on a clothesline to flap in the wind like useless rags. His mind throbbed with rage. He wanted to scream at the strong young men who would return to play another game, "Look, damn it, look. Look at Ben. Look at me."

He caught the handle of the bat in his hands, curling his fingers for the warm feeling of the wood. He looked at the pitcher for the Seagulls, who seemed small and frail. Foster wondered if the pitcher was also on trial, if the manager of the Seagulls had judged and condemned him. He rolled the bat in his hands. A taste of bitterness filled his mouth. The game he had loved with such passion had betrayed him. It had teased him, and now it was taking the last measure he had to give. He glanced back to the shelter. He could not see Ben. Then he looked automatically to Arnold Toeman and he saw Arnold Toeman's lips barely move, mouthing the word: bunt.

Foster stepped away from the batter's box. There were two outs. He could not run against a bunt. He knew it. Arnold Toeman knew it. Goddamn it, he thought, swallowing the bitterness in his mouth. His leg was on fire with pain. He reached to rub it. His hand moistened with blood, oozing through his uniform. No, he said to himself. No, goddamn it.

He eased to the plate and tried to set his right leg against the pain. Perspiration rolled from his hair, across his face. He saw the pitcher from the Seagulls balancing in his motion, and he saw the ball spinning toward him. He pushed back on his left leg as the ball exploded into the catcher's mitt behind him. He heard the umpire bellow the strike call. He shook his head. It couldn't be, he thought. No. It was inside. A ball. He heard the boy catcher for the Seagulls laugh lightly. He ran his sleeve across his face. Behind him, he heard Arnold Toeman's snarling voice: "Lanier."

The pitcher was moving again on the mound, his arm falling forward over his head. Foster saw the ball leave the pitcher's hand, saw it roll from the fingertips, saw it rising. His mind snapped suddenly clear and he felt his shoulders turning as the bat cut into the air. Then he felt the ball against the bat, solid, jolting, and he heard a chorus of screams from the Hornets' shelter. The bat was out of his hand and he was limping, dragging, running toward first base, watching the ball rise higher and higher into deep left field. A rush of exuberance chilled Foster. The pain was gone from his leg. And then he saw the left fielder for the Seagulls, a boy, blond as a palomino, running, racing the ball, and he heard the players for the Seagulls whipping their teammate into a final sprint with their boyish cries. Foster slowed near first base. He saw the boy left fielder dive high against the plank fence, saw him juggle the ball as he fell, and then saw him pull it to his chest.

Foster stopped at first base. He touched the bag with his right foot, almost tenderly. He looked around the infield, toward second base. Once, he had played second base with the grace of a god, he thought innocently. He inhaled deeply, filling his lungs with the hot dust of a baseball field, and then he turned and walked away, past Arnold Toeman and out of the ballpark.

THE TRAIN THAT ran from Augusta to Jericho, then west to Athens and Atlanta and north into Tennessee and Kentucky and finally into Ohio, was scheduled to leave at nine thirty-five in the evening, four hours after the game between the Augusta Hornets and the Savannah Seagulls had ended.

Ben sat in the train station and waited. He was numb weary, his eyes still blurred from the crying that had spewed from him after the game. He had promised Milo that he would stay in Augusta for a few days, but he could not stay. He wanted to leave, to be home. He would tell them at home that he had discovered he did not care for professional baseball, and that he had spoken frankly with Arnold Toeman, the manager, and Arnold Toeman had advised him to follow his conscience, although he would be giving up an almost-certain opportunity.

Milo would not contradict his story. Milo would understand. They had always been friends. Milo would know how he felt. Besides, there was a chance that Milo, too, would fail and return home and he, too, would need the comfort of a secret.

Ben watched the people around him. He wondered where they were going and why, and if any of them had been at the ball game to see the remarkable catch he had made before Arnold Toeman cut him from the team.

No, he thought. None of them had seen him.

Across from him, two children sat with a mother, drawing pencil pictures on tablets. The mother wore the black clothing of a mourner, her eyes vacant.

A man wearing a rumpled suit, a bowler hat tilted over his eyes, slouched against the back of a bench, sleeping.

A man and a girl sat near him. She was young, with hair the color of soft bronze, large, wondering eyes, and the prettiness of an unfolding flower that promised a golden face. There was no youth in the man's face. Still, they sat close, touching hands, smiling, whispering to one another. The man and the girl seemed suspended in their togetherness and in their aloneness.

Ben pulled from his pocket the watch his father had given him. He snapped it open and looked at it. It was ten minutes after nine. He closed the watch and turned it in his hand, slipping his fingers over the slick, warm metal. His father had advised him not to follow Milo Wade to Augusta. It would be a hard chase, his father had said. And it could be dangerous business. Yet, his father had embraced Ben on the day of his leaving, wishing him well, whispering that he understood. In his youth, Ben's father had also been an athlete, good enough for people to still talk of his feats, and Ben knew his father would have been pleased if he had become a baseball player. Even more, he would be pleased with Ben's safe return to Jericho.

He thought of Foster Lanier, wondered if Foster would leave that night for Kentucky. He did not want to see Foster, for Foster would tell him consoling lies.

He pushed his watch back into his pocket and pulled his suitcase nearer to him. His baseball glove was tied by a cord to his suitcase. Ben touched the glove lightly. He could feel the sting of an imaginary baseball against his hand and he could hear the swish of grass beneath his feet. It had been so right, so comfortable, in the outfield of a baseball game. Ben shuddered with hurt. God, he thought, fighting tears. I tried. I tried.

A hand touched his shoulder and Ben turned. It was Milo. Beside him stood Nat Skinner.

"Ben, what're you doing here?" Milo asked gently. "You said you'd stay a couple of days."

Ben stood awkwardly. He looked at the crowd in the train station, gathering their belongings for the waiting train. "Yeah," he mumbled. "I—I thought I'd better get on back home, though. I tried to find you, to tell you."

"We checked your room. They said you'd left," replied Milo. "I figured you'd be down here. Me and Nat wanted to take you to supper."

"On us," Nat said, smiling.

"Yeah. Uh, I—got me a bite," Ben lied.

"Look, Ben, I'm sorry it happened," Milo told him. "It won't be the same, you not being out there with me."

Ben reached for his suitcase. He forced a feeble smile. "Shoot, Milo, you got some pros now. Won't be no need to cover for me like you always had to."

Milo laughed. "You hear that, Nat? Me cover for Ben? Other way around, if you ask me. Nobody in Georgia's fast as Ben in the outfield. We been playing together since we was twelve, and I guarantee you he's the fastest I ever saw."

"Me, too," said Nat. "Never saw nothing like that play you made today, Ben."

"Takes more than being fast," Ben said. "Anyhow, it don't make much difference. I had my fun trying it. Tell you the truth, I'm kind of glad it happened. I got me a pretty good job lined up back home."

"Doing what?" asked Milo with surprise.

"Clerking in the dry goods store," answered Ben. "Mr. Ledford offered me the job before I left. Him and Daddy's big friends. He told me George Hill was quitting to go to school over in Athens."

"That's a good job," Milo said. "Mr. Ledford's a good man. You better keep your eye out for me, Ben. I may be joining you in a few weeks."

Ben did not reply. He began to move into the flow of the crowd, staying close to the young girl and man. Milo and Nat followed him.

"You give my best to your folks, Ben," Milo said.

"Yeah, I will, I will," Ben stammered. "Train's about ready to leave."

Nat offered Ben his hand. "I'm glad I got to meet you, Ben Phelps, and to play some ball with you."

"Same here, Nat. Good luck." Ben's voice was weak and unsteady.

"Ben, we're friends," Milo whispered. "I reckon I just got lucky."

Ben could hear the noise of the train building steam and the light, happy voices of its passengers. He could feel Milo's hand tighten on his arm. He was crying, but he was no longer ashamed.

"We had some good times, Ben," Milo said softly. "C'mon, Ben—"

"I'm not crying because I was cut," Ben blurted. "It's—it's knowing I'm not gone be there to see you make it."

"Ben, I'm not going nowhere but Augusta."

Ben shook his head. "You wrong. You going places nobody's ever been."

The steam from the train whistled its restless warning. A rough-dressed man pushed between Ben and Milo, rushing along the train, peering into windows, calling in a loud voice, "Lottie! Lottie!"

"I'll be keeping up with you, Milo," Ben said. "I promise." He turned quickly and took the steps leading into the train. He did not look back, but he heard Milo's voice: "I'll be seeing you, Ben."

The train began its crawl away from the station.

"I don't see him," Nat said, searching the windows.

"You won't," Milo replied evenly. "He'll stay out of sight until they're out of the station."

"I feel sorry for him," Nat said.

For a moment, Milo did not speak. The piercing squeal of metal curled in the air and the train's smoke rolled ghostly over the station.

"Me, too," Milo said at last. "But he just wadn't good enough. He never was. I just couldn't tell him."

BEN SAT ALONE on a back seat in the last car of the train, across the aisle from the girl and the man he had watched in the train station. He stared at the night through a window that reflected him grotesquely, like a mirror of moving water. He ached. The train was loud and brutal. It was not delivering him home; it was removing him from all that mattered. The night flickered before him from behind the window. In the window he saw again the ball screaming off the bat and spinning crazily downward behind second base. He felt his legs moving and the lightness of his feet as he sprinted, leaning forward, already in the dive. And then, from a spectator's distance, in the astral projection of a vision realized, he saw himself in flight—off the ground, suspended—with his left arm thrust forward and his glove open like a mouth.

"Ben, you got it! You got it!"

"Goda'mighty, Ben! You got it!"

He had never been so magnificent. He knew he would die with that vision in his eyes, like an aged cataract, with the sound of voices screaming in praise: *"Ben, Ben, you got it! You got it!"*

He closed his eyes and leaned against the seat and reached instinctively inside his coat and touched his baseball cap. Everything about him had changed, and he knew it. He could feel the boy he had been passing out of him, dissipating in the steam and smoke of the train. He did not care. For one moment, quicker than a breath, he had been magnificent. Magnificent.

EVEN WITH HIS eyes closed, Ben knew when Foster Lanier stumbled past him in the aisle. Foster was drunk, had been drunk since early evening, Ben guessed. He pretended sleep. He could sense Foster leaning forward, toward him, and he was afraid that Foster would speak. The train swayed. He heard Foster mutter something and then stagger away.

"What was wrong with him?" Ben heard the girl ask the man from across the aisle.

"Drunk," the man answered. "You could smell it. Smelled like he'd slobbered some down his shirt, or something."

Ben listened, straining to hear the conversation.

"You don't drink much, do you?" the girl asked.

"Not much. Won't at all, if you don't like it."

"Just so it's not much."

"Not much. You got my word on it," the man said.

"All right," the girl said simply.

Ben could hear the man shift in his seat. His voice lowered. "Some folks say a man that drinks can't last laying up with a woman."

The girl did not reply.

"Depends on the man, I'd say," the man said confidently. "Now, me, it don't bother me none. You didn't hook up with no quitter. I'll say that much and leave it there. No need to start bragging." There was a pause and more shifting in the seat and the man added, "You see that boy sleeping over there?"

"What about him?" the girl asked.

"You think he could last with a woman?"

For a moment, the girl did not speak, and Ben believed she was looking at him. Then: "He looks nice to me."

"That boy," the man declared, "get one look at you in the flesh and he'd faint dead away. I guarantee it. He wouldn't last two minutes with you. That's the difference between a man and a boy."

"I don't know," the girl said absently.

"Damn," the man exclaimed quietly. "Damnation."

"What is it?"

"Just thinking about it makes me fidgety."

Ben wondered about the girl and the man. Why was she with him? He was older. Where were they going? Where did they meet? He heard a low sigh from the man, heard the girl whisper, "No, not here."

The man said, "I never been good at waiting."

"When will we be in Knoxville?" the girl asked.

"Tomorrow, sometime."

Ben wiggled in his seat and opened a slit in his eyes, playing his eyelashes like a shade. He could see the man trying to fondle the girl's breasts and the girl resisting him with her hands. He thought the girl saw him watching through the slits of his eyelash shades. Thought the girl looked directly at him and smiled. He closed his eyes again and rolled his head sleepily toward the window and opened his eyes and looked into the mirror of the darkened window. He could see the man and the girl behind him, and the girl was pushing away the man's pawing hands. Then he looked deeper, through the abstract, pale images of the mirror, and in the distance he saw a forest of pines with feathered tips. He wondered if Milo would miss him. No, he thought. No, Milo would not miss him. And knowing it, he began to ache.

———

BEN DID NOT know how long he slept. A few minutes perhaps. He woke to the monotonous droning of the train, steel speeding on steel, and to Foster pulling at his arm.

"C'mon, Ben, damn it, wake up," Foster said in a loud voice. "God-o-mighty, you can sleep anytime."

Foster's felt hat was pushed back on his head. His face was limp, his eyes filmed. Ben could smell the strong bourbon Foster had been drinking.

"Foster," Ben said. "What—what is it?"

"Nothing. Damn noisy train. Can't sleep a dab," Foster said. He settled into the seat beside Ben and pulled a bottle from his inside coat pocket and offered it to Ben.

"Me and you, we ought to be toasting something," Foster said. "Old Arnold Toeman, by God." He laughed easily. "All my years of ballplaying, Ben, and I never seen a son of a bitch like him."

Ben refused the bottle. He said, "I'll be getting off before long. Wouldn't help to go home having whiskey on my breath."

Foster nodded his understanding and drank from the bottle. "I was that way, first time off from home. God-o-mighty, that was a long time ago." He drank again from the bottle. "Old Arnold Toeman," he added. "Yes sir, Ben, when he dies, won't be a decent maggot in seven states crawl near him. That's worth toasting, Ben. Damned if it's not. I'll toast it for me and you both." He swallowed again from the bottle.

"You ought to go easy on that stuff, Foster," Ben advised. "Make you sick."

Foster held up the bottle and gazed at it. "Guess you right, Ben," he said philosophically. "Does that sometimes. Makes me piss a lot, I know that. Piss the same, exact color in that bottle." He shook the bottle. "What it looks like, Ben. Piss. Maybe that's what I been drinking. Piss. Maybe that old nigger pissed in a empty bottle and sold it to me, knowing I wouldn't know the difference. Well, it's not Kentucky-made, but that's all I know."

Foster's voice had become louder as he talked and Ben could see the girl and the man staring at them. He whispered, "Foster, better hold it down. They liable to throw us both off this train."

Foster laughed. "Not enough people on it to throw nobody off, but they may try to, Ben. They may. God-o-mighty, I may have to walk my way back to Kentucky. Crawl, I guess. Goddamn leg." He looked over to the man and the girl and smiled. "Offer you a little drink, friend?" he said, extending the bottle across the aisle.

"That cheap stuff or premium, neighbor?" the man said.

"Cost a penny, got a bite. Give you plenty, treat you right," Foster recited. He smiled happily.

The man laughed. "I heard that one. Drunk my share of it, too." He accepted the bottle from Foster and drank tentatively, getting the taste on his tongue. "Taste good enough to me," he judged. "Fact is, I'd call it some cuts above decent." He swallowed hard.

"Just not Kentucky," Foster said. "Your lady, there. She want some?"

"Don't know," the man said. He turned to the girl. "Want to try it?"

The girl shook her head and let her eyes float to Ben.

"Young folks," the man said, drinking again. "Guess they got time to learn what's what, but they don't know what they missing." He handed the bottle back to Foster.

"That's true," Foster agreed. "Ben, here, and me, well, we're baseball players. He's starting and I'm quitting. He's hell in the field, even if he can't hit the ground with a stick and don't drink a drop." He punched Ben gently, laughed at his own humor.

The man's face brightened. "Baseball players. Well, by shot. What's your name, friend? Maybe I saw you somewhere. I'm a traveling salesman. I been to lots of games, all over hell and half of Georgia."

"Lanier," Foster answered. "Foster Lanier."

The man's eyes widened in surprise. He whistled softly and then he said, "Well, I'll be damned." He caught the girl's arm and pulled her up to face Foster. "Honey, this man's Foster Lanier. I saw him in Louisville. By God, you was something, friend. Something else, all right."

Foster beamed. He jabbed Ben with his elbow. "Now here's a man who knows a baseball player when he sees one, Ben. Not like Arnold Toeman." He stood in the aisle and extended his hand to the man. "What's your name, friend?"

"Norman Porterfield," the man said, standing. "This is Lottie Barton." He grinned. "She's a special friend of mine."

The girl nodded to Foster.

Foster removed his hat. He said, "Glad to meet you, little lady. Glad to, indeed." Then: "Norman, I'm about to step out at the back of the car and obey the urge. Let's me and you drink to the night and leave the teetotalers to themselves."

Norman looked hesitantly at Lottie. She said, "Go on. I'm tired, anyhow."

"Be back in a few minutes, honey," Norman said.

"Take all night. I don't care," Lottie told him.

"Ben, you mind your manners," Foster said.

Norman laughed and followed Foster through the rear door of the car to the platform, and the two men stood urinating into the night and the wind, splattering the tracks below them. When they had finished, Foster handed the bottle to Norman and watched him drink.

"No need to worry none about the boy in there with your lady friend," Foster shouted over the noise of the train. "He just got cut from a team. He don't feel like nothing. He's lower than a pile of worm shit."

"Don't matter," Norman called back, handing the bottle to Foster. "She don't mean nothing. Just a stray I picked up at one of the river houses in Augusta. Started to whore a little bit, but she don't know nothing yet. I told her I'd take her with me. She's got a body that'd stop old Satan in his tracks. Woman like that can be an asset in a traveling man's business."

"God-o-mighty," exclaimed Foster. "Whoring? That young? She must be a nimpo."

Norman smiled broadly. He said, "We working on it. Yes sir, Foster, we working on it." Then he added, leaning close to Foster, "Look, if it wadn't for the fact I just met her a couple of days ago—"

Foster waved away the thought with his bottle.

"Truth is, Norman, I'm not up to it, not that she's not pretty enough to be tempting. I been a little under the weather and drinking too much of this damned stuff takes the want right out of a man."

Norman remembered what he had said to Lottie about drinking men not lasting. Maybe he should have said they can't even start, he thought. He laughed aloud and reached for Foster's bottle.

BEN TRIED NOT to look at the girl. He sat erect, as an adult would sit, and stared into the back of the seat in front of him. None of the seats around him was occupied, and Ben felt trapped. He turned his head to the window, and in its mirror finish he saw the girl. She was gazing at him with a curious expression. Ben knew she was his age, perhaps younger, yet she seemed older, as much woman as girl. She wore perfume. He was sure of it. Perfume the odor of flowers. He could smell it, thin in the warm air of the train. She was pretty, he thought. Pretty in a sad kind of way. He had never seen anyone with eyes as soft. He guessed the color of her eyes to be brown, though the light in the train was too dim for knowing.

The girl said, "Ben. That your name?"

Ben turned to her and nodded. "Ben. Ben Phelps."

"I'm Lottie," she said. "Lottie Barton. My mama thought Lottie was pretty, and she could say it easy with my sister's name. She's Lila. Lila and Lottie." She moved to the seat near the aisle.

"Glad to meet you," Ben said.

Lottie looked at him and smiled. She thrust her face into the space that separated them. "You drink whiskey?"

"Uh — no," Ben stammered. He remembered the conversation he had overheard between Norman and Lottie. "Well, I tried it one time. Made me sick. Somebody said it was bad makings."

"Norman — he's my friend — drinks too much," Lottie confided easily. "I don't know him that much, but I can tell. Says he don't, but I know he does."

Ben nodded politely. He did not know what to say.

"I think I'll let him go his way when we get to Knoxville," Lottie added. "He's a lot older than I want, anyhow. Ever notice how old people seem to dry up? Like some old leaf hanging up on a tree. Just hanging there."

Ben did not answer.

"They all right, I guess," Lottie said after a moment. "I mean, they can't help it, I guess. They got their place, but they don't never seem to know when they get old. I don't ever want to get old like that. Do you, Ben?"

"Uh, I guess it happens," Ben said. "Not much a person can do about it."

Lottie smiled at him patiently. "That's right," she agreed. "A person can't. You're a smart person, Ben Phelps. It's easy to tell that."

Sitting close, she smelled of sweet strong perfume. Ben squirmed in his seat and glanced out the window.

"I never been on a train before," Lottie said quietly. "It's pretty out there. Nothing but nighttime going by, like it's water that we swimming in. You ever wonder who lives out there in all that night-time, Ben Phelps?"

Ben answered without looking at her: "Just people, I guess."

"What kind of people, you think?"

"Farmers, I guess. About all there is around here. Farmers."

"My granddaddy's a farmer," Lottie said. "I'm glad I never lived on a farm. All that work to do."

"It must be hard," Ben mumbled.

"They don't never do nothing but work. All day. Work. I never heard nobody in my granddaddy's whole family ever laugh out loud. They all look like they just waiting around to die, or something."

"Uh-huh," Ben said.

"You really a baseball player, Ben Phelps?"

The question made Ben ache again. "I play some," he answered. "Not good enough for the professionals, like Foster was, but I play some."

"You like it?"

Ben thought about the question. He did not want to like baseball. The game had betrayed him, hurt him. He did not want to need the game, but he knew the game was in him like a terminal disease that could not be seen, only felt.

"It's all right," Ben said softly.

Lottie stretched in her seat and looked back toward the closed train door. She could see the outline of Foster and Norman, huddled close on the platform. They were drinking and laughing. She turned back to Ben. "What did you say?"

"I said baseball was all right," Ben told her.

"Oh."

"It's nothing but a game, but it's all right."

"I never saw a baseball game," Lottie said. "My daddy used to go see them, I guess. He never said much about where he went to."

"Sometimes you get tired of it," Ben said.

"Sometimes you get tired of everything, Ben. That don't mean it's all bad. That's what my mama keeps telling me." She looked thoughtfully past Ben to the sheen coating of the window. "I guess she was talking about my daddy. He's not much of a man, to be honest about it."

Ben did not know how to reply to her. She was not complaining. Was not angry. She was merely talking, as casually as she would talk about a dress. She was a woman, not a girl, Ben thought. A woman would know such things as the worth of a man.

"Where you getting off, Ben Phelps?"

"Jericho," Ben said. "Not much longer to go, I'd guess."

"Jericho? I never heard of it. Sounds like it's from the Bible."

"They say it is," Ben said. "It's not too big."

"Must be little," Lottie said. "I never heard of it. Must be a train stop and not much more."

"Just about that," Ben admitted. "A little bit bigger. Not much."

"I said I was going my own way in Knoxville, but I probably won't," Lottie said with a sigh. "I guess I'll stay with Norman a little while. I never been nowhere and he's been all over."

"Why'd your folks let you go off like that?" asked Ben.

Lottie shrugged slightly. She lifted her hand to touch her face. "I just left, way my sister did. One day, Sister just wasn't there. Her name's Lila, like I told you, but I always just call her Sister. Didn't nobody hear from her for two years. Then she come home one day and Mama said, 'Where you been?' and Sister said, 'Out.' And that was the end of it. Sister's not left for nowhere since then. Just sits on the back porch in a rocking chair and looks at that old river. All day. All day rocking and looking at that old river, like she's on a boat and it's taking her somewhere she's never been to. Don't have good sense, I guess."

Ben started to speak, but did not. He watched Lottie, as though expecting a fuller explanation. He could not comprehend anyone leaving home so casually, strolling away without guilt or fear. But there was no guilt or fear in Lottie's eyes. She seemed aware only of the space immediately around her, and that space seemed innocent and pleasant.

"I kind of think my daddy found out I was leaving," she said after a moment. "When we was pulling out of the train station, I thought I heard him calling me."

Ben remembered suddenly the man at the station, running beside the train, looking into windows. He was shouting, "Lottie, Lottie, Lottie . . ."

"But maybe it wadn't him," Lottie added. "Maybe I was just hoping it was." She paused, gazed out the window, and then she said in a small voice, "It's funny what a person wants sometimes."

Ben nodded. He wondered if he should tell her about the man calling for her, decided against it.

Lottie peered toward the train door. "Wonder what's keeping them," she said. She looked back at Ben and smiled. "Getting drunk, I'd bet. Me and you, we'll wind up taking care of both them before morning."

"Not me," Ben said. "I'll be getting off before long."

"They'll be drunk soon."

"Maybe," Ben said.

Lottie leaned against the headrest of the seat and closed her eyes. Ben wondered if she was thinking of her father, or her sister. Or if in the clouds of memory she was listening again to the close-whispered promises of Norman Porterfield. Promises of seeing places she had never seen, places too grand to imagine. Norman Porterfield was a salesman, with a salesman's quick step and a salesman's catchy song, and he had a salesman's way of building castles out of air. And Ben believed that Lottie wanted to live in castles, even those made of air.

The train roared across a trestle bridging a river, and the echo from the river flew up like a scream.

IT WAS AFTER one when the train pulled to a stop in Jericho. Ben slipped quietly from his seat and looked at the sleeping Norman Porterfield and Lottie Barton, her head nestled against his chest. He wondered if she would leave Norman in Knoxville and if, someday, she would reappear at her parents' home and sit with her sister to watch the river.

He took his suitcase and moved down the aisle. Foster Lanier was sprawled across two seats, his head tilted awkwardly in his drunk-sleep. Ben paused and looked at Foster with pity. Foster was a sick, broken man. He had been a god and now he was a mortal with a mortal's deathmask clouding his face. Ben turned and hurried down the quiet aisle. He stepped from the train. A conductor asked, "This your get-off place?" Ben replied, "Yes sir. This is home." And the conductor said, "Wish I was getting home."

Ben walked away hurriedly, holding his suitcase tight in his hand. In ten minutes, he was at his home. He tried the door, but it was locked. He rapped lightly on the door. Inside, he heard the bark of his dog, Paws, and a moment later he saw light streaming out of the cracks of the doorjamb and he heard his father's voice: "Who's there?"

"It's me," Ben answered.

His father opened the door and stood looking curiously at Ben.

"Hello, Father," Ben said.

"Why, son, what're you doing here?" his father asked.

"I come home. I quit the game," Ben said.

Elton Phelps stepped forward and embraced his son clumsily. He said, "Well, I'm glad you did. Come on. Go see your mother. She's been worried about you."

THE VISIT WITH his parents was short. Ben explained that he had decided to give up baseball and return to take the job that Arthur Ledford had offered. "I talked it over with the manager," Ben lied, "and he said he thought I could make it, but if I wanted to take a good job, he understood it. So, I just got on the train tonight, before Milo or some of the others could change my mind."

"How's Milo doing?" asked his father.

"Doing good," Ben answered. "He'll make it all the way. Milo's the best they've got in that league. I heard the manager tell somebody that Milo might make it all the way up to Boston in a year or so."

"Well, I'm glad for him," Ben's father said. "Maybe that's what he ought to do, but I'm glad you're home. This is where you belong, Ben."

When Ben left his parents, he went into his room and unpacked his suitcase. He then took the steps leading to the attic and went into the room that had been his private world, the repository of his grandest moments since childhood. He sat in a chair and looked around the attic at the artifacts of years of play—skates and kites and wood guns and wood swords—and he could hear Milo Wade laughing. Milo belonged to the attic, also. He wondered if Milo had lain awake in the room they had shared in Augusta, thinking about him. And he wondered if someone else—Nat Skinner, perhaps—would move into the room with Milo. He looked at the baseball glove he held and the splendor of the catch in Augusta flashed into his vision and the voices filled the attic:

"*Ben, you got it! You got it!*"

He took the glove and placed it in a trunk his mother had given him for his fifteenth birthday, one with a lock. Then he left the room and closed the door. He would never again touch the glove.

T H R E E

FEW PEOPLE SPOKE to Ben about his experience in Augusta. He had been away three weeks, and three weeks was not enough time to consider as leaving and returning. He had been away and now he was home and he was working for Arthur Ledford in the job that George Hill had had before deciding to attend the University of Georgia to study chemistry. If anyone had left Jericho, it was George Hill.

Only Coleman Maxey seemed interested in Ben's short career in professional baseball.

Coleman operated a shoe repair shop and was the catcher for the Jericho Generals baseball team. He was a squat, crude man with a fondness for humor that hinted of unhealthy sex and, occasionally, he would binge-drink, two faults that were patiently tolerated by the citizens of Jericho because Coleman could take a pair of walked-down shoes and make them look new, and he could hit a baseball lopsided. Such a man was valuable, even if his manners lacked sophistication.

One week after Ben's return from Augusta—and on the third day of his employment at Ledford's Dry Goods—Coleman stopped him on his way to lunch at Brady's Cafe.

"I heard you was back," Coleman said. "What happened down there?"

"Just decided to give it up," Ben answered quietly. "I had the job with Mr. Ledford waiting, and I thought I'd better take it before he gave it to somebody else." And then he repeated something his mother had suggested: "Good jobs don't grow on trees."

"You got that," Coleman said. "What about Milo?"

"Milo?" Ben said. "You don't have to worry about him. He's the best player on the team. There was talk about him making it to Boston or one of the other big teams in a couple of years."

Coleman wagged his head in amazement. "That right? He's good, all right, but I never thought he was any better than you, except maybe in hitting, and he's a born natural at that. But you're not far behind. Guess that's why I was surprised when I heard you'd come home."

Ben shrugged uncomfortably and looked away. He thought of Arnold Toeman and the silence of his teammates when they learned he had been cut from the team. "I thought about staying around awhile," he said. "Some of the other players talked to me about it, but I had the job waiting."

"Like you said, Ben, good jobs don't grow on trees."

"I learned a lot, though," Ben said. "It's a different game in the professional leagues."

"Well, you got a place on our team," Coleman told him. "I guess you know that. We playing the Anderson team on Saturday."

For a moment, Ben did not speak. He shifted uncomfortably from foot to foot, tugged at the bow tie around his neck. Then: "I'd like to, Coleman, but I guess I'm through with playing ball."

"Why?" Coleman asked incredulously.

"I got the job now, and Mr. Ledford stays open late every Saturday. I can't go asking for time off, just getting started like I am."

"Well, damn," Coleman mumbled.

BEN'S EXCUSE TO Coleman Maxey was only partly true. When he spoke to Ben of duties for the clerk's job, Arthur Ledford had suggested that most of the better citizens of Jericho believed professional baseball was a sport for hardened men with habits of coarse language and drinking and dark living.

"In time, I think you'll know you made the right decision," Arthur had gently lectured. "Copy after your father, and you'll be a man people look up to. Your father was good at baseball, too, when he was a young man. In fact, your father was one of the best athletes we ever had around here. Nobody was as fast. But he quit all of that when he took a job and a family."

"Yes sir," Ben had replied.

"I know you and Milo have been dreaming of playing baseball for a long time," Arthur had continued. "And that's fine. A person needs a good dream. I used to dream about sailing on the ocean, and that was before I ever saw it. I still think about it, but I've never been out of sight of land. It's all right to dream. You just can't let it get the best of you."

No one in Jericho disliked Arthur Ledford. He was thought of as a kindly man who deserved every good word said about him, a diligent, almost obsessed worker, and a crusader for progress. He was driven, people believed, by an ambition to live up to the expectations of his late father, Alexander Ledford, who had established Ledford's Dry Goods and had been counted as one of the ten most influential citizens of Caulder County in the nineteenth century—a questionable selection to many who had known him personally. Alexander Ledford had been a severe, unforgiving man who wielded the power of his presence like a weapon. Arthur was the opposite. Remembered by his contemporaries as a shy, gentle child who occasionally stuttered, he had become forceful enough to assume his father's business only by patience and determination.

"You're a good person, Ben," Arthur had added. "From the best family I know. They're proud of you."

"Yes sir," Ben had said earnestly.

STILL, BEN COULD not desert the sport he loved so intensely. He could not play, but he could watch and dream the dream of his childhood.

In late afternoons, after work at Ledford's Dry Goods, Ben would go to the park where the baseball team practiced and played, and he would sit under the gray shade of a sycamore tree far away in the outfield and watch as the team paraded before him in the exuberance of the game. He was eighteen years old. Except for Spencer Franklin and Wade Pilgrim and Charles Hill, the men he watched playing his game were all older—some in their thirties—and Ben knew that none of them had his skills. None were as fast or had made a catch such as the catch he had made in Augusta. None knew the secrets of the game he had learned in three weeks from Arnold Toeman. The Jericho Generals were a team of men crudely playing a game of grace, and Ben yearned to be among them, to shout at their blundering, to show them the game as it could—as it should—be played.

Each day Ben went to the park and watched and each day he found himself wandering nearer the field and nearer the players. He did not want to be so near them, but their presence was powerful, luring him with their teasing chants and with their oaths. It was a song of romance and Ben was in love.

"Damn, Ben," Coleman Maxey said one day. "If you not gone play, at least come on down here and give us some of them tips you learned down there in Augusta."

It was a joke, but Ben thought Coleman was serious.

"Well, maybe a couple of things," Ben said cautiously.

Coleman winked at Bill Simpson, who played first base. "Anything you got," he said to Ben in a grave voice.

"Yeah," Bill Simpson said. He coughed to cover a laugh.

And Ben went among the players, talking to them, eagerly sketching in the red clay of the field the plays he had learned in Augusta, glaring at their failures with condemnation.

To the men of the team, Ben's presence was grand amusement. They mocked him and he did not know it was mockery. He was eighteen. A boy. The men of the team listened with controlled delight to Ben's instruction and then performed stupidly and then laughed secretly as Ben demonstrated again and again the art of bunting, of double-play pivots, of base-stealing. The players did not want Ben's advice. They wanted his jester exhibitions.

"Goda'mighty, Ben," Coleman would say, feigning frustration. "Damned if I know why we can't do nothing right. Looks so easy, way you do it."

"That's all right," Ben would reply. "It just takes work. Takes doing it over and over. That's the secret. Do it over and over."

"I guess you right," Coleman would concede, clucking his tongue behind a buried smile.

Ben's tragedy was classic, and it was universal: he believed he was unique among them.

He was eighteen. A boy.

He did not know the men of the team were making him their mascot fool.

Each week, he wrote a letter to Milo Wade in Augusta, describing what he was doing and how the men of the team were amazed.

Ben ended each letter in the same manner: *Stick to it, Milo. Don't come back home unless you have to.*

He signed each letter: *Your friend, Ben Phelps.*

IN LATE AUGUST, the fifth month of his return to Jericho, Christine Wade invited Ben to supper. Ben accepted reluctantly. He knew he would have to talk of Milo, and he knew Martin Wade would question him carefully. He had never been comfortable around Milo's father. There was an aura about Martin Wade, a quiet, serious superiority. He had worked at the bank founded by his late father following the Civil War, earning respect as a man of integrity, dignity, and fairness. He was also the most handsome man Ben had ever seen, and that handsomeness had caused the citizens of Jericho to jest among themselves that too many good qualities had been wasted on one man.

The men of Jericho also said that Martin Wade had met his match in Christine Cox Wade. She was feisty, the men contended in their gossip, saying the word crudely, with an emphasis that implied more than the word merited.

Milo was the only child of Martin and Christine Wade. From his birth, Milo's father had believed his son to be gifted. His son had promise, he privately asserted to friends. His son was bright and inquisitive. His son had the eyes and hands—the eyes and hands mattered—of someone who would accomplish great things. Hands meant for a musician, perhaps. The eyes of a statesman able to see visions of change and progress. No question about it, Martin Wade had pronounced: the mark of greatness was on his son. He had the eyes and hands for it, and the spirit. "All of them from his mother," he confessed. "He's got her in his blood, all right. But there's more. I don't know what, but I can sense it in him."

In the presence of Martin Wade, Ben had always felt that he was inferior, a tolerated outsider, though there had never been anything specific to justify his suspicions. Milo's father had always been kind to him, had always included him in special moments to celebrate

Milo's special achievements, and when Ben had succeeded in the small school competitions of childhood, he had always been generous in his praise. Still, Martin Wade awed Ben, as he awed everyone.

The supper was as Ben expected—a strained formality, a stagy rite of passage. Christine Wade fluttered with the serving of the food, her gay, bright voice urging Ben to overeat, reminding Ben of simple episodes of the childhood he had shared with Milo. Martin Wade listened politely, his eyes avoiding Ben. He was, Ben thought, unusually subdued.

When the supper was over, Ben and Martin Wade retired to the living room in the ritual of men. It was a ritual Ben had never experienced as a guest, and he felt uneasy. He sat erect, in his best imitation of a man's posture, and waited for Martin Wade to speak.

Martin Wade packed a pipe and lit it. The odor of the burning tobacco was sweet.

"Ben," Martin Wade said at last, "Mrs. Wade and I invited you to supper to share something with you, something only two or three people in town know about at this time."

"Yes sir," Ben said.

"I have been given an opportunity to assume the presidency of a bank in Athens," Martin Wade replied calmly. "Mrs. Wade and I have decided to divest ourselves of the interests we have in Jericho and move."

"To Athens?" Ben said.

Martin Wade bobbed his head and drew from his pipe. "We wanted you to know because you've been very much like a son to us all these years."

Ben was startled. "When?"

"Within the next month," Martin Wade told him.

Ben slumped in his chair. He said, "I'm sorry to hear that."

"Of course, we've had grave reservations about leaving Jericho," Martin Wade said. "We were both born here, and this is where we raised our son, but we also realize what we've been offered is the kind of challenge we both enjoy. Sadly, it means leaving our home."

"It's not too far away," Ben suggested.

Martin Wade sucked on his pipe. "No, it's not. Mrs. Wade keeps reminding me of that. I expect we'll make frequent trips back."

"Does Milo know about it?" asked Ben.

"He does," Martin Wade answered. "I'm not sure how he feels about it. His letter to us simply said he wished us good fortune. But I also have some news about Milo that we haven't shared with anyone, because we wanted to share it with you first."

"Sir?"

"We received a cable yesterday that he's been sold to the Boston Pilgrims, and he'll be reporting to them in a few days."

"The Pilgrims," Ben said in a stunned voice. "I—I knew he was doing good."

"Apparently, they've had some injuries on the team and they wanted a young man who wouldn't cost too much as a beginner," Martin Wade replied. "Good business, I suppose, and I'm proud of him, although I must confess I'd like to see him get over this obsession for baseball and come home. I only hope he's not too young for the experience in Boston."

Ben forced himself to sit forward in his chair. "No sir," he enthused. "There was talk about it before I left Augusta. Lots of people thought Milo was the best player on any team in the league, and they were right. He'll be playing right off, you wait and see."

Martin Wade smiled.

"You think he'll stop off on his way to Boston?" Ben asked eagerly.

"I'm not sure," Martin Wade answered. "Maybe. I'm not sure when he's leaving Augusta. Not for a few days, as I understand it. If he decides to stop here on his way, we'll let you know."

"Yes sir. I'd like that. I'd like to see him," Ben said.

Martin Wade dipped his head in a nod. His gray eyes were focused on the window. A pause billowed in the room.

"Yes sir," Ben said after a moment. "I'd sure like to see him."

Martin Wade's eyes blinked. He turned his face to Ben. "I understand you've quit playing the game."

"Uh—yes sir. Since I took the job with Mr. Ledford. Not enough time to do the job and play."

"But you go watch the games? And the practices?"

"Uh—sometimes. Yes sir."

"Ben, you need to be careful about that."

Ben blushed again. He could feel his body sinking in the chair. He did not speak.

"I was talking with Mr. Ledford in the bank this week," Martin Wade continued. "He told me that he planned to speak with you about consorting with the older members of the team. He doesn't think it's appropriate for someone in your position, and with the future you may have there."

"Sir?"

"Seems he overheard some of the men talking about it. Now, you know how I feel about you, Ben. Like a son to me. Personally, I never had a gift for the playing of sports. Not like your father. In his youth, he was quite heroic, especially in the running matches we had. No one ever beat him, as I recall. He was quite good at baseball, also."

"I don't know much about that," Ben said. "He doesn't talk about it."

"He wouldn't," Martin Wade said. "That would be boasting, and he's too good a man for that." He tapped his index finger over the tobacco in the pipe's bowl and stared thoughtfully at the string of gray smoke, thin as a spider's silk, that wiggled off his finger. "I always admired the skill and gamesmanship it required to be an athlete,

Ben. Yet, I do have to say I've never cared very much for baseball. I've always been afraid it promoted the wrong influence. Of course, Milo's playing, and I have to accept that, and I was always proud of you and Milo when you played together. You were good players, but you were also young. Some of the older men on the team are not the best citizens we have."

"Yes sir," Ben said timidly. He added, "But Spencer Franklin plays, and so does Wade Pilgrim and Charles Hill. They're younger than I am."

"And their parents keep a good eye on them, as we did on you and Milo, but not so close that you'd know it."

The admission surprised Ben. He had never realized that he and Milo were being watched from a distance by their parents.

"I'm telling you this, Ben, so you'll know. That's all. I've heard some talk about Coleman Maxey making fun of you behind your back."

"Sir?" Ben said in a weak voice.

"He's that kind of man, Ben. Enjoys embarrassing people, and I don't want to see you embarrassed. You're a young man now. You'll have to make your own decisions, as Milo is making his. Just be careful that you don't put your job in jeopardy. You've got a fine future with Mr. Ledford."

"Yes sir," Ben said softly. "I appreciate it."

The conversation ended with the appearance of Christine Wade. She swept energetically into the room and sat near Ben. She said, "No more men-talk. I want to know all about you, Ben. How's your mother?"

"Uh—fine," Ben said.

"And your father. How's your father?"

"He's fine, too."

Christine Wade looked at her husband. "Did you explain things to Ben?"

"I did," Martin Wade answered. "I told him about the move and about Milo."

"I'm sure sorry about you leaving," Ben said to Christine Wade.

"Oh, we'll be back all the time," Christine Wade replied happily. She reached to touch Ben on the hand. "And you'll have to come to see us. We're going to have enough room in that old house Martin's buying to open a hotel. I can just hear Milo complaining about it, saying we're giving up good enough for more than we could ever need."

Ben smiled.

Martin Wade rose from his seat. "If you two will excuse me, I need to attend to the horse." He extended his hand to Ben. "It was good to see you, Ben. I'm sure I'll see you in town before we move."

Ben stood. He knew it was the signal for him to leave. "Yes sir," he said. "It was a good supper. When you write to Milo, tell him I said hello. Tell him I hope he stops by on his way to Boston."

"Has he not written to you?" asked Martin Wade.

"No sir. I know he's busy. Just tell him hello for me."

Martin Wade frowned, then nodded once. "I will." He turned and left the room, and Ben could feel a chill following him. It would be the last time Ben would ever see Martin and Christine Wade, except in photographs in newspapers. They would seldom return to Jericho. Martin Wade would become a state senator and a failed candidate for governor of Georgia. Christine Wade would die of a fall during a mountain climbing vacation in Colorado in 1915.

———

THE NEWS OF Milo Wade going to Boston to play for the Boston Pilgrims moved over Jericho like a flash fire from a comet that had tumbled unexpectedly out of a night sky. The Pilgrims, with the great Cy Young, had won the first American League Championship in 1903, and had beaten the Pittsburgh Pirates of the National League in the first World Series between the two professional leagues. The Pilgrims were again leading their league, but had suffered from injuries to key players. Milo Wade, eighteen, strong, aggressive, a talented hitter and runner, was cheap insurance.

"Not been playing a whole year," the townspeople bragged, "and he's going to the Pilgrims."

"Word is, they've been planning on this since the first few weeks after Milo got to Augusta."

"If anybody can make it, it'll be Milo. He don't like to lose."

"Not many boys his age can play like a man, but Milo's different."

"Once he gets there, they'll have to drag him away with a team of horses."

The talk was lively, bright, jittery with excitement. From the talk it seemed that Milo Wade was not going to Boston alone; he was taking an entire town with him.

To Ben, it was proof that he had prophetic vision. Milo Wade wore the destiny of greatness like a dazzling garment, something spun from threads of light. No one could see it as clearly as Ben. No one had been as close to it. When people asked him about the news, Ben answered proudly, "I always knew it. Always."

"You think he's going to stop off for a little while when he comes through on his way to Boston?" the people asked Ben.

"I'd guess so," Ben told them. "I don't know. Takes a long time to get to Boston. Maybe he won't have a chance to, and with his mama and daddy getting ready to move to Athens, maybe it won't work out."

"Sure hope he does," the people said wistfully.

"Me, too," Ben agreed.

Each day, Ben checked the schedule at the train station, annoying Akers Crews, the stationmaster.

"Ben, it's the same as it was yesterday and the day before," Akers

griped. "Only thing I can tell you to do is meet every train. I can't
go looking for him and drag him off."

When his schedule at Ledford's Dry Goods permitted, Ben was at
the station for each train. He stood on the station platform, watching
the doors of the passenger cars, excited, but also apprehensive. He
had written to Milo faithfully, but had not received a response to
any of his letters. At first he had dismissed Milo's failure to write as
the stress of playing ball and traveling, yet he knew it was a feeble
excuse. In the three weeks he had been in Augusta, he had written
daily to his parents. There was time to write.

His mother had cautioned him, "Ben, maybe Milo's decided to
cut the apron strings and start out on his own without looking back.
A lot of people do that, and we just have to accept it when it happens." It was an ancient apology to explain the conduct of people
who left their homes and refused to communicate with their families.
From all the stories he had heard, Ben believed that every Southern
family had such a person. In his mother's family, it was her brother
Wendell. Wendell had disappeared in 1897, telling a friend that he
wanted to go to California to find gold. He had never written, and
no one knew where he was.

"Milo wouldn't do that," Ben had insisted. "We been together too
long."

"Sometimes people change overnight, son," his mother had replied gently. "If that's what he's done, you have accept it and go on
with your life."

Sometimes, standing on the station platform, the words of his
mother would come to him and Ben would realize that he had
stepped into a shadow, out of sight.

ON THE FIFTH day of waiting and watching, Ben saw Milo Wade.

It was early evening, the eight-twenty stop.

Milo was sitting deep in his seat in the last passenger car, his face cloudy behind the window glass. He was gazing expressionless at the station.

Ben hesitated in the shadow. He looked around, but did not see Martin or Christine Wade, and he wondered if they knew that Milo was on the train.

Could have been a change in schedule, he thought.

Or maybe Martin and Christine Wade were in Athens, at their new hotel-big home.

Ben did not move. He saw Akers Crews busy with the loading of boxes on one of the boxcars. Akers was a small man who suffered from arthritis in his bowed back. The aggravation of pain colored his scowling face.

Steam hissed from the engine. A thundercloud of black-gray smoke boiled up like a tornado's funnel, spread open in the humid air, settled around the station. Ben could smell the acid of the smoke.

In the train car, Milo turned away from the window.

And then Ben heard Akers shout something to the engineer. The engineer waved a hand from the cab of the engine.

Ben moved quickly, impulsively, from the shadow and stepped from the platform and crossed rapidly to the passenger car where Milo was sitting. He saw an older man, wearing a felt hat, peering at him from the seat opposite Milo.

"Milo!" Ben called over the noise of the train.

Milo did not look at him.

"Milo!" Ben called again. He waved his hand. He saw the older man lean toward Milo, reach for him, say something, and Milo turned to look through the window.

The train began to pull away.

"Milo!" The call became a shout.

Milo moved toward the window, then settled back. He lifted his hand.

"Good luck, Milo," Ben bellowed. "I'll be keeping up with you."

The train lurched forward and Ben began to walk rapidly with it, waving to Milo. "Good luck," he cried again.

IN THE TRAIN, the older man said to Milo, "Somebody you know?"

Milo glanced again out of the window. "We grew up together."

"Looked like he was trying to tell you something."

Milo turned back in his seat.

"That your hometown?" asked the older man.

"Was," Milo said.

"Was?"

"My folks are moving," Milo answered. He added, "So am I."

"They still live there, your folks?"

"They do now, but not for long."

"You didn't get off," the older man said. "They know you were coming through?"

Milo shook his head. "Didn't tell them. Didn't have time to stop off."

"Well, they'll know about it soon enough, I'd guess," the older man observed. "Word gets about in a small town like that, and you being seen by your friend—"

"It won't matter," Milo said abruptly. "My folks are busy enough."

The older man sat back in his seat. After a moment, he picked up the newspaper he had been reading and ducked his head to stare at it. The young man sitting across from him seemed detached and angry. Cold. The young man seemed cold.

"YOU SEE HIM, Ben?" asked Akers Crews.

"Yes sir, he was on the train," Ben said.

Akers wagged his head in disbelief. "That boy should've got off that train, even if it was just for a minute. This is his home, where he grew up. A man ought never get too big to stand on the ground of his home."

"I guess he didn't have time," Ben said softly.

"Time's got nothing to do with it," Akers argued. "He's just got the big head because he's going to Boston. You lucky you got out of that game when you did, Ben. Nothing worse than somebody that gets too good for his own kind, and that's what's happened to that boy." He watched the train disappear around a bend. "I wonder why his mama and daddy wadn't down here to see him?"

"I don't know," Ben said.

Akers began to climb the steps to the platform. He muttered, "Can't understand why people turn against their home. Can't understand it at all." He stopped and cocked his head to look at Ben. "You not thinking about playing again, are you?"

Ben could hear the fading sound of the train vibrating in the tracks. After a moment, he said to Akers, "No sir. I gave it up. All that's behind me."

"Son, once you been somewhere, you don't never leave it out of sight behind you," Akers said solemnly. "You just drag it along with you, like a cranky old dog on a leash. You just better hope he don't get to snarling and decide to bite you in the ass when you not looking."

Akers Crews's words were more prophetic than either he or Ben knew.

———————

THE CARNIVAL HAD unfolded its worn canvas tents in a pasture near the train depot and had begun to play its beckoning calliope music — lively and shrill — and the enticing spell of the music began to pull the people of Jericho and Caulder County to the wonders of a traveling event advertised by posters as the Marvels of the Earth Exhibition.

It was not a great carnival, not like the spectacles of Barnum and Bailey, with jungle animal acts and beautiful women doing acrobatics on the backs of white horses, or daredevil men walking steel cables that swayed in the high, trapped air of tents, or sideshows of part-people, part-something mutants.

Still, it was a carnival — game tents and food tents, the scent of fresh sawdust and peanuts and cotton candy, the yodeling singsong of show barkers, the yelping of children — and Ben walked alone among the late-afternoon crowd that moved languidly along the street of tents. He liked the closeness of the crowd, the gentle nudging of arms, the courteous sidestepping, the darting, wiggling bodies of boys chasing amazement. He liked the lavish, moving colors of dresses and ribbon streamers—ambers and reds and blues and yellows—swimming in the September sun.

Ben also liked the tricksters behind the booths and at the canvas tent doors, babbling like excited auctioneers—daring, inviting, promising. He liked the absurdity of the aging tiger, tail-swatting at flies like a drowsy cow, located next to the tent of scientific oddities that were certain to change mankind in the electric age that Thomas Edison had fathered. It was the twentieth century. The motorcar was real. George Franklin owned one and Branson Quitman had ordered one. The Wrights had flown an airplane across the sands of a place called Kitty Hawk in North Carolina. Men with genius, or madness, had predicted that voices would be picked up from the air—from the *air*, not from the wires linking telephone to telephone. At the Marvels of the Earth Exhibition, the twentieth-century world was on display in illusions of magic and in spectacular renderings of imaginative paintings and in toys of fantasy far grander than the grandest of dreams.

The crowd moved with the motion of a slow body of water, lapping in waves to the tents, and at each tent, the alluring oddity hidden inside was more splendid, more incomprehensible, than the oddities in the nearby tents. It was song and dance and laughter that flowed along the street of tents.

Ben followed the festival, permitting himself to float like a leaf in the gentle current of the onlookers. He did not enter any of the tents or stop to play their games. He watched and listened and wandered leisurely, speaking politely to people who floated with him, or against him. He could feel, in the heat of the late-afternoon sun, an almost surprising mood of relaxation. When he laughed at something unexpected or amusing, he could sense the weight of his hurt over Milo Wade leaving him.

And then he was at the end of the street of tents, moving with the crowd to a cleaned-off cornfield beside a single large oak. It was where he and Milo and other townsboys had played choose-up games of baseball as children. In the distance, he could see people pushing into a half-circle around something that commanded their attention.

"Ben, Ben, you got to see that," a boyish voice near him cried.

The voice belonged to David Grubb, who was young and blond and often sang solos with the Presbyterian church choir. David would be the first man from Jericho to die in World War I.

"What's going on, David?" asked Ben.

"They got a baseball-hitting contest going on, that's what," David said excitedly. "Anybody that gets a hit off that fellow gets fifty cents. Cost a nickel for three strikes. I'm going to find my daddy, see if he'll let me try." He ran away, dodging into the flow of the crowd.

Ben could hear the unmistakable slap of a baseball hitting a leather mitt, and the gasps of awe from onlookers. He could feel his throat tighten. The muscles in his arms quivered. He moved toward the sound of the ball striking the mitt, a sound that called to him out of the crowd.

He stood at a rope line that fanned in a V, like the first and third base lines of a baseball field, and watched Frank Mercer standing at a wood home plate, waving a bat in the air, stretching the muscles of his shoulders. The man behind the plate wore a bleached baseball uniform and a mask that covered his bearded face. He was sitting on a stool. He looked awkward and deformed.

"What's the matter with the catcher?" Ben asked a man standing beside him.

The man chuckled. "Looks like he's about to topple off, don't it? He's just got him one leg."

Ben looked more closely. The catcher's right leg was missing at the knee. He could see a pair of crutches beside the stool.

"Well, you right," Ben whispered.

"Shoot, that's nothing," the man beside him said. "Take a look at the fellow throwing the ball. Just got one arm."

Ben turned to look at the pitcher. He did not have a left arm. His shirtsleeve had been pinned or sewn to the face of his shirt. He stood majestically, staring down at the catcher and Frank Mercer. Ben was stunned by his size. He was a giant. And then Ben saw his face. Scars. White ridges of flesh against a burning red skin. It was a face to turn from, to fear, to remember.

"All right, all right, all right," a skinny man wearing a black suit and a top hat chortled through a megaphone. He was standing near the catcher. "This looks like a strong fellow. Maybe he'll do it. Maybe he'll get a hit off the One-Armed Wonder of Tennessee. But take my advice, folks, and don't make any side bets on it."

"Hit him, Frank!" someone crowed from the crowd.

"You can do it, Frank!"

"I'm adding fifty cents to the pot if you do," someone else called.

Frank smiled and lifted his hand to the voice. He stepped into the batter's box, waving the bat in showmanship.

Ben watched the giant roll the ball in his bare hand, examining it. Then he saw the slow rocking of the giant's body and the one full turn of the arm and the slight, graceful twist of his torso and the sudden whip of motion. Ben did not see the ball. He heard it splatter against the mitt of the catcher, saw the catcher recoil in pain. He saw Frank Mercer stand motionless, staring in disbelief at the giant with the face of scars.

"Strike one," the barker sang.

"You got to swing the bat, Frank," yelled Coleman Maxey, laughing happily.

"At what?" Frank called back. "I never seen nothing to swing at."

"I got him figured," Coleman bellowed. "You swing when I tell you."

The pitcher took the ball and stared coldly at Coleman, standing behind the rope near the catcher. He then turned back to Frank and started his rocking motion.

"Now," Coleman shouted.

Frank swung viciously. The pitcher still held the ball. The crowd laughed joyfully and booed Frank.

"Damn," Frank muttered, smiling sheepishly.

"Best wait to he throws it, mister," the barker advised, tipping his hat to Frank.

Frank struck out on the next two pitches and dropped the bat. He said, "That's it. Great Goda'mighty, I never saw nothing like that."

"Try again, friend?" the barker teased.

"You got two dimes out of me for trying it too many times already," Frank said. "Won't find me wasting no more money."

"Who else?" the barker called through his megaphone. "Tell you what we're going to do. We're going to raise the prize. One dollar to the man that gets a hit, fifty cents for even touching the ball."

The crowd murmured.

"Hey, you," the catcher said suddenly in a gruff voice, muted by the mask he wore. He was pointing his mitt toward Ben. "You look like a player to me. Cost you a nickel."

Ben smiled and waved away the offer.

"C'mon, Ben, give it a try," Frank Mercer urged in a mocking voice. "You used to hit pretty good. Shoot, boy, you were a pro."

"I gave it up," Ben mumbled. He stepped back into the crowd.

"You ever see anybody that good down there in Augusta?" Coleman asked.

Ben looked at the giant, holding the ball, glaring at the crowd. He shook his head.

"What you think that fellow you was telling us about—that Arnold Toeman—would tell you to do, hitting against somebody like that man out there?" Coleman pressed.

Ben did not answer. He knew he was again being played the fool by Coleman, though he had long given up going to the Generals' practices or the games. He turned his head toward the tents, made a move to leave.

"Used to hit pretty good, did you?" the catcher called. "You look like you still can. Look like somebody that's been around the game. C'mon, boy, give it a try."

The crowd around Ben began to push him forward.

"Go on, Ben, try him."

"Yeah, Ben. Everybody else has."

"Shoot, Ben, I'll pay the nickel," Frank thundered. He flipped a coin to the barker.

"You can't back out now, Ben," someone said merrily. "Cheap as Frank is, he'll hound you to your grave over owing him."

Laugher rippled over the crowd. "You get a hit, Ben, I'll throw in a extra dollar," Coleman chortled. He held up a dollar bill. "In fact, I'll put my mark on it to prove it's mine, if you get a hit." He took a pencil from his pocket and with showmanship, marked an X in the corner of the bill.

"Well, if Coleman's gone throw in a dollar, by shot, so will I," Frank declared. "So will I."

Another voice: "Me, too, by God."

Another voice: "Count me in. Shoot, I'll even let Coleman hold my dollar right now."

Another voice: "I'm in for it."

The voices around him became louder. Money was passed to Coleman. Hands pushed Ben to the rope, pulled the rope up, nudged him beneath it. He stood and looked at the pitcher. The pitcher stared angrily at him.

"I got the money right here, Ben," Coleman called, holding fanned-out dollar bills over his head, waving them. "Ten dollars, boy.

Ten dollars. And just for the hell of it, I'll throw in a new set of soles for them shoes you wearing. Let's see what old Arnold Toeman taught you, boy."

The crowd hooted.

"Bat's right here," the catcher said.

Ben walked slowly, self-consciously, across the field. He picked up the bat, rolled it with his fingers. It was hard ash, turned for a thick handle. He waved it once in the air, weakly, feeling the weight. Then he stepped to the plate and twisted his feet into the grass. His heart was thundering and his mouth was dust-dry. He closed his eyes and rolled his head, and for a stunning moment the wondrous exhilaration of the game flooded him, filled him.

"Well, well, well. We got us a player," the barker boomed, his voice echoing through the megaphone.

A cheer flew up from the crowd.

"Ben," the catcher whispered under the cheer. "You just stand there and do what I tell you, boy."

Ben's head jerked toward the catcher. He looked into the gray eyes behind the mask: Foster Lanier.

"Don't say the first goddamn word," Foster warned. "I'm fixing to make you a hero, boy. They'll tote you out of here on their goddamn shoulders."

"Fos—"

"Shut up," Foster growled. "Turn back in the box and listen."

Ben obeyed.

"Take you a couple of swings," Foster said quietly. "He's gone throw two balls you not even gone see, then he'll float one in and you better, by God, hit it out of sight."

Ben raised the bat, balanced it above his shoulders. He saw a small smile ease into the face of the pitcher, and then the smile vanished, and the face turned cold. He watched the rocking motion of the pitcher's body, the turn of his arm, the long, hard step forward. He saw the ball for only a fraction of time, a blink of white across space, then he heard it explode into Foster's mitt. The crowd screamed at Ben.

"Hit him, Ben!"

"Watch out, Ben! He could throw it straight through you if he hits you!"

Ben heard Frank and Coleman laughing.

Behind the plate, Foster oohed joyfully. He said in a low voice, "You ever see anything like that, Ben? Damnedest pitcher alive, I swear it. Ugly, too. Watch this one, Ben. It's gone miss you by two inches."

Ben looked quickly to Foster and Foster lobbed the ball back to the giant.

"Hell, don't worry none," Foster whispered. "He's not gone hit you. It's just gone rile up the crowd a little bit, and then you'll get your hit and they'll think one of their boys kicked the shit out of us. Good for business. We do it everywhere."

Ben could feel the ball that missed him by two inches. He fell away instinctively as Foster leaned dangerously from his stool to catch the pitch.

"God-o-mighty," Foster cried. He looked at Ben sprawled in the grass. Ben could see him wink from behind his mask. "You all right?" he said in a voice loud enough for the crowd to hear.

The crowd hissed angrily.

"Now, don't get upset, folks," Foster pleaded. "Once in a while, one slips. Looks like the boy's all right."

Ben pulled himself to his feet and picked up the bat. He stepped to the plate and lifted the bat to his shoulders. His heart was racing.

"Hit the son of a bitch, Ben," someone yelled. And then a chant began: "Hit him, hit him, hit him . . ."

Foster leaned forward on his stool. "It'll be belt-high, Ben," he whispered. "No curve, just straight. Swing easy."

The pitch glided in, exactly as Foster had promised. Ben could feel the hit as he turned the bat, could feel the rhythm of his muscles, like a rehearsed dance, and the splendor of the shock rushing through him. He looked up and watched the ball lifting high into the bright, angled rays of the sun, flying beyond the crowd. He heard an eruption of voices screaming his name, and he heard again the cries in Augusta:

"You got it, Ben! You got it!"

The giant pitcher stood unmoving, glaring at Ben with bitterness. He did not like the artless game of deceit that Foster Lanier had commanded him to play. In every place they stopped, he threw the pitch that would be hit, but he did not like it. Foster called it the business pitch. "Let one hit it and every man and boy in the crowd's got to give it a try," Foster had said. Foster was right, but the giant did not like it.

The crowd spilled over the V of the rope, threw itself into a circle around Ben. They slapped gladly at him. Coleman shoved a wad of money into his hand with a yodel of joy. "By God, you done it," Coleman shouted.

Ben looked at Foster, who sat relaxed on his stool, holding his catcher's mask. A playful smile fluttered across Foster's face. He winked at Ben.

"By God, Ben, I'm gone give it a try," an older man declared, reaching for the bat.

"Wait a minute, friends," Foster called. "Quiet down just a minute." He caught one of his crutches beside his stool and struggled to stand. "Wait a minute," he repeated.

The crowd around Ben became silent.

"They calling you Ben," Foster said. "What's your name, anyhow?"

Ben answered, "Ben Phelps."

Foster whistled softly. "Well, no damn wonder," he said in astonishment. "I know you. Watched you playing down in Augusta earlier this year. Ben Phelps. No damn wonder."

"You know Ben?" Coleman asked with surprise.

"Know him well enough," Foster said. "I can't believe he's here and not off playing somewhere with the professionals." He hobbled to Ben and extended his hand. "It's a privilege, Ben Phelps," he said earnestly. "I saw you make a catch down there in Augusta — it was against the Savannah team, I believe — that was the best I ever saw, and I'm a man that's played and watched baseball all over this country."

Ben said nothing. He stared at Foster quizzically. The crowd remained quiet.

"I'm telling you, folks," Foster continued, "you'd of been proud of him. Ben here looked like he was flying that last ten yards. Caught that ball a half-inch off the ground. Nobody alive could of done it but Ben."

Ben could sense the people looking at him curiously. He mumbled to Foster, "Thanks."

"How come you not playing somewhere?" asked Foster.

Ben licked his lips. He crossed his arms and shook his head.

"Yeah, Ben, how come?" someone asked.

"Guess you learned it wadn't all that it was made out to be. That right, Ben?" Foster said.

"Well, I—"

"I don't blame you," Foster said, laughing merrily. "Wish I'd of done the same thing when I got started. Lost this leg trying to play baseball. I'd lots rather been working at a good job somewhere. I'd be dancing if I'd of done that."

"Ben can play, all right," Coleman said. "I been trying to get him to come back and play for the town team, but he won't do it."

"You got a job, Ben?" asked Foster.

Ben nodded.

"Well, there's your answer, friend," Foster said to Coleman. "A good job's a lot more sure than baseball, I'll tell you that for God's truth."

"I can't argue that," Coleman admitted. "But Ben can play, and that's a fact. I never saw him hit one like he just did, but I guess he picked up some good pointers down there in Augusta. He's always been the fastest man around here."

"Yeah," Frank said. "Him and Milo Wade was two of the best we ever had on the town team, that's for sure."

"Milo Wade?" Foster said, wiping his face with a handkerchief he had pulled from his pocket. "I know that name, too." He looked at Ben. "He was down there in Augusta too, wadn't he?"

Ben nodded.

"He's up in Boston now," Coleman said. "Doing good, too, from what I hear."

"He's good, all right," Foster said, "but I'd take Ben here. You saw what he just did, and I guarantee you they's not a half-dozen men a month even come close to hitting my man."

"I—was lucky," Ben protested meekly.

"Everybody's lucky and everybody's unlucky," Foster replied, dangling the stump of his right leg. "But luck's got nothing much to do with it. You hit the ball, Ben Phelps. Hit it better than anybody since I put this show together. That's all I'm saying. These people here got a reason to be proud of you."

"Well, we are, mister," Coleman said enthusiastically. "Wish we could get him back playing with us."

"Maybe he will now," Foster said. "But I wouldn't advise him to quit on his job." He stepped back on his crutch and the crowd closed around Ben.

"You get a chance, you come back tonight and talk some baseball with me, Ben," Foster said. He smiled again and winked at Ben. "Who's next?" he sang. "Who's as good as Ben Phelps?"

———

IT WAS DARK when Ben returned to the Marvels of the Earth carnival. The street of tents was empty except for carnival people moving about lazily, gathering beneath orange moons of lights from lanterns. Ben could hear the mumbled talk and tired laughter, could see silhouettes of their faces in the orange lights, could smell their cigarette smoke and the meat-rich odor of their cooking. The people of the carnival were exhausted, and Ben knew it. They had arrived in Jericho by train, had raised a small city of canvas, had begged and teased to make their daily wage, and now they were exhausted.

As Ben passed among them, they stared absently at him, and he wondered if they had homes or if their tents were their homes and they were merely nomads of slow travel, like Gypsies who transported their nations in brightly painted wagons. Most likely there were Gypsies among the carnival people, Ben thought. Gypsies possessed by spirits too mystic to understand. He paused at one tent advertising the telling of fortunes, found himself gazing at the chipped-paint canvas face of a woman peering through jeweled fingers into a chipped-paint crystal ball, and he wondered if Gypsies were standing behind the dark slits of the closed tent flaps, watching him from black eyes. If they could see into the beyond, into days that had not yet been lived, what would they see for him? A chill rushed through him and he pivoted quickly to walk away. He did not see the giant one-armed man standing in the shadows near the tent, or the stubby, broad-faced midget sitting on a table.

"Boy," the man said in a coarse, low voice.

Ben did not answer. He stood, unable to move, staring at the man, the blood of his heart driving painfully against his chest. The vivid white scars of the man's face were almost fluorescent in the dim light.

"You didn't hit me, boy," the man growled. "I give you that."

"Yes—yes sir," Ben whispered. "Foster told me."

The midget giggled.

"Won't no way you hit me," the man said.

"No sir."

"Never."

"I—I was looking for Foster," Ben said.

"Be by the tree, in the field," the man said.

Ben looked toward the tree. "Thank you," he mumbled. He turned to leave.

"Boy."

Ben stopped and turned back. The man held a baseball in his hand.

"Next time, I bust you in the skull," the man said.

A peal of laughter squawked from the midget's throat, a cry of a predator bird. He crossed his chest with his hands and the laughter collapsed into a hacking cough.

Ben walked away quickly, away from the street of tents and into the field where Foster Lanier's game of baseball chance had been played. Under the oak, he saw the light of a lantern and, behind it, the outline of a tent. He found Foster sitting against the oak, drinking. The stub of his right leg was propped on a blanket. In the night light, Foster looked very old.

"I been waiting," Foster said. "Didn't think you was coming."

"Took some time finding you," Ben lied. His eyes fell on Foster's half-leg.

Foster laughed wearily and slapped the leg at his thigh. He said, "Not as much of me as they was the last time I saw you."

"What happened?" asked Ben.

"Found me a crazy doctor up in Knoxville," Foster said easily. "Took out his handsaw and cut it off like it was a plank."

"Why?"

"Said it was me or the leg. Hell, the leg wadn't worth much nohow," Foster said. He shrugged. "Sit down, boy. We got some catching up to do."

Foster had not made it to Kentucky. He had stopped in Knoxville with Norman Porterfield and Lottie Barton, and there he had become ill and the leg had been amputated. While recuperating, he heard tales of a one-armed man who could throw a baseball through the side of a barn. The man made wagers that no one could hit a ball thrown by him, but few people were willing to try, because there was a story that the man had killed someone by hitting him in the face after the challenger had tormented him for his deformity.

"Truth is, he knew the man," Foster said. "Had something to do with how that man treated his daddy." He shook his head. "I guarantee you it was on purpose. My man can throw it where he wants to."

Foster had met the one-armed giant, watched a performance, and then offered the proposal of a one-armed pitcher and a one-legged catcher, and they had begun touring with the Marvels of the Earth carnival.

"Ben, he's the meanest son of a bitch I ever saw," Foster confided.

"Got his face cut to ribbons in a razor fight with some nigger in St. Louis when he was a boy, and his arm was cut up so bad they had to take it off. God only knows what he could of been if he'd had two good arms. No man alive born to throw baseballs like him."

"I never saw nobody that big," Ben said.

Foster giggled the giggle of a drunk. "You know what his name is, Ben? Baby. Baby Cotwell. That's it, by God. His real name is Baby. I call him Cotwell. Let it out that he may be on the run from the law, and we do a couple of tricks to keep people wondering."

"What kind of tricks?" asked Ben.

"Well, like today," Foster explained. "We didn't do a thing until the sun got behind this tree and that give us a shadow between where Cotwell was throwing and I was catching. Ball disappears in that shadow, fast as he throws it."

Ben laughed softly with Foster. He sat and looked into the night sky and remembered the drunken Foster on the train ride from Augusta.

"I was reading somewhere that Milo was doing all right," Foster said.

"I guess so," Ben said solemnly.

"Aw, shit, Ben, just forget it," Foster said. "I told you before, it's not much of a life. Let Milo do it. Hell, it'll happen to him, too, sooner or later. The ax falls on everybody."

"I don't know," Ben said.

"Well, by God, I do," Foster insisted. "I damn well do. C'mon, let's have us a drink to Milo." He handed the bottle to Ben. "C'mon, Ben, one swallow. It's not gone kill you, not one swallow. It's Kentucky-made. Last bottle I got like it."

Ben took the nearly empty bottle and sipped from it. The bourbon burned his lips and throat. He handed the bottle back to Foster, and Foster drained it in one swallow.

"Tell you what, Ben, I got a surprise for you," Foster said. He shifted against the tree and motioned with the bottle toward the carnival. "Look coming yonder."

Ben turned and watched the girl crossing the field, a slender figure against the dull steel of the sky.

"Don't go to thinking nothing, Ben," cautioned Foster. "It's purely a working arrangement."

"What is?"

"You'll see."

She was only a few feet away before Ben recognized her. He looked with surprise at Foster. "Lottie?" he said.

Foster grinned. "In the flesh," he answered. "I told her you'd be by."

Lottie walked into the light of the lantern. She smiled warmly at Ben. "Hello, Ben Phelps," she said.

Ben stood. He said, "Uh, hello."

"You bring it?" asked Foster.

Lottie pulled a jar of corn whiskey from the fold of her arm and handed it to Foster.

"That's the arrangement, Ben," Foster said. "Lottie here, she's my nurse. I got her a job working the carnival and she looks after me."

"Oh?" Ben said foolishly. "What do you do? With the carnival?"

Foster snickered. He slapped the ground with the palm of his hand. Lottie glared at him.

"Depends on where we are, and what tents they throw up," Foster said. "That right, Lottie? Take here, it being a small, God-fearing town, Lottie works one of the food tents." He glanced up at Lottie. "They call them 'joints,' don't they, pretty girl?"

Lottie did not reply. She sat on the ground and tucked her dress beneath her knees.

"But in them big towns, like Knoxville, she works the girlie tent," Foster continued. He opened the jar of corn whiskey, tasted it, frowned in disgust, recapped it. Ben stood uncomfortably, looking from Foster to Lottie, Lottie to Foster.

"Now, don't get me wrong," Foster said. "She's not no main act, or nothing like that, even if she is the finest-looking woman they got. She just sort of stands around the stage, looking good, in one of them barely nothing costumes, making every man and boy in the county howl at the moon. Am I telling it right or not, Lottie?"

Lottie shrugged nonchalantly. She looked at Ben and then across the field to the tents.

"They keep trying to put her in the middle of things, make her do things that run a man's blood up, but I won't let them," Foster declared. "I told her I was taking her home — even trade for helping me out — and, by God, I aim to do that, without her head turned to fancy thinking. Then I'm going home, Ben. Going home to Kentucky, and, by God, that's where I'm gone stay."

"Home?" Ben said to Lottie. "So, you're going home?"

"I guess," Lottie told him. She pushed her hand through her hair. "Norman, he left," she added. "Said he had to go on working."

Foster nodded gravely. "Good man, he was, Ben. Found me the doctor. Stuck around for the cutting and a little drinking after it was over. Wouldn't see me staying by myself. Made Lottie stay with me. Good man, he was."

"I'm glad you made it through all that, Foster," Ben said.

"I'm fine as one leg can make a man," Foster said in a slur. He lifted the jar to Ben.

"Uh, no thanks," Ben said. He glanced at Lottie.

"Aw, shit, Ben, Lottie don't care if you take a drink, do you, Lottie?"

Lottie shook her head lazily. She hugged her knees and gazed at Ben.

"He took one before you come up," Foster said. "Bet it was the first time, wadn't it, Ben?"

Ben shifted on his feet. He could feel his face coloring. "Not the first," he said. "I had some before. Milo and me."

"Well, God-o-mighty, that offends me, Ben," Foster replied indignantly. "Maybe the last time I'll ever see you again on this earth, and you turning down a drink with me." He again offered the jar. "You ought to like it. It was made somewhere around here."

"Maybe a sip," Ben said. He took the jar and opened it and tipped it to his lips and swallowed. The taste was sharp and sour. He swallowed again. A shock tickled his skin.

"Now, that's being a friend," Foster said, taking the jar from Ben. He capped it, then reached for his crutches and pulled himself up.

"Where you going?" asked Ben.

"For one thing, I'm gone find me a bush and take me a long, yellow piss," Foster said. "Then I'm gone find Cotwell and give him his cut for the day. I don't, he'll get drunk and come bulling in here in a little while and want to fight me over it. Crazy bastard when he's cold sober, Ben, but you ought to see him when he's been drinking some."

"I'll go with you," Ben said quickly.

Foster smiled. He leaned on his crutches and moved his face close to Ben. "They's nothing on earth Baby Cotwell would like better than squeezing your head like it was a grape, Ben. Besides that, you wouldn't want to leave Lottie out here by herself, now would you?"

Ben looked at Lottie. Her eyes were dark in the orange light of the lantern. She said nothing.

"Uh, well, no," Ben stammered. "We'll—we'll wait here for you."

Foster pushed away on his crutches, swinging the stump of his right leg. "Well, I'll be a little while. Help yourself to a drink, you want one. Just don't leave it empty." He moved laboriously across the field, toward the carnival.

Ben sat near the tree. He opened the jar of corn whiskey and sipped from it—a bare sip. He could hear grass insects singing around him.

"You doing a good thing for Foster," Ben said at last. "I can tell." He touched his lips again to the mouth of the jar, pretending to drink, then he asked, "You really going home, like Foster said?"

"Maybe," Lottie said. Her voice was soft. She watched as Foster disappeared into the darkness.

"Maybe?" Ben said.

"Maybe I'll stay with the carnival. It's all right. We get to go places. Better than sitting around at home, looking at that old river like Sister does."

Ben picked up a small rock and rolled it in his hand. He lifted his head to the voices of the tent people drifting across the field, voices underplayed with laughter. He knew that Lottie was watching him.

"Don't think I'd like that, all that traveling," Ben said.

Lottie did not reply. She pushed up on her knees and brushed the front of her dress. She looked again in the distance, toward the tents.

"What is it?" asked Ben.

"You think Foster's going to die soon?" she said.

"I don't know. He drinks a lot. Drinking can kill a man," Ben answered.

"Sometimes he says he loves me. You think he does?"

Ben did not answer for a moment. Then: "I don't know. He says so, I guess he does."

Lottie shook her head, flinging her hair. She slapped at something in the air. "He don't say it unless he's been drinking." She paused. "That's like my daddy was." She stood and extended her hand to Ben. "C'mon, Ben Phelps."

"Where we going?"

"Just come on," she said casually.

Ben took her hand and she tugged him up, then she turned and started walking toward the tent.

"Lottie—"

"C'mon, Ben."

Ben stared at her in confusion. He could taste the corn whiskey on his tongue.

"Ben—"

"All right," he answered.

At the tent, Lottie threw back the flap and motioned Ben inside. She stepped in behind him and pulled the flap closed.

Inside, the tent was tinted with the light of a small lantern, and in the pale amber of the light, Ben could see a mound of quilts spread across the ground. A large and a small valise had been pushed into one corner. An ivory-handled fan was spread open on the top of the small valise. A painting of tiny, delicate red and yellow flowers, dangling from dark green stems, flowed across the fan's face.

"That's pretty," Ben said. He gestured with his face toward the valise. "The fan. My mama's got one almost like it."

"Foster bought it for me," Lottie said. "It's the prettiest thing anybody's ever give to me."

Ben twisted back to face Lottie, who stood against the tent flaps. "Why—am I here?" he asked in a weak voice.

"It's what Foster wants, Ben," Lottie said calmly. "Foster likes you. Said it was all you needed to be a man."

Ben watched her fingers moving down the front of her dress, slipping buttons.

"What—what're you doing?" Ben whispered.

Lottie did not answer. She reached down, crossed her arms and caught the hem of her dress and peeled it over her head. She stood nude before him.

"I'm going to make love to you, Ben Phelps. I'm going to make you a man. Me and Foster, we talked about it."

Ben was frozen. He had never seen a woman who was nude.

"Foster said you'd be scared," Lottie murmured. "Said you'd want to leave. Said you'd be scared somebody would find out. Nobody will, Ben. Not ever. We'll be leaving after tomorrow. Nobody'll know. Foster wants me to do it." She stepped to Ben, touched his face with her fingers. The protruding nipples of her breasts were tan in the light of the tent. "But that's not why I'm doing it, Ben. I'm doing it because I want to."

Ben could not move. He was terrified. He felt her hands playing across his chest, slipping the buttons of his shirt, pushing it back. Her fingers danced lightly over his stomach, skimmed his belt line, flashed along his ribs to his armpits. He could feel himself growing, and he moved to relieve the tightness.

"Touch me, Ben," Lottie said quietly, taking Ben's hands and guiding them to her breasts. Her breasts were firm and smooth. She pushed her nipples between his fingers and forced him to squeeze them gently. A great flood of blood exploded in him, weakening his legs. His fingers circled the erect tips of her breasts and she lifted and pushed against him.

"Lottie—"

She fell to her knees on the quilts and pulled him down with her.

"Lottie—"

She raised her hands slowly over her head in a dancer's pose.

"Look at me, Ben," she said.

Ben tried to speak. His mouth was dry. He could see the pumping of her heart across her abdomen, and the dark, feathered pit of curled hair at her legs. Perspiration oozed from his neck and shoulders. He pushed back, his shoulders rubbing against the canvas of the tent.

"Look, Ben, look."

She began a slow, sensuous weaving of her body, her knees spreading, her hands leaving shadows against the trapped, amber light of the tent. A muted sound of music—barely audible—played in her throat.

"This is how I dance in the show," she whispered.

"Lottie—"

"Hush, Ben, hush."

She moved to him again, her fingers skimming his stomach, circling down over his belt and his trousers. Her hands found the rigid bulge of his penis and she began to knead it softly.

"Lottie, no—"

"It's all right, Ben. Nobody's here but me and you."

"I—can't," he whimpered.

"Yes you can, Ben. You can."

"No—" He caught her hands, held them. "It's not—right."

A sudden, quizzical expression blinked in Lottie's eyes. "Don't you want me, Ben?" she asked softly.

"It's—not that," Ben whispered. "I just—can't."

For a moment, Lottie did not speak, then she said gently, "It goes against the way you was raised. Is that it?"

Ben nodded.

"It's all right, Ben," she said. She leaned forward and kissed him gently on the forehead. "I'll tell Foster we did it. That'll make him happy." She began to button his shirt. "You're a good person, Ben Phelps. I knew that the first time I met you. Foster knows it, too. He's always talking about you, saying how hard you tried when you was playing baseball." She paused, buttoned the last button on his shirt. "You know what I wish, Ben? I wish Foster could still be playing baseball. I never saw nobody miss something as much as he misses baseball."

"I guess he does," Ben mumbled.

Lottie reached for her dress, paused with it in her hands, gazed thoughtfully at the lantern. She did not seem conscious that she was nude. "Sometimes I think I love Foster," she said quietly. "Do you think that's wrong, Ben? Him being so much older, I mean."

Ben shook his head. "No," he told her. "If you love somebody, I don't see that it matters too much."

Lottie slumped on her knees, still holding the dress, still gazing at the lantern. She smiled. "He don't know what to do with me, he says. Says he don't know if he ought to marry me or put me on the next train home. Says he'd probably put me on the train, but he don't trust me to stay on it past the first stop down the road, unless he's on it with me. Says he plans on walking me up to the front porch of my mama's home to make sure he's kept his bargain." She turned to face Ben. The smile grew. She opened her arms to expose her body. "Do you think I'm pretty, Ben Phelps?"

Ben bobbed his head once. "Yes, I do. You're very pretty."

She pulled the dress over her head. "I'm glad," she said. "I like to be pretty." She began to button the dress. "When I was little, I used to think Sister was the prettiest person I'd ever seen. I always wanted to be pretty like Sister." She touched her hair with her hand. "But she's not pretty anymore, Ben. It's like she poured all her prettiness in that old river and she just sits there watching it wash away."

"You won't do that," Ben said.

She looked away. "I don't want to, Ben. I don't ever want to do that."

FOSTER LEANED ON his crutches in the shadow of the tiger's cage and drew from a finger-rolled cigarette. He stared across the field to the faint light of the tent that he shared with Lottie.

"That's a good boy," Foster said to Baby Cotwell.

"You done wrong, giving her to him," Baby Cotwell said bitterly.

Foster drew again from the cigarette and dropped it to the ground and clumsily crushed it with the tip of one of his crutches.

"It's what I want," he said evenly. "That boy means something to me. Damned if I know why, but he does."

"He's nothing," Baby Cotwell growled.

Foster looked solemnly at the giant standing beside him. He said in a low voice, "Listen, you son of a bitch, I know what you thinking. I see you around that girl. You ever touch her, by God, I'll kill you."

Baby Cotwell sneered. He spit a laugh and walked off into the night, weaving among the tents. Foster saw the midget leap from a nearby table and waddle after the giant, like a dog following its master. Foster rolled his shoulders against a chill. He had not seen the midget huddled on the table, his body folded tight like a sleeping bat.

BEN DID NOT want to see Foster. Foster would be drunk. Foster would preen proudly, would tease him about the remarkable gift of Lottie Barton, would try to force him to drink more of the corn whiskey as celebration. Without meaning, or meanness, Foster would make him feel like a small boy. Most damning, Foster would believe he had taken the gift of Lottie as his initiation into manhood. If he told Foster the truth, if he said that he had left Lottie's tent without making love to her, Foster would be astonished, would think him a weakling, and he did not want Foster to turn against him.

Lottie would lie.

Lottie would tell Foster that she had done as he wished, and Foster would be happy.

Ben avoided the street of carnival tents, moving cautiously along a worn path at the tree line that surrounded Jericho. The path was a shortcut to the school and the playing fields and had been used by every child in the town for as long as Ben could remember. He and Milo had used it a thousand times. Maybe more, he guessed. He believed he could walk it blindfolded.

It was a dark night, the slivered moon dangling at treetop like a pale-bronze Christmas ornament. He could hear a soft babbling of voices from the carnival, sleepy, barely different from the voices of cicadas and owls and distant, barking dogs. The night smelled of summer, of field dust and honeysuckle and pine.

He would be glad when the carnival left, Ben thought. He did not believe he would see Foster and Lottie and the one-armed giant named Baby Cotwell again. Not seeing them would be best. To the people of Jericho, Foster and Lottie and Baby Cotwell were like outcasts. Being seen with them would create whispering gossip, and with his new job at Ledford's Dry Goods, Ben could not afford gossip.

He wondered if Foster or Lottie would talk about him to the townspeople the next day.

No, he thought. No.

He was near Ford Street, which led from James Howe's home to Main Street. A sound, like a footstep on dead leaves, popped behind him, and he turned. He saw nothing but the trunks of trees. A shiver rippled down the back of his arms and he shook them to shake away the odd chill. He turned back to the street. He could see a light burning in James Howe's house.

And then he heard the sound again, louder. He started to turn. The shadow of a tree seemed to move over him and a blow caught him in the back, low on his ribs. He could feel them breaking, feel the air of his lungs blowing through his mouth. He heard a sharp cackling laugh, a harsh cawing. A roiling purple bubble of pain exploded in his brain and then he lost consciousness.

BEN AWOKE TO pain in his back and in his face, and to a searing white light that hurt his eyes. The white light was the sun streaming through a window. He moved his head and a shock flew up the stem of his neck, making him gasp. He closed his eyes. He could feel puffed flesh on the left side of his face.

"Ben?"

It was his mother's voice.

He licked his lips, tried to speak, but could not.

"It's me, Ben. Your mother."

He moved his head in a slight, acknowledging nod. The pain in the stem of his neck was excruciating.

His mother's hands touched his face carefully. Her voice trembled: "Thank God you're alive."

Was it a surprise that he was alive? he wondered. If so, how near to death had he been?

"Some water? Do you want some water?"

His mouth was dry. He dipped his head once.

"All right, be still," his mother said anxiously. "I'm going to pour some on a cloth and let you suck from it. That way you won't have to sit up."

Ben could hear movement at the bed, then the sloshing of water. He heard his mother say, "Go tell the sheriff that he's awake, Elton."

He heard his father's mumbled reply, "Maybe I'd better wait a few minutes." The water-soaked cloth was on his lips.

"No," his mother commanded. "Go now."

He felt his father's hand on his own hand. "You'll be all right, son," his father said. "You'll be fine. Your mama's right here." He heard his father leave the room.

He took water from the cloth and listened to his mother's purring voice: "Just a little at a time, son. That's it. Good. Does it hurt to swallow?"

He shook his head weakly.

"Can you speak?" his mother asked.

Ben licked his lips again. He opened his eyes, blinked, tried to turn his head.

"You're at home, son, in your room," his mother told him.

He forced the words from his throat: "What—happened?"

The sound of his voice startled his mother. She squeezed the cloth involuntarily, dribbling water across Ben's chin. "I'm sorry," she said, quickly wiping at the water with the dry end of the towel.

"What happened?" she said as she fussed over him. "Somebody almost beat you to death, that's what happened. Most likely that no-good carnival crowd. The sheriff's been talking to them all day, but he'll not find out anything. A bunch like that, they stick together like fleas. A lie means nothing to that sorry lot."

Ben thought of Foster and Lottie, wondered if the sheriff would talk to them.

"Whoever it was, they meant to hurt you," his mother said. "The doctor said that."

A moving shadow blinked in Ben's memory and he heard shrill laughter and he knew that he had been attacked by Baby Cotwell and he knew that the midget he had seen at the carnival had cheered the attack.

His mother spoke rapidly, telling him the story of James Howe finding him, called out of his house by the braying of his dogs, and of the doctor's treatment and of the sheriff's questions.

"Sheriff said he didn't find your wallet on you," his mother said. "He thinks they must have seen you walking on the path and decided to rob you." She took the cloth from his mouth, dabbed it lightly over his forehead.

"You'll have to stay as still as you can for a while," his mother continued. "Doctor says you have some broken ribs, and maybe even a broken jaw." She paused, took the cloth away from him, sighed sadly. "Oh, my baby, your face—"

Ben wanted to ask about his face.

"I swear they were trying to kill you," his mother said. She took his hand, stroked it. "But you rest now. You rest. The sheriff will be here soon. He'll want to talk to you, but if you don't feel like it, you don't have to."

Ben blinked a nod, then closed his eyes. He could sense his mother moving away from the bed and he realized how well he knew the sounds in his room. His mother settled into the rocking chair that stayed in a corner of his room, but had been pulled close to the bed. She said in a low voice, "Try to sleep some, Ben. That's what you need, some rest. You need to rest."

And he did sleep.

WHEN HE AWOKE again, it was his father in the chair beside the bed. By the tilt and color of the light in the room, it was late day. The pain in his back and neck and face was not as fierce as it had been.

"Your mother's taking a nap," his father told him. "She was up all night, right here beside you. Couldn't pry her away."

Jack Rutland, the sheriff, had come and gone, his father said. And the doctor had also visited, leaving some ointments for his abrasions, and several neighbors who had heard the news, leaving food, and the preacher, leaving a prayer.

His father shifted closer to the bed. He added, "And, Ben, there's a man and a girl outside on the back porch — that one-legged fellow who's with the carnival. Says the girl is his sister. Says he won't leave until he knows you're all right and he can speak to you."

Foster, Ben thought. And Lottie.

"Why'd he come by?" asked Ben.

"Said he'd seen you play down in Augusta, and just wanted to pay his respects," his father answered. "Said there was talk all over the carnival about what happened, and the sheriff believed that somebody with them did it. Said he hoped his bragging on you yesterday didn't have anything to do with it."

His father paused for a moment. Ben could smell the face lotion his father used after shaving, a faint, sweet alcohol scent.

"You got any idea who did this to you, son?"

Ben did not answer for a moment. Then he lied: "No sir." He moved slightly in his bed. He could not tell his father about the one-armed giant and the midget. If the sheriff arrested him, Baby Cotwell would tell the truth of Foster and the set-up baseball hit, and maybe even about him being alone with Lottie — if he knew about it, and Ben believed that he did.

"I didn't see nobody," he added. And that was the truth. He had seen only the movement of a shadow and had heard the laughter of the midget. He had not seen anyone clearly.

"I can tell him you're all right, but you're not up to seeing anybody," his father said.

"No sir," Ben said. "Bring him in."

His father wagged his head in indecision. He started to speak, stopped. Ben knew his father. His father was a patient, forgiving man. He could not turn away Foster and Lottie, because Foster and Lottie had had the dignity and the bravery to appear at his home.

"All right," his father said. "But just for a minute." A tired smile crossed his face. "I get the feeling if I don't, he'll be moved in by morning. Besides, if I'm going to do it, I'd better do it now, while your mother's sleeping. If she wakes up and finds them loitering around, she'll be fit to be tied." He left the room.

A few minutes later, Ben could hear Foster's crutch-step in the hallway, a cautious walk, a walk taken from a warning.

The door opened and Foster and Lottie stepped inside, followed by his father.

"Just a couple of minutes now," his father said in a low voice.

"Yes sir," Foster said gravely.

His father stepped out of the room and closed the door. Would be standing guard against his mother, Ben reasoned.

Foster was dressed in a wrinkled black suit, with the right pants leg pinned up, and a yellowed white shirt buttoned to the neck. Lottie wore a full-length, misfitting white dress with long sleeves and a high neck. Borrowed, Ben thought. Yet she was remarkably pretty. Her bronze hair had been delicately combed.

Foster hobbled to the bed and looked down at Ben. "God-o-mighty," he whispered. He shook his head. "God-o-mighty," he said again.

Lottie stood behind Foster, a puzzled look of horror on her face.

"He did you a job, boy," Foster said.

"I guess," Ben said. "I've not seen it. I just feel it."

Foster leaned close. "I come to tell you he won't get by with it," he said softly. "Now, you get yourself well."

"I'll be all right," Ben said.

"I guess so, but you sure as God not gone be as handsome as you was."

Ben smiled and the smiling hurt his face. He moved his head to look at Lottie.

"You got a pretty home, Ben," Lottie said. Her eyes wandered over the room, memorizing it. "Prettiest one I ever saw."

"Thank you," Ben replied.

"We got to be going in a minute, Ben," Foster said. "I promised your daddy we'd just speak. Just didn't want to leave without seeing that you all right."

"Thanks," Ben said. "Where you going next?"

"I got to take Lottie home," Foster said. "Like I promised. But we going back to Tennessee first."

"What for?" asked Ben.

"I figure that's where Baby went to," Foster told him. "Probably hopped the train out this morning. Him and the midget. Took some of our money with him—mine and Lottie's. And, damn his soul, he took my bat. I paid good money for that bat. I got to get it back, and I got to square what he done to you."

"It's all right, Foster," Ben said. "You don't need to square anything for me."

Foster glanced toward the door, then back to Ben. "Well, now, Ben, the way I see it, what he done to you was about the same as doing it to me." He paused, narrowed his look at Ben. "You didn't tell nobody who it was, did you?"

"No," Ben said.

"Good," Foster mumbled. "You keep it to yourself." He pushed back on his crutches and nodded to Lottie. She stepped close to the bed, took Ben's hand in her own hands, then leaned over him and kissed him gently on the forehead.

"You take care of yourself, Ben Phelps," Lottie whispered.

"I will," Ben said.

"I'm glad I got to know you," she told him.

Ben nodded. "Me, too." He added, "I hope you get home soon."

Lottie smiled. A hollow smile. "Someday," she said. "Someday."

———

JACK RUTLAND HAD been sheriff of Caulder County for three terms. By count of years, he was sixty, yet by the amount of death he had seen in his life, he was ancient. He had joined the Confederate forces at the age of seventeen and had fought in the battle of Atlanta, falling with a saber cut across his chest in an assault of Union troops. The blood that had poured from him was enough to pronounce him dead, but a doctor—a Union doctor, Jack believed—had stitched him together in the vestibule of a church using sewing thread, and, miraculously, he had lived. A ragged, thread-pocked scar running from his left shoulder to his right hip was his badge of honor, he proudly declared.

As sheriff, Jack had enjoyed the most peaceful employment of his life. In twelve years there had been only three homicides in Caulder County, all over gambling disputes.

Now, he had a fourth.

On the morning after the Marvels of the Earth Exhibition had departed for Atlanta, Billy Moorehead, who was twelve, found the body of Baby Cotwell in a thick privet growth behind the fairgrounds. His skull had been crushed by the baseball bat used in the act that he and Foster had performed. Ben's missing wallet was discovered on the ground beside him, empty of money.

"I know you didn't do it, Ben," the sheriff said easily, standing beside Ben's bed, "but I thought I'd come by and tell you about it, and bring back your wallet. Sorry it's empty."

Ben wiggled his head against the pillow to acknowledge the sheriff. He thought of Foster, remembered Foster's promise to square what Baby Cotwell had done to him.

"Your daddy tells me his partner—that one-legged fellow—come by to see you," the sheriff continued.

Ben nodded again.

"Had his sister with him, is that right?"

"Yes sir," Ben whispered.

"You don't reckon he had anything to do with it, do you?"

Ben shook his head. "No sir."

"Don't guess I do, either," the sheriff said. "Don't see how a one-legged man could handle crutches and a baseball bat at the same time, not up against somebody as big as that one-armed fellow was." He paused, rocked his body in thought. "From what I been able to tell, that one-armed boy was hooked up with a midget. At least, that's what I was told when I did my asking around about who might of beat up on you."

"You think it was the midget?" asked Elton Phelps.

"Good a guess as any," the sheriff said. "One thing I do know: that one-armed boy had enough liquor in him to float a boat. He had his pants pulled down around his knees, like he was about to take a pee, and from the looks of things, he was hit on the knee with the bat we found, and that must of knocked him over, and then he was cracked in the head. If I was a midget and wanted to get a man down to my size, first thing I'd do is take his legs out from under him."

"Did anybody see anything?" Elton wanted to know.

"One or two people I talked to say they saw some of them carnival folks walking around in that area, but it was at night, and they couldn't tell one way or the other who they might have been. There was some tents set up back there, so I guess it could of been anybody."

Ben pushed his head against the pillow and swallowed hard. He thought of Foster's tent, and of Lottie, and he wondered if anyone had seen him go into the tent.

"What're you going to do about it?" Elton asked.

"Well, Elton, I guess I'm just going to forget it, unless the people of Caulder County want to pay me to go chase carnivals all over the country," the sheriff said slowly. "And to tell you the truth, them people's not worth it and I'm not up to it. They can go kill each other off and charge admission to it far as I'm concerned. And between me and you and Ben, here, I lean to every town having at least one crime that's never been solved. Gives people something to talk about." He looked down at Ben. "You take care of yourself, young fellow."

"Yes sir," Ben said hoarsely.

———

TWO MONTHS AFTER his beating, when the healing was complete, leaving him with a thin scar over his left eyebrow and an occasional sharp pain under the ribs in his back, Ben received a letter from Lottie containing a clipping out of a Knoxville, Tennessee, newspaper. The clipping was the story of the death of a carnival midget named Joseph Callahan, who had committed suicide by hanging in a hotel room.

Lottie's letter said:

Dear Ben Phelps

Foster found this in the newspaper up here and said send it to you. This was the midget that was with Baby. We heard about what happened to Baby down there. How somebody killed him. Foster said he would have done it if somebody else didnt. Me and Foster are sure sorry about the money they took from you. Foster said he wished he never had seen Baby. So do I. I was scared of him. I hope you are feeling better now. Foster said him to. We still with the carnival but Foster dont have the baseball show now. I make most of the money now. Maybe someday we will come back to where you live. You have a pretty house.

Lottie

Things were square, Ben thought.

He wondered if Foster would ever take Lottie home.

———————

THE LIE THAT Ben Phelps would share with only one person before his death—his feat against the one-armed giant named Baby Cotwell—quickly became part of the lore of Jericho, making Ben a perennial legend, a reseeded story that sprouted in warm, moist fields of tongues with the greening of spring and the playing of baseball. Each season, each time the story was told, a thin veneer of exaggeration was wrapped around it, like the sap rings of a tree, refining it as heroic history.

"Got himself almost killed because of it," the tongues remembered. "And then somebody come along and killed the man that beat him up, and they still don't know who done it."

Ben spoke reluctantly of the feat, calling it luck.

"Nobody's that lucky," the people said. "You hit him, Ben. By God, you did, and nobody else even come close."

"Well, I guess I did at that," he admitted sheepishly.

Only when young boys of the town surrounded him on the streets and asked him about it would Ben retell the lie that made him uncomfortable, but the lie he could not forget.

"It was a curveball," he would say. "I saw it making its break and I remembered what they'd taught me down in Augusta about pulling my hands in a little bit, just to keep the bat on the ball."

The boys would gaze at him in wide-eyed amazement, picturing Ben as David and the one-armed giant as Goliath, and Ben would tell them that any of them could do the same thing. All they had to do was to keep trying on their own, and to remember that hitting a baseball was more work than dream.

The boys could see David hoisting the head of Goliath by the hair, blood dripping from the bottom of his neck, with the fowls of the air and the beasts of the fields waiting to devour the flesh of the Philistine.

"Show us how," the boys would beg.

And Ben would take one of their bats and swing at an imaginary ball, and he would talk of the advice that Arnold Toeman, the manager of the Augusta Hornets, had given him.

"I guess he knew more about baseball than anybody I ever met," Ben would say. "But the best thing I learned from him was, 'Do it again.' That's why Milo Wade is so good. Doing it over and over, until he got it down right."

To the boys, Milo Wade was a god, someone who had left their town and made it to Boston to play with the big leaguers in less than a year. They played on the same playing fields that Milo Wade had played on, their feet touching the same earth that Milo Wade's feet had touched. Yet Milo Wade was not among them; Ben Phelps was. Some of them had even watched Ben against the giant—David against Goliath—and among the eager boys who surrounded Ben on the street, they were counted as the privileged.

Over time, with season following season, Ben became so accustomed to the retelling of the story there were moments when even he believed in the legacy of splendor that Foster Lanier had created for him.

Foster had given him a gift.

No, two gifts.

He could not forget Lottie Barton.

Each spring he thought of Lottie and the train ride from Augusta. And he thought of Lottie and the amber-lighted tent.

Sometimes the memory of Lottie was heavy with guilt and shame, and sometimes it was distant, as though faded under the sun of many years, and he thought of her tenderly. Occasionally, without prompting by memory, he dreamed of her in the tent, dreamed of her earth scent and the amber light bathing her amber body, or he dreamed of her sitting on the porch of her home in Augusta, with her sister in a nearby chair, numbly gazing at the Savannah River. And in the dream of the river, her prettiness had faded and a sadness rested permanently in her face.

And Foster. He thought often of Foster. Once, in his unexpected dream of Lottie, he saw Foster with her, sitting in her sister's chair.

He wondered if Foster had killed the one-armed giant named Baby Cotwell before leaving Jericho.

SECRETLY, IF UNEASILY, Ben welcomed the annual story about the one-armed giant. It was the only break in what he thought of as the monotony of his life.

Yet the monotony was deliberate.

It was not easy for Ben to harbor a lie. His parents had taught him that a person too full of himself would surely make a slip and the lie would bring him down like one of those graven-image idols God was always smashing to bits in the Old Testament.

Ben did not want to shatter like a hollow-clay doll. His life was as carefully walked as a soldier on parade. Day after day, the same.

And it was all right, Ben believed. It was not a bad life. He was not isolated. People seemed to like him. If life did not change for him, he would not regret being who he was.

From 1904 until July 7, 1910, only three things intruded memorably on the monotony of his life.

On August 17, 1907, his father died of a sudden, violent heart seizure, a seizure so unexpected that he and his mother remained dazed over it, as though it might have been a dream that both had had, simultaneously. His father had been a strong, robust, happy man, a man whose smile was so permanently fixed on his face he smiled even in sleep.

In 1908, a reporter from the *Atlanta Constitution* named Ollie Miles arrived in Jericho to do a story on Milo Wade. Cliff Allen, the high school principal, directed the reporter to Ledford's Dry Goods, telling him, "Go talk to Ben Phelps. He knows more about Milo Wade than anybody alive, and that includes the Boston Red Sox." The interview had left Ben trembling with excitement and with a restlessness that tormented his dreams for weeks. Ben clipped the story and placed it in a scrapbook that he kept on Milo. Occasionally he read it, and the dreams would return. The man he had described for Ollie Miles was not simply Milo Wade, but the man that he, Ben Phelps, yearned to be.

In 1909, two days before Christmas, in the storeroom of Ledford's Dry Goods, Sally Ledford, sixteen years old, confessed to Ben that she loved him. Her words—whispered, trembling—left Ben weak and terrified and speechless. During the five years of his employment at Ledford's, he had barely noticed her darting-around presence. She was merely the daughter of his employer, a child growing into womanhood, promising beauty.

"I don't want to scare you off, Ben," Sally said bravely. "I just want you to know how I feel, how I've been feeling since I was thirteen, I guess."

Because he was standing near a doorway with mistletoe tacked to the top of the doorjamb, Sally tried to kiss him. Ben turned his face against her breath — warm, peppermint-scented — and her kiss was on the corner of his mouth.

"Are you afraid of me or my daddy?" Sally asked.

"Both," Ben answered honestly.

"I'll leave you alone, if that's what you want," Sally said softly.

"I — I got to think about it," Ben told her.

On Christmas Eve, he accompanied Sally to the Methodist church after giving his mother a stammering excuse about Sally tormenting him over the merits of the Methodist choir. "I told her I'd go hear them if she'd just quit trying to make them out to be better than the Presbyterians," Ben told his mother. "I promised I'd walk her over to the service," he added in a failed attempt at being nonchalant.

Everyone gathered at the Jericho Methodist church to celebrate the birth of Christ — including the entire nativity ensemble of Joseph, Mary, the doll Jesus, three Wise Men, and several shepherds — paused in stunned silence when Ben followed Sally down the aisle to sit in the pew beside her mother and father. Sally would later say to Ben, "It was like they were watching the Christmas star. I've never felt anything that special."

To Ben, it was like being before a firing squad.

At first, it was that way.

In February of 1910, again in the storeroom of Ledford's Dry Goods, he impulsively kissed Sally.

The Christmas star exploded inside him, and the plodding, dull routine of his life became a blur of day speeding into day, the time that he wanted to be with Sally colliding with the time that he was with her. His mind hummed with thoughts of her, and also with thoughts of Arthur Ledford watching them. He was not sure how

Arthur Ledford viewed the blatant affection his only child had for him. It would not be wise to toy with such affections, not under the constant gaze of a father who was also his employer.

At night, in his room, Ben wrote poems to Sally, sketched her likeness on paper, gazed out the window of his room to find the north star. The north star, Sally had proclaimed, was the star of her destiny. "As long as you can see it, you can see me," she had cooed to Ben late one afternoon. "Just look, Ben. Just look." And it was so. He could see her in the north star. The star had her brightness. He could breathe deeply, could feel the star's heat, the roiling firestorm of its light, warming his chest, and the gladness of it filled him.

And, at last, he could no longer keep secret what everyone knew, but had stayed quiet about.

"What would you think of Sally Ledford as a daughter-in-law?" he asked his mother two days after Sally's seventeenth birthday in June.

His mother smiled radiantly. "Nothing would make me happier," she said.

"I like to see you happy," Ben told his mother. "But it's nothing definite. I just wanted to know what you thought about it. Don't go talking about it."

"Not until you tell me I can," his mother promised.

At the Fourth of July celebration in Jericho, an evening of barbecue and drumbeat music and fireworks and field games, Sally said to Ben in a purring, dreamy voice, "I want it to be always like this."

"Don't know why it won't be," Ben said confidently.

A skyrocket exploded over the fairground.

"I don't want it to be like that," Sally said.

"It won't," Ben replied.

He did not know about the letter that had already been posted in Beimer, Kentucky.

ON THURSDAY, JULY 7, 1910, almost six years after the Marvels of the Earth Exhibition had boarded train cars for another city, Ben opened a letter addressed to:

BEN PHELPS
BASEBALL PLAYER
JERICHO, GEORGIA

The letter was from Lottie:

Dear Ben Phelps

Foster said for me to write you. Make it to Ben Phelps baseball player Foster said. Maybe you never got the story but me and Foster was married. Five years ago I guess it was. We had us a little boy. Hes three years. We named him Ben. Its what Foster wanted and I liked it. Foster said for me to write to you and say we live in Kentucky now. Its a place called Beimer. Hes sick and he wants me to tell you to come up to see him. Hes got something to say to you and he wants to say it when hes looking at you. I know its a long way off from where you live but I sure hope you can come. Foster says you are the only person he wants to see. Its a pretty place where we live. It gets cold in the wintertime but I dont much mind. I hope you can come up soon.

Your friend
Lottie Lanier

The letter deeply affected Ben. There was sadness in the news of Foster Lanier's illness—still young, in his thirties—and there was fondness in the memory of Lottie.

Ben had never told anyone about Lottie. He could have bragged suggestively of the night with her, as other men bragged of their nights with easy women, but he did not. He did not think of Lottie

as an easy woman, but as a girl going home. It did not matter to
Ben how many men Lottie had taken in a dimly lighted tent. She
was a gentle person, a good person.

And maybe that was why Foster had married her, Ben thought.
Foster must have had great needs. It must have been hard for Foster
Lanier, the great baseball player, a man recognized by strangers on
trains, to follow the carnival as a one-legged freak. Maybe Lottie had
believed him when he told her he loved her, and maybe she had
made him happy. Maybe she had taken Foster into the tent one
night, in some small town, and Foster had realized that Lottie was
all he needed, or wanted. Maybe it had happened that way, in a
fingersnap, like a religious healing. And maybe the son — Ben, the
son — had helped Foster forget his bitterness.

Other than Sally, or his mother, Lottie was probably the best
woman he would ever know, Ben thought. Foster was lucky. Foster
had Lottie.

Ben read the letter again and a dark loneliness settled over him.

THAT NIGHT, IN a small office he had fashioned for himself in the
storeroom of Ledford's Dry Goods, Ben sat at a rolltop desk and
wrote a letter to Lottie. He was sorry about Foster's illness, he wrote.
Foster had been good to him, a special friend. Foster had helped
him get over the hurt of not playing baseball. And he was glad about
Foster and Lottie being married and having a baby, and it was a
good feeling to have that baby named Ben, in his honor.

Yes, he wrote, he would make arrangements as soon as possible
for a trip to Kentucky to see Foster, as Foster wished. It would require
a few days of planning, but he would do it.

Most likely a week or two, he suggested.

As soon as possible.

In fact, he added, perhaps he would make the trip to Kentucky a
part of an excursion he had been planning for many years, a visit to

Boston, where he would see his boyhood friend Milo Wade play baseball for the Boston Red Sox. It would be a roundabout trip, but he did not mind.

Foster would remember Milo Wade, Ben wrote.

Things were going well for him, Ben included in the letter. A new granite quarry had been opened between Jericho and Athens and a lot of people — many of them Italian — had moved to the area to work the granite from the earth. His job was probably the best in Jericho, he suggested, and the way it looked, he would be running the store one day. And there was a girl he was seeing. Her name was Sally Ledford, the daughter of his employer. She was seven years younger than he, but very nice, the kind of girl that both Lottie and Foster would like. Might even be a wedding in the future. Near future.

Thank you for writing me about Foster. He's a great man.

BEN WALKED HOME in the hot summer evening, the odor of cut grass heavy in the watery glue of the humidity. He thought of his suggestion to Lottie that he would visit Milo Wade in Boston. It was an old boast, one freely offered to men who stopped in Ledford's Dry Goods, or took lunch at Brady's Cafe, or played baseball on the town team. Though Milo had never returned to Jericho after his parents' move to Athens, Ben had been faithful to the train-station promise he had made in Augusta and again in Jericho: he had followed Milo's career with a devotion that was maniacal. Each week during the baseball seasons, Ben monitored reports of the Boston Red Sox, carefully averaging Milo's at bats and hits in leather-bound record books. It was a solemn ritual exercised each Sunday afternoon in the privacy of the storeroom in Ledford's Dry Goods. Closed on Sundays, Ledford's was quiet, empty, the perfect place for ritual.

Each month, he wrote Milo a letter noting his tabulations — his tabulations, not the lies of sportswriters and faceless official scorekeepers.

Once, he had received a brief letter of appreciation from the business office of the Red Sox, and he treasured the letter. Milo had instructed them to write, he believed. Milo had not forgotten when they played baseball together in Jericho and in Augusta.

"One of these days, I'm going to Boston to see him," Ben said to the men who prodded him with questions about Milo.

"When, Ben?" the men asked.

"Someday, when I can work it out, I'm going," was Ben's answer.

Each year, Ben spoke of someday, and each year he took the excuse of pressing business, too little time. He had not seen Milo Wade in six years, had not heard from him. He knew only facts — that Milo had married a woman named Mary Bishop, that he played baseball with passion that was vicious and dangerous but brilliant, that he lived in Boston in the off-season, and that he rarely returned to the South until the spring training season.

Other than the facts, there were the rumors. Milo Wade, the writers of sports stories contended, was a madman, despised by his teammates and by opponents. He tried to hurt anyone who challenged him, fought with spectators, bullied game officials. And there were people in Jericho who believed the stories and made shaking-head opinions that had Milo betraying his refined Southern heritage and becoming a ruffian in Boston.

"He must of changed," they said gravely.

"Don't care if he never comes back here, if he's turned out that way," they said.

"He may know how to play ball, but he's not much of a man, the way he seems to be acting," they said.

"Hard not to be ashamed of him, if he's doing what they writing about," they said. "And him having such good folks."

Ben heard the comments and argued about them. "You can't believe all of that. Most of it reads like it was made up, if you ask me."

The people smiled patiently, knowing of Ben's boyhood with Milo. "Maybe you're right, Ben," they said.

To Ben, Milo was a player who gave and took in wars with men who were mercenaries, whose hire was for a season of victories and defeats, tallied and divided like pirate loot. Those who were the mightiest earned advertisements of their deeds in colorful stories written by imaginative men fond of hyperbole. The mightiest were giants, larger than life. Powerful. Indestructible.

Milo Wade was one of the mightiest.

And there was something else for Ben. Milo Wade was the magnification of what he might have become — should have become. In Augusta, the difference had been an inch or less — the space of a swinging bat missing a thrown baseball. Ben had been faster than Milo, faster than any of them. He had listened eagerly, learned quickly. He had tried. God in heaven, he had tried. He had been liked by his teammates. Yet he had failed. An inch of space. A half-inch. A quarter-inch. He had failed by such fractions of space, it seemed impossible to believe.

AT HOME, AFTER he had put away the letter he had written to Lottie, Ben ate his supper in a troubled mood that his mother had learned to tolerate with patience. She asked him, after a long silence, "Are you all right, Ben?"

"Just tired," Ben told her. "I had some things to take care of at the store."

"That why you're late?"

"I had some business correspondence to catch up on," Ben said.

His mother studied him closely. She knew he was not telling the truth, but she knew also that the lie was not dangerous. "How's Sally?" she asked.

"All right," Ben said. "I didn't see her today. Her mother's been sick again."

"I'm sorry to hear that," his mother said. "But I'm glad she's got Sally to help out. She's such a fine young lady."

Ben did not reply.

"Of course, when she's married, she won't be around so much."

"Mama, she's just seventeen, and barely that," Ben said.

"I was married at seventeen," his mother replied.

"Well, she's not," Ben said. He paused over his food, thought of Sally, and a smile that he tried to hide warmed his face. "Not yet," he added.

His mother pried gently. "You sure nothing happened? You look like you're upset."

"Nothing, Mama."

"Well, tomorrow'll be better," his mother said enthusiastically. "Always think that tomorrow'll be better, Ben."

"Maybe it will, Mama. Maybe it will."

ε I $\mathcal{G}$ $\mathcal{H}$ $\mathcal{T}$

FOR FIVE DAYS, Ben said nothing of the trip he would take.

He knew he would not go to Boston.

Boston would be his deception.

He would tell his mother and Arthur Ledford and Sally that he was going to Boston, because he could not tell them about Foster, about Lottie and the baby named Ben. They would not understand. They would lecture him sternly about the foolishness of such a trip, so far away to the backwoods of Kentucky, to see people they did not know and could only imagine as being low-class.

Even the lie about going to Boston would cause argument, Ben realized. Yet it was an argument he believed he could win. Milo Wade was in Boston, and Milo Wade was a part of his life. Everyone understood that. Everyone.

Each night, after work, he sat at his desk in his storeroom office and reread the letter from Lottie, and he studied train schedules and maps. On the maps, Ben had circled major train stops—Athens, Atlanta, Chattanooga, Nashville. From Nashville, he would go into

Kentucky, toward Bowling Green. He would depart the train at Bei-mer, only a few miles across the Tennessee border, and there he would find someone to direct him to the place where Foster lived.

He did not know how long he would be with Foster—a day, he reasoned. A day should be enough. And then he would return to Atlanta and stay another day, maybe two. Long enough not to inspire questions about the time needed to go to Boston and return.

He knew he would be asked about Milo Wade by the townspeo-ple. Had he seen Milo? Had they had supper? Had Milo introduced Ben to teammates? Ben guessed at the questions and made up an-swers. He and Milo never had a chance to talk person-to-person, he would say, but he was pretty sure Milo waved to him in the stands and made some signals that he could not understand. Mainly, though, the mix-ups were the fault of the office people for the Boston Red Sox.

It would not be hard to cover questions about Milo Wade, Ben believed.

On the map, a large black dot represented Boston, with a pen drawing of an ancient sailing ship anchored in its harbor. The At-lantic Ocean dipped against the dot, floating the ship, and Ben imag-ined foam-capped water slapping beneath piers.

Someday he would go to Boston, he thought.

Someday he would see foam-capped water beneath piers and ships on the ocean, and he would see Milo Wade.

ON THE SIXTH day after receiving Lottie's letter, Ben requested per-mission from Arthur Ledford to be excused from work for the fol-lowing week.

It was late afternoon. Only one customer—Beatrice Windom—was in the store, deliberating over the purchase of a new hat. Sally Ledford was waiting on her, enduring her annoying chatter.

He wanted to go to Boston, Ben said in a low, polite voice to Arthur Ledford, to see Milo Wade.

Arthur looked at Ben with a frown.

"I don't expect to be paid for it," Ben told him.

"Well, Ben, I don't think I need to remind you that you've got a job," Arthur said patiently. "When I hired you, it was because I needed you. Nothing's changed about that."

It was exactly what Ben had expected to hear.

"Mr. Ledford," Ben said, "I've worked for you for six years, six days a week, and only missed nine days of work, six of them when I was beat up and three of them when my daddy died."

"Now, Ben, how many days do you think I've missed?" Arthur asked.

"Yes sir, but it's your place of business. I only work here."

Arthur nodded. "That's true enough. What do you think your father would have said about this?"

"I think he'd be happy to see me go, sir. He knew me and Milo were friends."

"I think you're wrong," Arthur suggested tactfully. "I think your father would have put his foot down. I think he would have called it a waste of time and money."

Ben did not reply.

"What about Margaret? Have you talked to your mother?" Arthur asked.

"No sir. Not yet. I plan to do that tonight."

Arthur did a half-turn away from Ben. He looked across the store to Sally. Sally's smile was radiant. She seemed to be on tiptoe, like a ballerina. He turned back to Ben. "What about Sally? Does she know about this?"

"No sir."

"Why not?"

"Well, sir, I just don't think she'd understand it."

"I think you're probably right about that," Arthur said.

"Yes sir," Ben replied quietly. "It's—well, it's just something I always wanted to do and I thought I'd do it before—well, sir, before getting on with my life."

Arthur's eyes narrowed with suspicion.

"I guess maybe I take after my daddy," Ben added. "I know he took a train trip to Washington, D.C., when he was about my age. I guess I just want to go a few miles more up the track."

"I don't remember your father doing anything like that," Arthur said.

"It was right before he got married, the way I understand it," Ben said.

Arthur's lower lip curled and he began to scrape it with his upper teeth, a habit that telegraphed a test of his patience. He said to Ben, "Well, I guess we're at a stalemate. If you want to do this, then it's up to you. But I'll have to let you go and bring somebody else in to take your place if you do."

Ben dipped his head. "Yes sir," he said meekly.

Arthur mumbled something Ben did not understand, then walked across the store toward Sally and Beatrice Windom. "That hat looks nice on you, Beatrice," he said in a pleasant voice.

Ben watched the play between Beatrice Windom and Arthur Ledford. It was as old and as rehearsed as a scene from a play. He saw Sally glance toward him, flick a shy smile. He ducked his head and began to rearrange shirts on a display table. The face of his father flashed in his mind.

Arthur Ledford had wept openly at the funeral of his father, calling him a man of principle and fair play, a man he had used as a model for his own life.

"If you ever need to talk to somebody, man to man, you come to me," Arthur had said to Ben at the gravesite. "I know I'm not your father, but I'll try my best to fill in when you need it."

Ben turned and walked to the back of the store, to the storeroom and the storeroom office he had created for himself. The office was not an office, only a cleaned-out place with an old rolltop desk and a chair. The one expensive item in the room was a desk lamp with a large frosted globe that had a design of grapes circling it. He had bought the lamp with his own money.

He filled a box with personal items — his father's photograph, the record books on Milo Wade, the letter from Lottie, a watch fob given to him by Sally, his train schedules and maps — and he pulled down the desktop and locked it and left the key on the lip of the desk.

Sally stopped him as he walked through the store with his box of personal items.

"Ben," she said. "Where are you going?"

He paused, let his eyes sweep the store. "To Boston," he told her.

"Boston?"

Ben nodded, then he walked out of the store.

AT HIS HOME, Ben placed the box on the kitchen table.

"What's that?" asked his mother.

"Some things I've been keeping at the store," Ben answered.

"Why did you bring them home?'

Ben looked at his mother. "Because I'm not working there any longer."

His mother's face turned pale. She touched her throat with her hand. "What?" she whispered. "What — happened?"

"I asked Mr. Ledford about having a few days off," Ben said. "He said if I took them, I wouldn't have a job."

His mother sat heavily in a chair. "Days off? Why, Ben?"

"I want to go to Boston to see Milo play ball."

"But, Ben—"

"I've worked six years and just missed nine days time," Ben said firmly. "It's not asking for much."

"But, Ben, you've got to have a job," his mother said desperately. "Your father's will left us well off enough, but a man needs to have a job. You can't just walk out on Mr. Ledford. He's been good to you all these years."

"Yes ma'am," Ben said. "I know that. But I've worked for every penny, as hard as I would have if it was my own store."

"Does Sally know?" his mother asked.

"I told her," Ben answered.

"You know how Arthur is, Ben," his mother whimpered. "He may not let you see Sally again, and even if he would, Alice probably wouldn't."

"Mama, that's up to Sally, I guess," Ben said wearily. "If we ever get married, it'll be her I'm going to marry, not her daddy or her mama. She might as well know that now."

His mother put the palms of her hands together in a begging gesture. "Why now, Ben? Why do you want to go see Milo now?"

Ben looked away, through the window. He did not like deceiving his mother, but it was necessary. "I've been waiting a long time," he said. "I just keep feeling that time's running out." He swallowed away the shame that he could taste.

Margaret Phelps sat in silence, gazing at her son. He seemed more boy than man. She had heard the stories of his boast about going to Boston. Fence gossip. The laughing kind of tale that mothers often passed among themselves concerning something their children had said, or done. Ben planning to go to Boston was no more than that, the gossipers lightly suggested. A childish thing. When it got out that he had given up a good job to chase after a dream, he would always be treated with snickering. She could not let him live with such indignity, even if she had to lie.

"Ben, I want to tell you something I should have told you long ago," she said.

Ben looked at her quizzically.

"Before your father died, he talked to me about taking you to Boston," his mother continued. "He was keeping it as a surprise."

"He did?" Ben said.

"Yes."

Ben sat in a chair at the table. He shook his head in disbelief. "I wish I'd known."

"It's my fault," his mother said. "If he'd lived, it would've happened by now. But I know he'd still be happy if you went by yourself, so I want to know when you want to leave."

"I was thinking next week," Ben told her. "But as soon as I can."

"Tomorrow?" asked his mother.

Ben nodded yes.

"Good," his mother said. She stood. "See to what you need. We'll pack when I get back."

"Where are you going?"

"Out."

"You're not going to see Mr. Ledford, are you?"

His mother turned to him. "Only for a minute."

"Mama—"

Margaret Phelps moved past her son and out the door.

SHE WALKED WITH her shoulders erect, her face lifted, her arms swinging free, and she realized that she was not carrying her purse or wearing a hat. A flutter of gladness trembled across her chest. She could not remember walking into town without carrying a purse or wearing a hat—not since childhood.

She had read a story about a women's march for suffrage and remembered the name the women were called—suffragettes—and that was how she felt. A suffragette in march step, but not for the right to vote. The right to be a mother, perhaps. Her face was damp from the heat of the July breeze, and she drew her left index finger across her cheek, beneath her eye, rubbing away the moisture. She could feel perspiration at her neck, clinging to the white shirtwaist she wore.

She wondered how Arthur Ledford would react when she stepped into his store and asked to see him privately. He would be unnerved, she believed. He had always been tentative around her, even from their childhood together. Once, when they were very young, Arthur had tried to kiss her, and she had pushed him away. He had seldom looked directly at her since that day, even through the years of friendship that he had shared with her late husband. Secretly, she had always thought of his lookaway behavior as humorous, and had occasionally teased him about it, causing him to blush. The truth was, Arthur Ledford was a handsome man with impeccable credentials. He would have been a good choice for a husband, and she would have put herself in the path of his search if she had not fallen in love with Elton Phelps. Now, she pitied Arthur. He had married Alice Barber, and Alice Barber Ledford was a hateful, complaining woman. Everyone in Jericho knew the only thing that qualified as marriage between Arthur and Alice was Sally, their daughter, and she was far more the child of her father than the child of her mother.

She paused at the door of Ledford's Dry Goods. Across the street, she saw Frances Yerby going into Merriweather's Furniture and Appliance holding the hands of her five-year-old twin sons—Luke and Linton. The boys moved with her like listless shadows. Frances deserved sympathy, she thought. A sorry, quarrelsome husband, twin boys given to illness and injury. She wondered what sort of malady the twins were now suffering. Something. Later, after Ben left for Boston, she would call on Frances, she decided.

She stood for a moment, composing herself. She could feel the heat on her face. She inhaled deeply, then opened the door and stepped inside.

Sally and Arthur were behind the counter, talking. They turned in unison, surprised.

"Margaret," Arthur said uncomfortably.

"I want to speak with you, Arthur," Margaret told him. "Privately, if you don't mind."

Arthur looked away. "All right," he said.

"I've—got some things to do in the storeroom," Sally said timidly.

"It won't take but a minute, Sally," Margaret said.

Sally smiled a worried smile, then rushed away.

Margaret crossed the store to the counter. Arthur kept his eyes from her. He drummed nervously on the countertop with a pencil.

"Arthur, look at me," Margaret insisted.

He looked up. An expression of embarrassment clouded his face.

"I've come to tell you that my son is going to Boston," Margaret said calmly, "and when he returns, the job that he's had for six years will still be here."

———

HIS MOTHER WORRIED about him riding on a train.

There were train wrecks every day, she had said in a woeful voice. People killed by the thousands. Always something in the newspapers about it.

"Remember what I've told you about your great-uncle Abner?" his mother had asked.

Yes, he remembered. His mother had told the story often, with such dramatic intensity it left the impression that she had been on the scene, and the sight of it was seared permanently into her memory. "The most horrible death imaginable," she would say at the conclusion of each telling. "Just horrible." And she would bow her head and close her eyes and sigh like a stage actress. Sometimes she would whisper, "Horrible," a final time.

Abner Phelps had been killed in Pennsylvania in a train wreck in January of 1878, when a brushfire burned into cross ties and shifted the rails and the train tumbled down an embankment into a creek. A coal-burning stove in Abner Phelps's passenger car had broken apart, spewing fire, and all the passengers had died in the blaze.

Trains were not safe, his mother had declared.

"I'll be fine, Mama," Ben had said. "It's nineteen ten. They don't have coal-burning stoves on the trains I'll be taking. Anyhow, it's July, not January."

"I won't sleep until you're home," his mother had vowed.

He was dressed in a dark brown, well-tailored three-button suit cuffed at the sleeves and pants. He wore a matching vest over a high-collar shirt and a stylish tie. A new chocolate-colored felt hat with a narrow brim rested at a tilt on his head. His shoes were polish-bright. He had the look of a garment salesman setting off to invade a new territory, or of a politician on the speech circuit.

Inside the suitcase on the seat beside him were three additional shirts, two older pairs of trousers, another pair of shoes — broken-in and comfortable — underwear, socks, handkerchiefs, toothbrush, shaving needs, writing materials, Lottie's letter, an assortment of sandwiches his mother had prepared, and, in an envelope, money he had secretly put away, week by week, in a clothes trunk. He had no specific reason for saving it, other than habit, but now was glad for the habit.

In another envelope, kept in the inside pocket of his suit coat with his travel schedule, he had a letter from Sally, a letter written late at night and riskily delivered to the front door of his home. His mother had discovered the letter when she opened the door. The message was simple:

Ben, I love you. I'm sorry about how Daddy acted. I don't want you to go away, but if you do, I want you to come home to me. I already miss you. I already hurt so much I can hardly breathe.

The letter had made him ache, made him want to stay. He loved Sally Ledford. Knew that he did. Sally dazzled him, made him feel awkward, out of control, the same emotions he had heard others describe when they talked of being in love. He had lingered on the platform of the train depot, believing she would appear to tell him goodbye, to embrace him in public. Perhaps kiss him.

She did not appear.

He licked his lips over the thought of the kiss, imagined the sweet, peppermint heat of her mouth. A single glad heartstroke drummed in his chest and throat, and he swallowed it and swallowed also the imagined heat of Sally's mouth.

He sat near a window, resting comfortably, gazing at the scenery that seemed to move dizzily past the window. He knew that he, not the scenery, was moving, but he liked the thought of sitting still and having the countryside zip past the train window. It was like being on a merry-go-round at some carnival, riding to the thundering sound of the engine and the rhythmic clicking of wheels over rails, and, occasionally, the high, shrill scream of the steam whistle. Once his father had told him in secret that he had always wanted to be a railroad man, but knew better than to suggest it publicly. Uncle Abner's death, his father had lamented, had chilled any fancy he might have had for riding trains for a living. "Your mother would never have put up with it," his father had said in a voice that fathers used with sons when the story being told was mixed with humor or with cloudy instruction.

He leaned his head against the headrest of the seat and thought of his mother. She had marched off to Ledford's Dry Goods with so much righteous anger it steamed from her, and she had returned home as a one-woman parade, with the gladness of music and song curling from her voice, and with the promise of Ben's job when he returned from Boston.

Later, when the euphoria of her bravery had subsided, she had begun her anguish over Ben's long train ride.

"I just know I'm going to dream about Uncle Abner," she had said woefully.

It was Ben who had dreamed of Uncle Abner. A dream of fire and screams. A dream so vivid it might have been a premonition.

He took his written-out travel schedule from his coat pocket and studied it. Athens and Atlanta in Georgia, Chattanooga and Nashville in Tennessee, Beimer in Kentucky. And between them, so many stops at so many small·places. He had sketched out a crude map from the atlas, and he touched the names with his fingertip, following the pen line of his drawing. He would travel through late afternoon and night before reaching Beimer in midmorning.

Across the aisle, he saw a man and a woman and a girl, perhaps thirteen or fourteen. Farm people, Ben thought. They wore washed-thin Sunday clothing, with an after-rain scent of lye soap that was suspended faintly in the train car. The man and woman sat statue-erect, motionless, a glazed expression in their unblinking eyes. Ben knew it was the first time they had been on a train. Could tell by the way they sat, by the way they did not seem to breathe, as though the great speed of the train had siphoned the air from their lungs. The girl was not afraid. She wiggled restlessly in her seat and gazed in wonder at the illusion of the moving countryside.

He thought of Lottie.

So long ago.

So long ago.

The girl in the aisle across from him laughed sharply, suddenly, her face glowing. Her head turned against the motion of the train, and she watched wide-eyed as something remarkable, or humorous, disappeared from sight. Her parents did not move.

There would be a thirty-minute stop at the Athens depot for

adding freight, the conductor announced. It was all right to get off the train, he conceded, but anybody wandering too far away would be left if he didn't pay attention to the time.

Ben saw the man and woman across from him glance at one another in confusion.

"Let's get off," the girl said.

"We're not there yet," the man said gruffly. "Best to stay put to we get there."

"Where you headed?" Ben asked.

The man looked at him suspiciously.

"I'm going up into Kentucky," Ben said.

"We going as far as Chattanooga," the man answered. Ben recognized the faint trace of an accent—German, he thought.

"That's a pretty long way to go," Ben replied. "Where'd you get on?"

"Down to Augusta," the man said. "We come from down near there."

Ben stood. "Well, I think I'll stretch my legs a minute. Don't like getting too cramped on one of these things. Makes it feel a little funny trying to walk on the ground again, after you been on a train a long time. A little like having sea legs." He tipped his fingers to his hat and left the train.

There were many people in the Athens depot. Passengers and well-wishers, businessmen, train workers. The noise of voices rode over the hiss of steam. A small commissary sold coffee and cakes, and Ben pressed himself in the line of buyers, bought a coffee and a cake, and found an out-of-the-way place to have his refreshments and still be close to the train.

The talk around him was lively.

Spirited debate over the vote to ratify a federal income tax.

Men in awe of Barney Oldfield driving a Blitzen Benz more than one hundred and thirty miles an hour at Daytona Beach.

Matching stories about seeing the rooster tail of Halley's Comet.

Declarations of surprise over the recent parade in Athens by the Colored Knights of Pythias, a spectacle unlike anything ever witnessed by the city's citizenry.

Laughs spewing up from a knot of men talking in whispers, and Ben knowing that a traveling salesman's joke had been told.

It was talk that Ben never heard in Jericho. In Jericho — especially in Ledford's Dry Goods — conversations were guarded, and as repetitious as a parrot's jabbering.

He saw the man and woman and young girl exit the train. The man stepped tentatively onto the platform, stood for a moment, tested the weight of his body on the wood flooring, then took a careful, comical step, his face furrowed in worry. Ben smiled. He knew he had frightened the man into believing it would be impossible to walk on firm ground after riding in a train. He turned his face. He did not want the man to see him, to see the smile. It would be embarrassing to the man.

On the wall of the depot, Ben saw a poster promoting the reelection of Martin Wade to the state senate. The pen-and-ink drawing of Martin Wade showed the face of a darkly serious man, a brooding man. His mother had said to Ben, "If the train stops long enough in Athens, you should try to see Martin and Christine Wade, or call them on their telephone. Maybe they could tell you how to get in touch with Milo in Boston."

Ben did not want to see the Wades, or to talk with them.

The Wades were like occasional memories — distant and vague. Ben had always been uncomfortable in their presence, and from the pieced-together gossip that had wandered into Ledford's Dry Goods over the past six years, Martin Wade had changed since being elected a state senator. "I could have told you," the people said as they accused Martin Wade of an arrogance that many people in Jericho had always suspected. Or said they had. Ben had learned from working in Ledford's that many people had the gift of knowing when the knowing was obvious and safe enough to say aloud.

He heard the call for the train.

The man and the woman and the young girl rushed back across the platform of the depot, the man pushing the woman and the girl in front of him like someone guiding a cart or a wheelbarrow.

Ben smiled again. He liked the man and the woman and the girl. They were not arrogant. They were merely going to Chattanooga, Tennessee, probably on a mission that involved family. A simple trip, yet it would be one of the most unforgettable experiences of their lives.

It was like the trip he had taken from Augusta, on the night that he met Lottie Barton.

Ben stepped into the train, found his seat, nodded to the man. The man returned the nod, then set himself rigid, waiting for the train to move.

Between Athens and Atlanta, Ben wrote two letters—one to his mother, one to Sally. Both warned that, once in Boston, he might find himself too busy to write. In the letter to his mother, he told of the man and the woman and the young girl. In the letter to Sally, he confessed that he missed her and that he believed they needed to do some serious planning for the future when he returned to Jericho.

I'm almost tempted to get off in Atlanta and catch the next train home, he wrote. He added, *But I've come this far and I guess I need to go the rest of the way, so I'll just mail this letter instead.*

He did not tell her the rest of the way was no farther than ten miles across the state line dividing Tennessee and Kentucky.

BEIMER, KENTUCKY, WAS in a wide, cleared-out valley between two mountain ranges. A narrow, quick-rushing stream called Long Rock River cut in wiggles through the middle of the valley. The railroad followed the riverbed, though not in wiggles. Seen from the window of the train, the water of Long Rock River ran silver over gray and had the look of water cold as dripping ice. Years later, when he told of first seeing the river, Ben would vow he could see foot-long fish leaping up and over the water's spew, their flesh-colored bodies flashing like shooting stars. It was a tale doubted by those who heard it.

Beimer, itself, was not a town. It was a place, a train stop. It had a small depot, a water tank, and a one-room store that was located across a wide dirt road from the depot.

The store did not have a posted name.

"Don't need one," said the man who sat on an empty nail keg near the front door of the store. "Only store around here, almost to Bowling Green, I reckon. Everybody just calls it the store."

"Just wondered," Ben said. "Didn't see a sign."

The man was lanky and thin, his shoulders narrow and up-pointed, like a buzzard's wings when the buzzard is on the ground. He wore overalls and a dingy cloth shirt buttoned at his throat and work shoes with dry, cracked soles. A felt hat was pulled oddly low on his head, touching his ears. His hair was dark and long. A beard grew wild over his face, but could not cover the wrinkles that eroded his cheeks. Thick eyebrows nested over his eyes. He had a smile that seemed friendly enough. No teeth. None up front, at least. To Ben, he favored a caricature of Abraham Lincoln.

"Don't see many folks getting off the train here," the man said. He laughed a quaint, giggly laugh. "You the first this whole year, I reckon. Old man Clifford Cooley's boy come last Christmas. Come all the way from Atlanta, by God. Him and his wife and kids. Three of them. Boys, I reckon. They was so blame covered up against the cold, I was hard up to tell. By God, they didn't stay no longer than they had to. Couple of days later, they was back on that train, going back to Atlanta. Reckon they'd had all they wanted off old man Cooley."

The man again laughed his giggly laugh and covered his toothless grin with the back of one hand. He added, "Old man Cooley's not got the sense God put in a pile of dried-up cow shit."

Ben acknowledged the man's description of Clifford Cooley with an accommodating nod.

"You got folks up here?" asked the man.

"No sir," Ben said.

"Who you be?" The question was easy, not threatening.

"My name's Ben Phelps, sir," Ben told him. "I'm from down east of Atlanta."

"Well, God-o-mighty," the man whispered in awe. "That's a piece away. Yes, it is. A piece away." He extended his hand to Ben.

"Name's Henry Quick. My daddy was Gurney Quick. I run this store."

"Yes sir, I guessed so," Ben said.

"Who you up here to see, Ben Phelps?" Henry asked.

"I'm looking for Foster Lanier," Ben answered.

Henry Quick's head jerked up in surprise. His small, nut-colored eyes fanned open. "Well, by God," he exclaimed. "Foster. By God. Foster. You not one of them baseball fellows, are you?"

"Sir?"

"One of them baseball fellows, come to try to get Foster to play some more," Henry said. "Foster's not got but one leg. Can't hardly walk no more, even with them crutches he got for hisself. Used to be, they was baseball fellows in here all the time, looking for him, not knowing he's not got but one leg."

"No sir," Ben said. "I'm not looking for him to play ball. We're just friends. We used to play ball together."

The news excited Henry Quick. "Well, by God. That right? Me and Foster played some when we was just young'uns. I wadn't much, but Foster, he was something to behold, I tell you." He looked at Ben with admiration. "And you played with him? Don't look like you old enough."

"Last year he played," Ben said. "It wadn't for long. Just a few weeks."

"By God," Henry said again. "What you come to see him about?"

"He sent me a letter," Ben replied. "Just thought I'd pay him a call."

Henry wagged his head gravely. He said, "Foster's not doing too good." He looked at Ben. "You know his woman?"

"Lottie?" Ben said. "Yes sir, I've met her."

"She sure is a pretty thing."

"Yes sir."

"She comes in sometimes when they need something. Brings her boy in with her. They got a old buggy and a horse that's not fit to feed."

"She been in lately?" asked Ben.

Henry cocked his head in thought, stroked the beard that dangled below his chin. "Can't say that I seen her in a week or two. But it's a pretty good way up to their place. Two, three mile, I reckon. Maybe more."

"You guess you could tell me how to get there?" Ben said.

"Guess so," Henry answered. "Not hard to find." He pointed south. "You go on down the road there for about a half mile, down to where they's a little knoll covered up with rocks about the size of a shoe box. My daddy used to say it was where some Indians was buried, but nobody ever dug up no bones that I know about."

Henry laughed, rocked back on the nail keg. "Anyways, they's a little wagon-track road going up in the hills. You follow that, you gone come to where Foster lives. Got him a little log cabin up there. Pretty sight. Reckon it's pretty as any place you'll find around here. Used to be, leastways. Not been up there in close to a year, myself. Me'n some others that live hereabout went up there and cut up a stack of stovewood, and I guess we'll be going back before too much longer, before winter sets in. All that land back up there used to belong to the Laniers. Foster's sold off some of it, I hear, and I expect that's right. Don't know how they'd make out otherwise."

Ben shifted his suitcase in his hand and glanced inside the store. "You think of anything they might be needing, since I'm going up there?"

Henry's laugh turned to a cackle. He stood, unfolding a body that was well over six feet tall. His head seemed to bob between his up-pointed shoulders.

"Can't carry much if you walking around with that valise," Henry advised, "but I'd guess they could use some chicory coffee, and, knowing Foster, he'd be happy over a bottle of good makings."

"You got some?" Ben asked.

Henry cackled again. Cackled like a man who has been told a new and surprising joke. "Son, you in Kentucky," he said.

———

FINDING THE KNOLL covered in shoe-box-size rock was easy. The tale of an Indian burial ground was most likely true, Ben reasoned. He had read of such rituals from stories of archaeologists—how Indians, for some reason no one really understood, made little mountains for burial grounds. Carried the dirt, handful by handful, or vessel by vessel, from one place to another, tamping it down to make it look like just another hill. Yet, if you dug into those hills you would find pottery and arrowheads and tomahawks and clay dolls and beads. Anything Indians used. And bones. You would find bones of Indians dead hundreds of years. It awed Ben that archaeologists could take a bone fragment and say that it was the remains of a warrior or an old woman or a baby. And from his reading, it seemed to Ben that what the archaeologists really wanted to find was the burying place of a chief. A chief's grave would be so full of treasure they would have to dig it out with their fingertips, or with spoons, or with brushes.

He would have enjoyed being an archaeologist, Ben thought. Finding things that had been buried for hundreds of years. Bones and beads and flint knives and maybe gold bracelets or onyx and amethyst stones washed up from the creek beds. Sweeping the dirt off the grave of an Indian chief had to be better than sweeping the dirt from the floor of Ledford's Dry Goods.

The wagon-track road was grass-and-weed-covered. Not often traveled by anyone other than Lottie driving the buggy, Ben guessed.

The road had the look of trying to disappear, or to heal itself of the wounds of travel from years back. Only the thin, hard-packed tracks of the buggy's wheels left marks.

Watch for snakes, Ben thought. Timber rattlers probably. He had never been to the Kentucky mountains, but the look of the land in the long-shadow hour of the day made him think of timber rattlers. Maybe hiding in the ruts of buggy tracks, colored like the dirt, like leaf rot.

The train from Chattanooga had been delayed five hours. A late-afternoon wind blew across the valley and skated up the green-needled backs of hemlock and pine and red cedar, a racing, yowling, playing wind, and the feel of it and the sound of it pushed a chill through Ben's body. Must get cold in the mountains at night, he thought. Even in summer, it must get cold.

He stopped his walk beside a stream that nudged close to the road, its water lashing at an outcropping of gray, flat rock wedged solidly into the creek bank. He judged that he was better than halfway up the wagon road from the Indian mound. If Henry Quick had the wits to run a store, he would not be too far off on his estimate about the distance to Foster's home. Another mile should do it, Ben reasoned. Soon, he hoped. The climb had taken energy, and he could feel an ache in his chest and a tenderness in his throat, and he wondered if the summer cold he had had a few weeks earlier was making a return.

He cupped water from the creek in the palm of his hand and drank from it. The water was cold and tasted of moss and, curiously, cinnamon. Whiskey-making water, Foster would call it. Ben wondered if the jar of whiskey that he carried with him, the jar bought from Henry Quick, had been made from the same water, and if it tasted of moss and cinnamon.

A crow cawed from the top of a pine. Another answered from nearby, hidden by limbs.

Ben inhaled slowly, taking the air deep into his lungs. Clean. Cool. Not thick with humidity. A scent of woodsmoke, he thought. Maybe from Foster's cabin. Or maybe it was not woodsmoke, but the scent of the woods damp with water from rain or from seepage puddling into shallow pockets of springs. Still, he was close to the cabin. He could sense it.

THE CABIN WAS in a clearing on a shoulder of land that bulged up from the road and curved into the side of the mountain. A stand of hemlock, large at the base, sky-tall, surrounded the cabin at the edge of the clearing.

From the road, with the sun's slant crossing its roof in a bright ribbon through the dense trees, Ben thought the cabin looked like a painting he had seen on the cover of a magazine. A string of smoke rose from a chimney, waved ghostly in the air—smoke arms and smoke legs swimming out of the string—and Ben believed it was the woodsmoke he had smelled, or thought he had smelled. Smoke arms and smoke legs slithering over the mountains, becoming invisible, leaving only their scent.

A small barn was behind the house, a rail fence disappearing into the woods, into a growth of rhododendron and sassafras. The fence was draped with bushes of climbing red roses, heavy-flowered, their petals the color of blood. A horse, back-bowed, thin, a scabbed coat, stood listlessly near the fence.

Ben slowed his walk. He had risked his job because Foster had summoned him, and now, on the yard road to the cabin where Foster lived, Ben was unsure he had made the right decision. Foster and Lottie shared part of his life that he could never share with his mother, or with Sally, or with anyone. They knew the secret of his hit against Baby Cotwell. They knew of his night in the tent with Lottie. They knew of his weakness and his shame. Maybe he had been wrong in answering Lottie's letter.

He was at the cabin. It was too late to turn back, to undo what he had done.

The door to the cabin opened and Lottie stepped onto the porch. She had not changed, Ben thought. Thinner, perhaps, but still girl-pretty. A small boy moved like a shadow from the cabin and ducked behind her, clutching to the dull cotton dress she wore. The boy had a wreath of blond hair.

"Hello, Ben Phelps," Lottie said softly. She smiled. A smile of gladness, of relief.

"Hello, Lottie," Ben said.

"You sure look nice, Ben."

A blush swept over Ben's face. He glanced at the suit he wore, felt foolish. "I kind of overdressed," he said. He added, "For the train ride."

"I like it," Lottie told him.

The boy peeked from behind her, tugged at her dress.

"Ben, stop it," Lottie said. She pulled the boy from behind her, holding him by his hand. "This is Ben," she said. There was pride in the way she said the name of her son.

"Hello, Ben," Ben said. "That's my name, too: Ben."

"This is the man you was named for, honey," Lottie said. "Now when I say Ben, I guess you won't know who I'm talking to."

"Maybe you better call us Big Ben and Little Ben," Ben suggested.

"I like that," Lottie said. "Big Ben and Little Ben."

"He's a fine-looking boy," Ben said. "Looks like you."

Lottie shook her head, then ran her fingers through the blond hair of her son. "Looks like my daddy, some. Like my daddy looked when I was little. Got Foster's eyes, though."

"How's Foster?" asked Ben.

"He's inside," Lottie said. "Just waiting for you. Come on in. See for yourself."

The cabin had a large center room with a stone fireplace on the back wall. An open-frame door led to the kitchen. Another door, closed, led to another room, a bedroom, Ben guessed. The shade-dark center room was sparsely furnished with a table and four chairs, a rocker near the fireplace, and a bed against one wall. Foster was in the bed, propped against pillows, a quilt covering him at the chest.

"Well, by God," Foster said in a hoarse whisper.

Ben blinked in surprise. The man in the bed did not look like Foster Lanier. The man in the bed was a skin-covered skeleton. The skin was pale, the color of old straw. A film of perspiration glistened on his brow. His eyes were dull, drawn into his skull.

"Hello, Foster," Ben mumbled.

Foster laughed weakly, then coughed. He lifted a hand, let it drop back to the bed. "God-o-mighty, Ben, you look like Arnold Toeman." His voice was like escaping air.

Ben forced a smile. He touched the front of his suit.

"It's his train-riding clothes," Lottie said.

The sound from Foster was like a sigh: "Uh-huh." He scrubbed his head against the pillow. "Come over here, boy. Let me get a look at you."

Ben put down his suitcase and removed his hat and moved to the bed. Foster's eyes seemed to float over him.

"Put on a few pounds, it looks like," Foster wheezed.

"Some," Ben said.

A sad smile lifted in Foster's face. "I lost a little bit," he said.

Ben did not reply. He reached across the bed and touched Foster's hand.

"Last time I seen you, you was in bed and I was the one standing by it," Foster said.

"That's right," Ben replied.

Foster took Ben's hand in his own and squeezed it lightly. "Glad to see you, Ben. Damn glad. Glad you come."

"I'm glad to be here, Foster."

There was a pause. Foster's hand went limp on Ben's hand and then he said, "No, you not." He paused again, rolled his head away from Ben. "Hell, I wouldn't be. You looking at a dead man, Ben. Been dead for a long time now. I just keep breathing, and Lord only knows why."

"Maybe you better see a doctor," Ben suggested.

The smile returned to Foster's face. "Well, they's not one close by, but it won't do no good if he lived back there in the barn. Don't take no doctor to know what's going on here, Ben."

Ben could hear Lottie move behind him.

"I—bought you something," Ben stammered.

"What's that, Ben?"

"I was talking to the man down at the store—"

"Henry Quick," Foster said.

"That's right. Mr. Quick. Asked him if he had a bottle me and you could share."

Foster coughed a laugh.

"I thought it was about time I did the buying," Ben added.

Foster nodded wearily. "I'd be proud to take one with you," he said.

———

BEN WAS SURPRISED at the supper Lottie prepared. Garden beans and squash, tomatoes, onion, slices of cured ham, cornbread, tea from sassafras roots. Foster called it preacher food, but ate only a small piece of cornbread soaked in bean juice that Lottie served him in his bed.

His mother had taught Lottie to cook, Foster said. His mother had died a year earlier, only a month before his own illness became serious.

"But I swear, Ben, Lottie's better at it than my mama was. My mama cooked the taste out of things."

Lottie smiled at the praise.

It was after the supper, blue-dark outside, a cooling ground wind stealing down the spine of the mountain. Inside, a small fire burned in the fireplace, giving off heat and the aroma of hickory wood. Weak bubbles of yellow light came from two kerosene lamps. Ben had helped Foster move from the bed to the rocker and had tucked a quilt around him; then he had taken a straightback chair and placed it near the rocker, sitting close enough to hear the whispering that had become Foster's voice. Lottie sat in another chair, holding Little Ben.

"Did Henry Quick tell you how my mama saved his life?" Foster said in his whisper.

"No," Ben answered. "How'd that happen?"

"Me and Henry was born a couple of months apart," Foster said. "His mama died about a week after Henry showed up, and they wadn't nobody to nurse him, so my mama done it. Nursed us both." He paused, smiled. "Henry turned out ugly enough." His smile became a coughed laugh. "Ugliest fellow I ever saw, I guess. Always told him he got the ugly tit and I got the good one. But he's a good enough man, Henry is. Folks around here depend on him."

"He said he'd played ball with you," Ben said.

Foster bobbed his head. "Wadn't much of a player, Ben. We put him over on first base since he was so rangy and had them long arms, but, Lord, he couldn't catch much."

"I've seen some fellows like that," Ben said.

"What about your friend—Milo, wadn't it? What's he doing?"

Ben was puzzled by the question. Anyone who followed baseball knew that Milo Wade was one of the great players of the game. He said, "Milo's doing good. He's with the Red Sox."

Foster frowned a question.

"Used to be the Boston Pilgrims," Ben added. "They changed the name a few years ago."

Foster nodded once.

"And Nat Skinner's playing up there, with the Philadelphia team," Ben said. "You remember Nat? He pitched."

"Uh-huh," Foster replied.

"Nat's doing good, too. About the best pitcher in the big leagues."

Foster sat, staring into the fire. In the firelight and the lamplight, Foster's skin seemed as brittle as old parchment. After a moment, he said, "I miss it, Ben. What about you?"

"Some," Ben told him. "But I stay pretty busy at the store."

Foster inhaled sharply. He quivered under the quilt. "Lord, God-o-mighty, Ben, I miss it," he said in a desperate, shrill cry.

"Foster," Lottie said quietly. "Don't get worked up. It'll start the coughing." She looked at Ben. The look begged him not to talk about baseball.

Foster bobbed his head again. He closed his eyes and began to breathe in even, deep sips of air.

Lottie moved Little Ben in her arms, began stroking his hair with her fingers. She said to Ben, "How's your mama and daddy?"

"Uh, fine," Ben said. "Mama is. My—my daddy died a few years back."

Lottie glanced quickly at Foster. "I'm sorry about that. He was a nice man."

"It's all right," Ben said awkwardly.

Foster laughed softly. He pulled the quilt up, under his chin. "You remember Baby Cotwell, Ben?"

Ben shifted in his chair. "Sure do."

"Somebody killed him."

"I know," Ben said. He wondered if Foster remembered that Baby Cotwell had been killed in Jericho.

And then Foster answered his thought. "Wadn't me, in case you ever wondered. We'd already left when they found him. I thought he was headed back up to Tennessee with the midget. We heard about it later, and then the midget hung hisself."

"We sent Ben the story out of the newspaper," Lottie said to Foster. "Remember?"

A puzzled expression crossed Foster's face, then vanished. "We did, didn't we?"

"Sure did," Ben said.

"He was a mean little bastard, that midget," Foster said.

"Wadn't as mean as Baby," Lottie said.

"Sure wadn't as big," Ben said. "And I kind of doubt that he could hit as hard as Baby did."

Foster laughed softly. "I guess you ought to know. Lord, boy, you looked like they'd scraped you off a cowcatcher."

"But he didn't get away with it, did he?" Lottie said. Then: "They ever find out who did it?"

"No, they didn't," Ben answered. "They didn't look too hard, I don't think."

For a moment, no one spoke, and then Foster said, "When we started out, me and Baby, we had us some times with that show. They wrote big stories about us in some of them towns, bigger than anything I ever got when I was playing for real. If Baby hadn't been crazy, we could of made a wagonload of money." He wiggled his head in memory. "But after that, me and Lottie, we saw some places, didn't we, little girl?"

Lottie did not answer. She continued to stroke Little Ben's hair.

"You never saw Lottie dance, did you, Ben?"

Ben flushed. He remembered Lottie in the tent, Lottie nude, Lottie in her dance.

"She'd make men howl at the moon, by God," Foster continued. "Lord, she was something. I'm telling you, Ben, she was something. Figured I'd better marry her, or have her walking off with somebody up to no good."

"All that's over, Foster," Lottie said simply. "All behind us. Best not to talk about it."

Foster lifted his eyes to Lottie, held them on her, and Ben watched their eyes speaking, saying words they did not need to utter, words that had already been said. Bitter words, Ben thought. Quarrelsome words. And he knew there had been great sadness as well as great love between them.

A piece of the burning wood hissed and broke, and a spit of smoke, blue-gray, curled gracefully up the stone chimney.

And then Foster said, "Ben, I want you to take Lottie home."

ELEVEN

BEN KNEW THE bed was Lottie's bed. The scent of Lottie, a clean scent, a flower scent, was in the bedclothing and in the pillow, and, Ben believed, he could feel the heat from her body, a lingering, soft heat. It was her bed, and the bed of Little Ben.

He had offered to sleep on a floor pallet in the center room with Foster. Could keep the fire stoked, he had said.

No, Lottie had told him. She and Little Ben would stay in the room with Foster. It was the way she wanted it, and the way Foster wanted it.

"Sometimes he gets a coughing spell at night," she had quietly explained. "I make him some hot tea and put in some of his drink. Makes him sleep better."

"I could do it," Ben had volunteered.

"No," Lottie had replied.

IT WAS PAST midnight, and still he was awake. There was a chill in the room, surprising to Ben, though he had guessed that nights in the Kentucky mountains would be cooler than in Jericho. In the Lottie-scented bed, he pulled the covering up to his face and lay still in her imagined body heat, and he thought of Foster's request of him.

Take Lottie home.

"Always promised I'd take her home," Foster had said. "Can't now. Not now. You the only one I know I can count on for doing it."

Ben had protested gently. "You're going to get better, Foster. You'll do it."

"No, Ben, I'm not. No more going. Gone my last place."

"I just got a few days, Foster."

"Leave when you got to," Foster had replied. "They'll be going with you."

"We can't leave you here," Ben had argued.

Foster had turned his face to Ben. "I got kin. They'll be looking in on me."

Lottie had not said anything. She had merely gazed into the fire, holding Little Ben, stroking his hair, and Ben had known that what Foster asked was a frayed agreement between them. Probably something they had talked about, quarreled over. And from the look on her face, Ben had guessed that Lottie had more to say, but would be quiet until she needed to speak.

"Will you do it, Ben?" Foster had asked in his whisper.

And Ben had answered, "Yes."

It was the only answer he could give.

And in Lottie's bed, in the ghost space of her body, he could feel the weight of his promise settling on him. He thought of Sally and of his mother. How could he tell them of such promises?

He closed his eyes, determined to dream of Sally. He did not. He dreamed of Lottie. Lottie before him in the tent, amber-pale light on her face and shoulders and breasts. Lottie had his hands in her hands, guided his hands to the nipples of her breasts, leaned to him, kissed him with her fire mouth.

BEN AWOKE TO the touch of Little Ben's fingers on his face. A horizon of sunlight cut across the bedroom from the window, and Ben realized he had overslept.

"Breakfast," Little Ben said softly, in a voice that was both baby and boy, the first words Ben had heard him speak.

"Be right there," Ben said. He could smell the odor of chicory coffee and fatback and biscuits from the kitchen.

"Breakfast," Little Ben said again.

Ben pulled himself from the bed and dressed quickly in a pair of older trousers and shirt, and he wiggled his feet into the shoes that were comfortable. Little Ben stood at the bed, leaning against the bedpost, and watched.

"Breakfast smells good," Ben said, tying the laces of his shoes.

Little Ben did not move or speak. His large blue eyes did not wander from Ben.

"Your mama's a good cook."

A smile, almost imperceptible, posed on Little Ben's mouth.

"C'mon, let's go have some breakfast," Ben said.

"Breakfast," Little Ben repeated. The smile broke free, grew into a happy laugh.

BEN WAS STUNNED to find Foster sitting at the kitchen table with a blanket around his shoulders, feeding himself from a gravy-covered biscuit. A shine was in his eyes, his voice stronger: "Well, you look like you slept all right."

"Sure did," Ben said. A fire was in the fireplace, warming the room. He could see Lottie in the kitchen.

"Take a chair," Foster told him. "There's some of that coffee you brought us. I almost forgot how good coffee was."

Ben sat at the table. He took the coffee and sipped from it. Stronger than his mother made, he thought, but he liked the taste.

And maybe it was the water the coffee was made from, the same water that made the bourbon Foster had bragged about.

"That's good," Ben said.

Foster leaned to him, stole a glance over his shoulder toward the kitchen. "Had to show her how I liked it," he said in a deliberate whisper. "Used to make it weak as well water." He coughed a laugh, pulled the blanket tight to his shoulders. Under the blanket, he looked diminutive, a draped skeleton.

Lottie came from the kitchen, carrying a plate of food—gravy biscuits, fatback, a hard-fried egg with the yellow yolk broken and spread over the white. "Foster wanted gravy this morning," she said, placing the plate on the table in front of Ben. "Hope you like it."

"Sure smells good," Ben said.

Lottie sat near Foster. "Sometimes that's all he wants all day— gravy and biscuits."

Foster coughed again, tucked his head, nodded agreement.

Little Ben slipped near Ben's chair, watching him curiously.

"You eat?" Ben asked Little Ben.

Little Ben nodded a shy nod.

"Two whole biscuits," Lottie said proudly. "One with gravy, one with brown sugar." She motioned Little Ben to her. "Let him eat in peace, honey."

The breakfast was good and filling, and Ben ate slowly, took a second cup of coffee offered by Lottie, listened to Foster tell of his ancestors who had moved into the Kentucky territory in 1823. His ancestors had fought Indians, Foster vowed. Fought them until they began to marry them. Why, his bloodline was as much redskin as white. Why he had been blessed with such good eyesight for playing baseball.

"Used to dream that's what I was," he said. "Indian. Used to dream I could shoot a dove on the fly with a bow and arrow."

"Don't overtalk," Lottie warned him. "You know how tired it makes you."

Foster ignored her with a shrug of his bone-sharp shoulders. He took more coffee, continued talking.

"One time, Ben, my people owned every inch of land on this mountain."

"That right?" Ben said.

"Cut my first baseball bat from a ash about a mile from here. Put it by the fireplace and dried it out over the winter and then whittled it out with a draw blade and pocketknife and rasp file. Rubbed it down smooth with a cow bone. Had a handle like a rock."

"What happened to it?" asked Ben.

Foster sighed, cleared his throat. His voice had become hoarse and he was forcing words. "Batted with it a long time, then broke it in a game we was playing against some team out of Tennessee, just over the line."

Lottie moved from her chair to Foster. She said gently, "All right, that's enough talking. You need to crawl back in bed and get some rest."

Foster did not reply, and he did not resist.

"Ben, you take his other arm," Lottie said.

"Sure," Ben said, and he helped Lottie guide Foster back to the bed. Then he stood back and watched as Lottie pulled the covers over Foster, purring to him as a mother would purr to a baby: "You sleep now. You sleep. We'll keep the fire up. Me and Ben. We're right here. Me and Ben and Little Ben."

Foster closed his eyes and in a few moments, his breathing became labored with sleep.

"He got himself all worked up," Lottie said softly, "but he'll be all right now." She turned to Ben. "I got to pick some beans from the garden."

"Why don't you let me do it?" Ben said.

"Maybe you can take Little Ben down to the creek and fish for some catfish. Foster loves catfish."

"Where do you keep the poles?" Ben asked.

"Right inside the barn. There's a shovel there for digging worms."

"You think it's all right to leave Foster?" Ben said.

Lottie looked back at Foster. Her gaze held on him for a moment, then she said in a whisper, "I got to."

THE GARDEN WAS below the barn, surrounded by a high barbed-wire fence. The fence was for deer and bear, Ben reasoned. It was a small garden, hoe-dug instead of plowed. A row of beans, one of squash, two of corn, four hills of cucumber, four of potato, a half-dozen tomato plants, eight of pepper, some flowers Ben did not recognize, a small grouping of herbs — chives and mint and sage and rosemary. Once his father had kept such a garden in the back-yard. His father had mastered the growing of tomatoes. Large, brilliantly colored, juice-filled. Too many tomatoes for the needs of the family, and so there were always giveaways to neighbors and friends.

"You stay where Big Ben can see you," Lottie said to Little Ben.

Little Ben was outside the garden, searching for small stones to throw against the trees.

"You hear me?" Lottie asked.

Little Ben nodded absently.

"When he was little, I used to think he never was going to talk," Lottie said. "I guess maybe he's just a little slow at it."

"I thought it might be because I was around," Ben said.

"Some, maybe. He don't see many people. Some of Foster's people drop by once in a while, but they don't usually have nobody Ben's age with them. Just men mostly."

"Maybe he's a listener, instead of a talker," Ben said.

Lottie smiled. "If he is, he gets a earful when all them men show up."

A SMALL BRANCH of spring-fed water coiled into the creek, sweeping away the sand bottom and leaving a pool that Ben guessed was five feet at its deepest. He had fished with his father and Milo on such creeks and had quickly learned the lesson every fisherman knew — catfish found such spots because the springs and the rain washed in food and the pools held it.

The creek bank around the pool had been walked down and standing places had been fashioned by fishermen patient enough to wait for nibbles to become gobbled-down bites. Ben was surprised by the well-used look of the spot. He knew that Foster was not able to fish, and he doubted that Lottie had been there often. Once or twice, maybe. With Little Ben, maybe. She was not the fishing type. She would not have looked at the water and wondered about the fish; she would have yearned to follow its flow. Must be other cabins nearby, he thought.

He had dug worms at the pasture edge, near a small, wet-weather spring, handing each worm to Little Ben to drop into the can half filled with moist dirt. Little Ben seemed mesmerized by the worms, by the feel of their wiggling over the palms of his hands.

"Worms," Ben had said.

"Worms," Little Ben had repeated.

And now he sat with Little Ben on the bank of the creek, their cane poles pushed out over the water, lines hanging limp over cork floats that bobbed playfully on the pool's dark pewter surface.

"When the cork goes under, you pull it up," Ben said to Little Ben, because it seemed he should say something.

Little Ben did not reply. He gazed expectantly at the water and at the bobbing cork.

"Like this," Ben added, and he demonstrated how to jerk on a line, setting the hook in the mouth of a fish.

Little Ben looked at him curiously, with amusement, Ben thought.

"Well, I guess you know how to do it," Ben mumbled. "Looks like you been here before."

Little Ben smiled.

"Worms," said Ben.

"Worms," echoed Little Ben.

BY ELEVEN-THIRTY ON Ben's pocket watch, they had caught six catfish that were of keeping size.

"Guess that's enough," Ben said. "Your mama may be wondering where we are."

Little Ben looked toward the path leading to his home.

"Maybe we'll come back later," Ben said.

Little Ben grinned.

LOTTIE WAS SITTING on the front porch as Ben and Little Ben crossed the pasture from the woods. She held a basket of beans in her lap. Ben lifted up the string of fish, still dripping water. He could see a faint smile flicker in Lottie's face, then fall away.

"She's probably wondering why it took so long just to catch a little mess of fish," Ben said. And then he offered Little Ben some advice: "Seems to me every woman on earth has a different idea of time when it comes to getting something done." He could feel a flush on his face. It was the first opinion regarding women he had ever given, and he had said it quietly to Little Ben, not wanting it to carry across the pasture to Lottie. Lord, he thought, that's the way my father used to talk to me, that half-whispering.

Little Ben ran ahead of Ben, reached his mother, wiggled himself up into her lap, put his head against her breasts.

"He's a good fisherman," Ben said, approaching. "Caught as many as I did."

Lottie smiled. She pushed her fingers through Little Ben's hair, kissed his forehead.

"I'll get these cleaned," Ben said.

Lottie looked up. Her eyes were dull. "It's all right," she said softly. She pulled Little Ben closer to her, then added, "Foster's dead."

————

THEY CAME SOLEMN-FACED, quietly, to bury Foster, wearing their church-and-funeral clothes. The clothes were scented with the faint odor of cedar from hot irons rested on cedar boughs.

They came bringing food and, with the food, mumbled regrets and low-voiced memories of Foster, who was a legend among them.

They came to see the little that remained of him in his pine-board coffin, but they could not. Lottie had had the coffin closed and nailed.

"No reason to shame him," she had said.

She had dressed him in the only suit that he owned and had placed his baseball glove into the coffin with him, and when it was known among the mourners what she had done, they bobbed their heads in approval.

"No need to shame him," they repeated.

Henry Quick and three other men had dug out a grave in the small family cemetery at the sideyard, and in late afternoon on the day after his death, the men set the coffin on ropes and lowered it into the ground.

A thin, back-bent preacher, with white hair that looked wind-whipped by the breath of God, stood at the head of the grave. He was dressed in a dingy black suit, with wool that had been picked by too much wear. His eyes were pale blue and small and carried an expression of sadness, as though sadness was pale blue in color. Yet, his voice was deep and rhythmic from the practice of making sermons, and the words he spoke were more like music than words. He recited the psalm about the valley of death, said that Foster was a gift from God and a man who would cause stories to be told until all life was dust, and then he prayed a gentle prayer of crossing over from world to sky. When he finished, he stepped back as Henry Quick and the other men began scraping dirt over the coffin with the sides of their shovels. A man with a mandolin began to play and sing "Amazing Grace," and the other mourners began to follow along shyly with the lyrics, and the song rose up into the trees and dangled on limbs like wind chimes.

It was, to Ben, a mysterious and unsettling occasion. Dreamlike. And he found himself wondering if it was a dream, something from a prolonged sleep that was, itself, like death. He was uncomfortable in his train-traveling suit that did not smell of cedar from hot irons.

Only Henry Quick had spoken directly to him. Everyone else backed away in his presence, somehow reducing their bodies with tucked-in arms and hands, keeping their heads dipped, their eyes dancing furtively to him and away from him, and he could sense what they had said among themselves and, having seen him, what they were now sure of: stranger off the train, dressed like a senator full of speech, asking the whereabouts of Foster Lanier, and Foster dead less than a day later. Only an agent of God, or of Satan, had such powers.

They had a right to their suspicions, Ben reasoned. It was odd, Foster dying so soon after his arrival. He, too, had wondered about it, had wondered if Foster's dying was from the weakness of his body, or from the helping hand of Lottie, the act of an agreement they had struck, an agreement as secret as any whisper ever passed between husband and wife.

He remembered going into the house after Lottie had told him of Foster's death. The body was covered with a sheet. A pillow was on the corner of the bed and Ben had picked it up. The face of the pillow had seemed moist, like the damp left by steam, and something in the touching of it told Ben that it held the last breath Foster had taken.

He knew he would never ask Lottie about it. If Lottie had stopped his breathing, it was because Foster had begged it, and it would have been done gently, with caring. It would not have been murder. Murder was something cruel.

The mourners seemed only to know that an agent of death had arrived on an afternoon train, and that Foster was dead, and, one day, another agent would arrive for each of them.

Ben watched as they drifted away from the burial plot. Watched as they gathered their leftover food and utensils. Watched them pull themselves up onto wagons and buggies. Watched them disappear around the bends of the road under the cover of tree limbs. Watched them vanish in the purpling of sunset.

Henry Quick had said, "Lottie says you taking her home. I guess you'll be going out tomorrow."

"I guess," Ben had replied.

"Won't need but two tickets," Henry had advised. "The boy goes free. Train stops at about two. Come on down in the buggy. I'll take care of it and the horse."

"What about this place?" Ben had asked.

"Somebody'll take it up," Henry had answered simply.

AT NIGHT, LITTLE Ben fell asleep early and Lottie put him in the bed where Foster had died.

"Do you think he knows what's happened?" asked Ben.

"I guess," Lottie said. "He's been seeing it a long time. I guess he knows."

"Does he know we're leaving tomorrow?"

"I told him," Lottie answered. "He never went anywhere, so maybe he don't know what it means."

"Do you have much packing to do?"

"Just one bundle," Lottie told him. "It's all done."

"Guess we'd better get some rest then," Ben said. "We got a long way to go."

"I guess," Lottie whispered.

BEN DID NOT know the hour that he awoke. Late, he guessed. Dark through the windows. He knew only that he had been sleeping soundly by the heaviness of his muscles.

And then he felt Lottie's body curled against his back, her arm resting on his shoulder, and he could hear her deep, even breathing. Sleep-breathing.

His body tensed, but he did not move. He listened. And the sleep-breathing made him close his eyes.

He was more removed from all that he had ever been than he would ever be again—locked in a cabin in the tree-thick mountains of Kentucky, on a night so dark not even God could see through the blackness of it. And there was something good about it, he thought.

AT DAYBREAK, WHEN Ben awoke, Lottie was gone from the bed. He dressed and went into the middle room, where Little Ben sat in a chair, eating a biscuit.

"Where's your mother?" asked Ben.

Little Ben looked toward the door.

"She's outside?"

Little Ben rocked a yes with his head.

She was at the gravesite, tearing apart a rose and dropping its petals over the dirt mound.

"Foster used to take rose petals and fold them up and make a little air pocket in them," she said without looking at Ben. "Then he'd smash them against his forehead, and if they popped it meant some-body loved you. If it didn't, it meant you was all alone."

She folded a petal and held it in front of her face and then, in a sudden, punching move, she hit her forehead with it. The petal popped sharply. She dropped it over the grave and turned to Ben.

"Does somebody love me, Ben Phelps?"

"Foster sure did," Ben said.

She looked back at the grave. "Yes, he did."

"And you've got a little boy in that house that does," Ben added.

Lottie smiled and tilted her head. "Do you, Ben?"

Ben thought of Sally Ledford, could see her face, hear her voice, feel her touch.

"Ben, do you?"

"You're my friend," Ben said after a moment. "I love you for being my friend, and for all you did for Foster."

Lottie smiled softly. She said, "Do you know why I got in bed with you last night, Ben Phelps?"

"No," Ben told her.

"I needed to be up against somebody who was warm. Foster hadn't been warm in a long time."

Ben did not reply.

"I just needed to be warm, Ben. That's all. I didn't mean nothing by it."

"It's all right," Ben said.

AT NOON, BEN hitched the horse to the buggy and put his suitcase and the tied sack bundle that Lottie had packed into the carriage space, and then he helped Lottie and Little Ben up to the seat.

"Are you ready?" Ben asked quietly.

Lottie took one gazing look at the cabin and Foster's gravesite. She nodded, folded her arm around Little Ben.

Ben clucked to the horse, tapped its rump with the line, and the horse strained against the buggy, its head lowered to the work of pulling.

At the road, Ben glanced back. He saw two gaunt, bent figures hobble-rush toward the garden—a woman wearing a ground-long cotton dress and a sunbonnet and a man in a black suit and dull white shirt, his white hair billowing over his head. The man was carrying a bucket.

"Somebody's at the garden," he said to Lottie.

She did not look back.

"Want me to go back and run them off?" asked Ben.

She shook her head. "It's just Miss Polly and the preacher. Their garden didn't make. I guess they hungry."

THE LETTER FROM Ben, arriving in Jericho two days after his leaving, was a giddy surprise for Sally. She read it again and again, as though the words were able to leap up from the page and fashion Ben's face and mimic Ben's voice. So many promises in the letter. So many.

Her own letters to Ben, written daily since his leaving, also had promises, though she knew she would not mail the letters because she did not have an address for him in Boston. It did not matter. She doubted she would ever show them to him, for she believed they were childish, the words dangerously revealing, words of romantic and erotic yearnings from a girl pretending to be a woman.

Her mother had noticed her behavior since Ben's leaving and had said, "What you're going through is the worst time of your life, and maybe the best. It's your in-between time, and you'll never forget it."

Her mother was right. "In-between" was the perfect word. Awkward, fragile, exhilarating. Her mother had said it was because her dreams had overflowed into her body like a summer flash flood and her body was struggling not to drown. And it did seem that way. Occasionally, thinking of Ben, something—some force—flew up in her body, pressing against her lungs, and she would gasp for breath.

She wondered how her mother knew such things. She loved her mother, yet also pitied her. Her mother was a bitter person who suffered from anemia and from resentment that no one understood. She seldom appeared at the store, seldom left their home, and, sadly, seldom smiled. It did not seem possible that such a woman had ever felt the joy of passion, or could recognize it in another person.

"Hold on to every second of it," her mother had advised. "It won't last long, and when it's gone you'll never get any of it back."

"What does that mean?" Sally had asked.

Her mother had turned away from her without answering.

On the night that she received Ben's letter, Sally closed the door to her room and pulled the drapes over the window. She removed her clothes and stood nude before the full-length mirror on the back of the door, gazing proudly at her body. She had heard girls talk of lovemaking, of how men behaved, and what a resourceful woman could do to keep men tamed to their touch only. Some of the talk was covered in giggles, some whispered in wonderment. Some believed lovemaking was a horror, some said it made a woman jittery with happiness.

Sally smiled at her reflection. She believed she would be jittery.

She lightly touched her breast, felt a shiver. Her breasts were small and sensitive.

She closed her eyes and imagined that she was in her wedding room on her wedding night, and that Ben was in the bed watching her.

"Mrs. Ben Phelps," she said in a soft voice.

She wrapped her arms in a hug around her body and thought of the promises in Ben's letter, and she remembered the first time she knew she was in love with him. It was a Saturday, one week before

her fourteenth birthday. She had carried lunch to her father, and as
he ate alone in the storeroom, she had helped Ben arrange a display
of dresses.

"You don't have to do this," Ben had said to her.

"Daddy says I have to learn about the store," she had replied politely but stubbornly. "When I'm sixteen, I'm going to start working
here so I'll know what to do when it's my store."

"It'd be better if he showed you," Ben had said.

"Why?"

"It's his store, you're his daughter."

"Does that matter?"

"I think so," Ben had answered. "If it's going to be your store one
day, he should be the one telling you about everything. I may say it
wrong."

"Well, what if I grow up and marry you?" she had said playfully.
"Then it'd be your store."

Ben had looked at her in disbelief, and then he had busied himself
again with the dresses, dropping one to the floor.

It was in that moment, as he stooped to retrieve the dress, that she
knew she was in love with Ben Phelps, and that one day she would
marry him.

She brushed her face with her fingers, pretending they were Ben's
fingers. The reflection in the mirror smiled back at her, and she
knew that she was beautiful and that her lovemaking would be beautiful.

"Mrs. Ben Phelps," she said again in her soft voice.

Before she went to bed, she wrote another letter to Ben.

My dearest Ben,

*Tonight, I believe you are here with me, so close that I can touch
the air and feel your face. I love you with every tender thought I
have ever had and wish for sleep only to dream of you, as I have*

every night that you've been away. Someday, I will tell you of those
dreams, or, better still, I will live them with you.

If you do not come home soon, I think I will die of loneliness.

But now, I will dream. And in my dream, you will be here.

I kiss the air that is your face, and hold the night breeze that
brings me your arms.

With my love,
Sally

———

THE TRAIN DID not arrive in Beimer until twenty minutes after
three, which did not surprise Henry Quick.

"Sometimes it don't get here to almost dark," he had said to Ben.
"Must've been some trouble on the track between here and Bowling
Green."

Ben and Lottie and Little Ben had waited on the porch of Henry
Quick's store, taking a lunch of baked sweet potatoes and biscuits
and water from Henry's well. After the lunch, Little Ben had curled
in his mother's lap and slept as Lottie fanned him with an ivory-
handled folding fan she had taken from her purse. Ben knew it was
the fan he had seen before, in the tent on the night that Lottie had
offered her body to him. The thought of the night made him blush.

"Guess the boy's wore out," Henry had suggested quietly.

Ben had agreed with a shake of his head.

"Looks like his daddy did when he was little," Henry had added.
"Got the same eyes. Maybe he'll be a baseball player, too."

"Maybe," Ben had replied.

"Foster was something else, he was," Henry had declared. "God-
o-mighty, he was something else." He had rooted his shoulders into
the chair back and had begun to tell stories of Foster.

The man that Henry Quick described was not the man Ben had

known in Augusta. The man in Augusta was old and tired and drink-addled, his skills eroded, his passion spent. The only thing that had seemed alive in Foster was his bitterness and his confusion over failure.

He remembered what Foster had said to him in Augusta, when Arnold Toeman had called him from the batter's box, sending in Foster to hit for him. Foster had said, "It's all right, Ben. It's not what it's made out to be, nohow."

Henry could have been talking about a god from Greek mythology, Ben thought as he listened, and he had imagined Foster wrapped in clouds with a crown of lightning bolts resting on his head, and in his hand he held a baseball bat as a warrior would hold a sword.

"Sometimes, when he was home, he'd sit out here at night with a bunch of us fellows, and he'd tell us about games he'd played in," Henry had said with a chuckle, "and he'd look up and say that playing a good ball game was a little like being a star on a black night. Said it was like being shot full of twinkle."

And maybe that is how he would find Foster one night, Ben had decided. As a constellation, a string of star-dots against the dark velvet of heaven, star-dot lines connected by memory, outlining Foster, the god, his body muscled with moons of distant planets.

WHEN THE TRAIN arrived, Ben and Henry put the luggage on the passenger car and Ben took Little Ben from Lottie.

"I'm glad you going home, Miss Lottie," Henry said. "But you always welcome up here."

Lottie shook Henry's hand. "Thank you for all the kindness," she said. She stepped up into the train, then turned back. "Sometimes, if you could put some flowers on his grave, I'd be grateful."

Henry nodded. He extended his hand to Ben. "Glad I got to know you, young fellow. Foster was a good judge of men, and I reckon he judged you right. You take care of them two."

"Yes sir," Ben said.

"You come through this way, you stop in," Henry said.

"I'll do that," Ben told him. He followed Lottie onto the train and took a seat across from her, still holding Little Ben.

"I'll take him," Lottie said.

"It's all right," Ben replied.

"He sure is sleeping hard," Lottie said. "Never saw him sleep this hard in the day."

Ben swept his hand across Little Ben's face. "He's a little hot."

Lottie frowned. "I thought he was, too," she admitted. "But I was thinking maybe it was because we was sitting outside."

"Maybe that's it," Ben said.

"Maybe," Lottie repeated. She reached across the space separating them and touched Little Ben's forehead. "Maybe it's just a summer cold," she added. "Mama said I used to get them all the time."

THEY RODE MOSTLY in silence, the train rocking over its tracks, lulling them with the clicking of wheels on rail, the Kentucky and Tennessee landscape spinning away from them in a blur of green and haze. It was the second time that Ben had been on a train with Lottie, but six years had passed and their lives had changed. She was no longer with a traveling salesman promising the quid pro quo of good times for good times, and he was no longer a baseball player wounded by dreams. She had married Foster, had had a child with him, had buried him. And Ben was a dry goods clerk in love with a girl who was seven years younger than he was. He had made a place for himself in Jericho. People liked him. Treated him with respect. He was no longer the boy played for a fool by Coleman Maxey and Bill Simpson and Frank Mercer. The only link to his youth was Milo Wade, and it was chain-strong, a link Ben could not break. As long as Milo Wade waged his wars on the baseball fields of America, Ben could daydream, could hold to wishes that were private and tender.

Still, Lottie was with him. And Little Ben, curled on the seat beside his mother, sleeping his child's sleep. And he had made a deathbed promise to Foster that he would take her home to Augusta. He could not turn away from such a promise.

It would not be easy. He had been away from Jericho for four days. By the timetable of his deception about being in Boston, he had three days before he needed to be home.

It was not the timing that concerned him. The timing would work. They would be in Augusta in less than a day, if there were no delays, and he could easily return to Jericho in another day.

He worried only that someone in Jericho would see him on the stop-through. It was a risk. He would have to stay on the train, hide himself from Akers Crews's annoyed eyes, and he would have to hope that no one from Jericho boarded the train for a trip to Augusta.

He rolled his head against the seat rest, looked at Little Ben, still sleeping, his face rose-blushed with the heat, and then he turned back to the window. He saw a grainfield, a pasture with grazing cows, a farmhouse on a knoll, a waterfall that poured from the hip of a mountain and tumbled over a rock wall and splashed into a narrow stream that cut a silver scar across the pasture.

If anyone from Jericho got on the train, he would tell him the near truth. He would say that one of the baseball players he had met had asked him to accompany his wife and child back to Augusta, and because the player was a friend to Milo, he had agreed. Lottie would not dispute him. Lottie would understand.

He thought: I have to buy newspapers at the stop in Atlanta. Have to find out the baseball scores, and how Milo played.

He did not need any other information. It would be simple enough to tell stories about the games. He had imagined being in

Boston at the Huntington Avenue Grounds ballpark for so many years, it seemed he had been there hundreds of times.

He would tell of other things, also. Of going to Boston Harbor to see the waters where American colonists, wearing the dress of Mohawk Indians, dumped three hundred and forty-two chests of tea in the year of 1773. Of visiting the Old North Church, where Paul Revere saw the lantern that would light the American Revolution. Of traveling one morning to Harvard University. Of walking the city until he was exhausted. He would say he stayed in a clean and airy boardinghouse and had fine meals and met good people. He would promise Sally that, one day, both of them would go to Boston. On their honeymoon, perhaps.

In Atlanta, he would buy a small gift for Sally and one for his mother. He would not say the gifts were from Boston; he would say they were from his trip.

Little Ben opened his eyes and looked quizzically at Ben. He moved against his mother's lap, waking her.

"Mama," he said weakly.

Lottie touched his face, felt fever. She looked at Ben. "He's burning up," she said fearfully.

THIRTEEN

THE MEDICAL CLINIC was only three blocks from the Nashville train depot, and Ben fast-walked the distance, carrying Little Ben, with Lottie keeping his stride. Worry was on her face.

"He'll be all right," Ben said over and over, as though muttering a chant that contained the power of healing. "He'll be all right. He'll be all right . . ."

Ben did not believe the words. He believed he was holding death. Little Ben's eyes seemed glazed. His body was limp, his breathing shallow.

And then in his mind—deep in his mind—Ben could hear the music of his church choir, and the words rushed silently into his throat, tangling with the muttering: *His eye is on the sparrow, and I know he watches me . . .*

Little Ben was sparrow-light.

"Sparrow," Ben whispered.

"What?" Lottie asked anxiously.

"He's like a sparrow," Ben said.

Lottie did not reply.

THE DOCTOR WAS young and handsome, with dark, darting eyes. He smelled of hospital alcohol and pipe tobacco. His name was Spencer Adams.

"Let's see about this little fellow," he said in a kind voice. He touched Little Ben's forehead, then his throat. His eyes dimmed, his lips wiggled.

"Get me some wet towels," he said to his nurse, "and chip some ice."

He turned to Ben and Lottie. "Best let us look at him," he said. "I want to take his temperature and try to work the fever down. The two of you can wait in the hallway. You'll find some chairs."

"I want to stay with him," Lottie said quickly.

"Best to let me do it," the doctor said. He looked at Ben. "I'm sure your husband understands."

Lottie turned to Ben, then back to the doctor. "He's not my husband."

The doctor's head ticked slightly.

"We're just friends," Ben said. "Her husband died a couple of days ago and I'm helping her and her son with their move down to Georgia."

"I see," said the doctor. "Still, I think—"

"We'll wait outside," Ben said. He took Lottie's arm. "Come on. He's with the doctor. Couldn't be in better hands."

Lottie did not resist.

"We'll take good care of him," Spencer Adams promised.

THE HALLWAY WAS wide. Benches and chairs were shoved against the walls, leaving room enough for walking without hindrance. Walking made heel-clicking echoes. All the benches and chairs were empty except for a man who appeared to be Ben's age, or younger. The man sat near the door leading into the doctor's office, hunched forward in his chair, his elbows on his knees, his fingers laced together, a look of anguish on his face. If he heard the heel-clicks of the people walking along the hallway, or the echoes, he did not acknowledge them.

Ben and Lottie took chairs that had a small table between them. A Bible was on the table.

"I think it's just a cold, like you said," Ben said quietly. "I had one a couple of weeks ago, sore throat and all."

Lottie turned her head to look at the man sitting near the door of the doctor's office. She said, "All his clothes are in my bundle."

"They're at the train station," Ben told her. "I left everything with the ticket agent. He said he'd watch after them."

"I don't know how I'm going to pay for all this," Lottie said fretfully.

"Don't go worrying about it," Ben said. "I've got some money."

A short, squat woman wearing the white uniform of a nurse came out of a room and hurried down the hallway and disappeared into another room.

"Do you know what I was thinking on the train, Ben?" Lottie asked softly.

"What?" Ben said.

"I was thinking about the first time I ever saw you — on that train from Augusta."

"That seems a long time ago," Ben said.

"Sometimes," Lottie whispered. "Sometimes it seems like it was yesterday, or last night." A smile warmed on her face. "You looked scared."

"Guess I was," admitted Ben.

"I was, too."

"We were both pretty young," Ben suggested.

"I almost got off when you did. Would have if I'd had any money to turn around and go back home," Lottie said.

"I thought you were asleep when I got off."

Lottie shook her head. "I was just pretending. I saw you. Even looked out the window at you. You looked lost standing there, watching the train pull off."

"Guess I was," Ben said.

"I remember thinking: How can he look so lost when he's at home?"

Ben's head rocked in a nod. "That's a good question," he said.

"I'm glad Foster was at home when he died," Lottie whispered.

"Me, too."

For a moment, Lottie did not speak. She gazed at the Bible on the table between them, reached to touch it with her fingertip, then pulled back her hand. "I don't think I'll ever have a home, Ben. Not a real home."

"You will," Ben said. "You'll see. Little Ben's going to be all right, and we'll get back on the train and you'll be back with your folks in a day or so."

Lottie looked up at him. "I don't even know if they're still alive, Ben."

"Didn't you write to them?"

"Some. But they never wrote back."

Ben could feel a flush on his face. He shifted in his chair. He had not considered the possibility that Lottie's family might have disappeared, and that he would be left with Lottie and Little Ben, standing in front of an empty house on the bank of the Savannah River. What then? he wondered. He could not abandon them. He knew that. Yet he could not return to Jericho with them — not without suspicion and questions he could never answer. He thought of the money he had in his wallet. Still a lot of it left, since he had not gone to Boston, and he could leave most of it with Lottie, but it would last her only a few days.

"I wonder how Sister is?" Lottie said absently. She paused. "Still rocking, I guess."

Ben tried a smile. It fell from his face. "Maybe so," he said.

The door to the doctor's office opened and the young man sitting near it looked up. An older doctor, balding, red-faced, approached him and spoke in a whisper. The color in the young man's face vanished and he dropped his head and began to cry. The old doctor reached for his arm, pulled him forward in the chair, and led him through the door.

"Somebody just died," Lottie said quietly.

Ben did not speak.

"Or maybe somebody was just born—his first baby—and he's so happy he just had to cry," Lottie added. "It's the way I was with Little Ben. I just had to cry. Foster was laughing like a crazy person, like he'd been there with God when God was making everything he put in the world."

Ben listened for the cry of a baby, but heard nothing.

They sat in silence for a long time, the silence broken only by heel-clicks in the echo chamber of the hallway, and by voices of passersby rushing from one door to another, voices like the humming of wings on insects. Ben knew that it was dark outside. A gnawing was in his stomach. He thought of the preacher and his wife raiding Lottie's garden, imagined them feasting on platters of vegetables. And maybe they had stopped at the fishing spot on the creek and had fished out a few catfish and that, too, was part of their meal.

He wondered what had happened to the catfish he and Little Ben had caught. He remembered dropping them near the house. Probably dragged off by the cat he had seen hiding at the barn. Or a raccoon.

He saw Lottie's body move suddenly, lift from the chair, and he turned to see the doctor coming from the door, heel-clicks sharp in the hallway. He stood and stepped close to Lottie. Touched her arm with his hand.

"He's better," the doctor said wearily. "Temperature's down some, but he's a sick little boy."

"Is it a cold?" asked Lottie.

The doctor shook his head. He fumbled a pipe from his jacket. "Not a cold. I'm only guessing, but I think it could be the first case I've ever seen of a disease called anthrax, or what some people call black bain or woolsorter's disease. I found a small carbuncle on his buttock, near the end of his spinal column, and that's a telling sign."

A look of confusion crossed Lottie's face. "He had a little sore," she said. "I thought it was like a risen."

The doctor dipped his head in understanding. He fingered the burned tobacco in the bowl of his pipe and judged there was enough left to light. "Almost the same, by the looks of it," he said. "Only a carbuncle's worse. I drained it best I could. I just wish I had the vaccine to give him."

"What's that?" Lottie asked.

The doctor lit his pipe and a whip of blue smoke wiggled from the bowl. He thought of his year's study in Paris and of the work of Louis Pasteur, whose discoveries had changed the practice of medicine. Anthrax was the first disease ever to be treated with vaccine. "Well, it's not easy to explain," he said. "Just say it's a way to handle some problems like your little boy may have."

Lottie looked quizzically at Ben.

"It's all right," Ben said to assure her. He had read of vaccines, but knew nothing about them. He also had read of woolsorter's disease, and he knew it was a disease of death.

"I could be wrong about this," the doctor said. "I hope I am."

Ben wanted to add, "Me, too." He did not. He swallowed hard, looked away.

"Where is he?" asked Lottie.

"He's asleep right now," the doctor told her. "We're not a hospital, but we've got a few beds for emergencies."

"Can I see him?" Lottie asked.

The doctor blinked a yes with his eyes. "Just for a minute. Just so you know he's all right. I want him to stay here tonight. We've got a nurse who's here, and I live nearby in case they need me."

"I want to stay with him," Lottie said.

The doctor shook his head. "It's best you get some rest. There's a boardinghouse just down the street, run by a fine Irish couple named O'Connor. I'm sure they'll have accommodations."

"He's my boy," Lottie said firmly.

"I think you better do what the doctor says," Ben said gently. "We can see him and then I'll get our things from the train station and we'll find you a place to stay. I'll come back and sit here, right outside the door. Anything happens, I'll let you know."

"That's a good thought," the doctor said.

"You sleep," Lottie said. "I'll stay here."

"You'll need to be awake for him tomorrow," Ben said. "That's when he'll need his mama and you don't want to fall asleep then."

Lottie knew he was right. She dipped her head in resignation.

"I'll check on him early in the morning," the doctor said.

"How long's he going to have to stay?" Lottie asked.

The doctor gazed the bowl of his pipe, frowning. If the boy had anthrax, he would likely never leave alive. Small as he was, he would likely die during the night. "We'll see," he said to dismiss the question. "But to be honest, I don't know."

Little Ben was sleeping peacefully. The color of fever was no longer in his face. Lottie stood beside the bed, looking at him, studying him, trying to read what the doctor could not know. And then she leaned to him and kissed him on the forehead, holding her lips to his skin, testing it for heat.

"All right," she said to Ben, stepping away from the bed.

———

THE ROOMING HOUSE was two blocks from the clinic, one block from the railroad station. It was named O'Connor's Inn. Its trade was mainly train travelers weary of hypnotic riding, opting to put earth under their feet and a standing-still bed under their bodies. The house was old and large, with small but comfortable upstairs bedrooms that had worn but well-kept furnishings. Downstairs, where Elizabeth and Ralph O'Connor lived, there was a living room suggesting a past elegance and a dining room with a table long enough for ten people, though more suited for eight.

Lottie did not argue with Ben about staying in O'Connor's. She was tired, and even if she did not sleep, the bed would be more comfortable than a chair.

"I'll be back in the morning," Ben told her. "Try to get some sleep."

"I never stayed in a place like this," Lottie said. "Never saw a place this pretty, except the house you live in, Ben. I remember how pretty it was. That porch that went all the way around it, and how white it was and big inside, and the way your mama had it fixed up with all her pretty things. Prettiest home I ever saw. Foster said so, too, and this place puts me in mind of it."

"It's nice, all right," Ben agreed.

She looked at him. "You get tired, you come on back here and I'll go take your place."

Ben thought of the cabin where Foster and Lottie and Little Ben had lived, and of the bed with Lottie's flower scent, and of Lottie's body next to him, needing warmth. It had only been a day, yet it seemed like a past life in an ancient time.

"I'll be fine," he said at last.

Lottie touched her hands together in front of her, palm to palm. Then she said softly, "Ben, will you hold me for a minute?"

"All right," Ben said after a pause. He extended his arms and Lottie stepped into them, easing against him. He could feel her hands embracing him at his back and her face nestled against his shoulder. She made no move, yet something seemed to leave her and enter his chest and throat. It was not lust. Trust, maybe. Or innocence. Not lust. In his arms, she felt very much like a child.

———————

BEN DID NOT want to sleep, but he did. Poorly. He tried to balance himself in the chair near the doorway leading into the doctor's office, but the weight of his body would pull him almost into a fall and he would jerk awake and bring his body back into a sitting position and clear the sleep from his brain to listen for sounds. Once he thought he heard the crying of a baby. Not Little Ben. A baby. And with the crying, faint footsteps. And then, for the rest of the night, he did not hear anything.

The hallway, without windows, was hot. Three electric lights burned dimly along its length, making weak umbrellas of light over the black-filled space.

Ben's shoulders ached. His eyes were dry and sleep-heavy. He thought of his own bed, of the night air that swept over him from opened windows. When they were young, he and Milo Wade had spent many nights at the windows, listening to neighbors who were sitting on porches in porch swings, talking in low voices. Sometimes they watched silhouettes behind curtains as neighbors prepared for bed. It had been Milo's desire to see Elaine Wallace nude, because

Elaine Wallace was the prettiest girl in Jericho. Also the most careful. Elaine prepared for bed in the dark, perhaps knowing her window was being watched.

He wondered if Milo had played well that day. Tomorrow he would find a newspaper and read about the game, and he would save the paper to record the results in his journal of Milo.

Once Sally had asked him about the journals that he kept locked in the rolltop desk. "Just business," he had told her. A gentle deception. When they married, he would tell her of the records he kept on Milo, and of the letters that he wrote. Or maybe she knew about the letters. Her cousin was the postmaster.

He thought of Sally sleeping. Thought of her letter. *I don't want you to go away, but if you do, I want you to come home to me. I already miss you. I already hurt so much I can hardly breathe.* He remembered her lips swollen against his lips. A tremor tickled across his chest and he could feel his heartbeat against his throat.

In two days he would see her.

In two days he would ask her to be his wife.

He touched his chest to quiet the tremor.

"Ben, will you hold me for a minute?"

The voice was so clear Ben turned to look down the hallway.

He touched his chest again. The warmth on his fingers was not his warmth. It was from Lottie.

FOURTEEN

THE DOCTOR WAS wrong about Little Ben. He did not have anthrax. At morning's light, he opened his eyes and said, as a question, "Mama?"

He was sick, still weak, but the fever had left him, and the doctor guessed that he only had an infection of the throat.

"There's so much we don't know," the doctor confessed. "So much we're just now learning about."

"Can we take him with us?" asked Lottie.

The doctor frowned. "He's still not well, and he's a little bit undernourished. I'd rather you let us watch him a while longer — this morning, at least. Let's try to get some food in him. Maybe you could leave this afternoon."

"Can I stay with him?" Lottie wanted to know.

"I'm sure he'd like that," the doctor answered.

OUTSIDE, IT WAS a bright, early-hot day. Ben moved sluggishly along the sidewalk leading to O'Connor's. "Go get some sleep,"

Lottie had insisted. "You paid for the bed, you might as well use it."

She was right, of course, Ben thought. He needed rest. There was still a long way to travel and he would need to be alert. He was not accustomed to going without his sleep. Still, he felt uncomfortable going to the bed where Lottie had slept. Her body would not be there, but her presence would be — her presence and the flower scent that seemed to be on her skin and in her hair.

In the room, he removed his coat and tie and shoes and fell across the bed. The scent of Lottie was in the pillow, and he pushed it away and closed his eyes. He thought of Sally, imagined her moving gracefully about the store, her smile breaking into laughter, her voice as merry as music. She was beautiful, so very beautiful.

And then he slept. Deep. Heavy. Hot. Floating in space that was absolutely black, space so thick it contained only a slow-moving dream, and in the dream he was again in Augusta, again in the centerfield grass of Hornet Field, again cawing in his boy's voice for Nat Skinner: *"You can do it, Nat! Bear down, bear down, bear down . . ."* He saw Nat's pitch, saw the swing of the bat from the Seagulls player, heard a sharp crack, saw the ball rising — small white dot against the black — and he could feel his body begin to move, the tension in his muscles uncoiling like a released spring. He could feel a hot wind slapping at his face. His heart thundered in his chest and the blood spewed in a flash throughout his body. And then he was in a dive, his left arm extended, palm up, and the hot wind that slapped against him seemed to cushion him, hold him. He looked up at the falling ball, and the ball became a shooting star, a slow, streaking fire across the absolute black of his dream space, and as the star fell toward him, he could see Sally's face in the red-orange of its kite-tail light. She was gazing at him, smiling. And then he could feel the star exploding in his gloved hand, shattering like fine glass, its light sizzling over his hand, and in the light he could see Lottie sleeping on the train. He heard voices from across the grass: "*Ben! Ben! Ben! You got it, Ben! You got it!*"

"Ben?"

Ben could hear his name, could feel the tug on his arm.

"Ben?"

He rolled his face, forced his eyes to open.

Lottie stood beside the bed, leaning over him. She looked frightened.

"You got the fever, Ben."

He opened his mouth to speak, could feel a swelling in his throat, a burning across his face and neck. His lungs ached.

"You lay still," Lottie said. "I'll go get the doctor."

Ben closed his eyes again. He could hear Lottie rush from the room, and after a few moments he could hear her voice downstairs and the voice of someone else, and then the closing of a door, a dull, faraway sound. He tried to raise his head, but could not. The stem of his neck throbbed with pain. His breathing was shallow and labored.

And then someone was in the room with him, and he heard a woman's voice: "Now don't go worrying, young man. You've just got a touch of something." There was an Irish lilt to the voice and he knew it was Elizabeth O'Connor. "Your lady friend's gone for the doctor, but we'll make you a bit cooler."

He could feel a damp cloth on his face, a gentle stroking over his forehead and eyes and lips.

"It's the heat, it is," Elizabeth O'Connor crooned. "Oh, yes, I've seen it many, many times. You get a bit of a cold and the heat drives it in you, and before you know it, you've got a full-blown fever." She pulled away the damp cloth. "Now, could you take a little sip of water?"

Ben nodded feebly. He could feel Elizabeth O'Connor's hand under his neck, lifting his head, and then the touch of a glass to his lips.

"Just a bit," Elizabeth O'Connor whispered. "Just a bit. What you need is a good swallowing of fine Irish whiskey, but I'm sure the doctor would faint away at such a remedy."

The water spilled over his lips, into his mouth. It was warm and tasted of tin. He tried to swallow and the glass moved and water trickled down his chin.

"Now, there I go," Elizabeth O'Connor complained quietly, removing the glass. "Trying to drown you." She lowered his head back onto the pillow. "But that's enough for now." She began to bathe his face again with the damp cloth. "The doctor will be here soon enough. You'll be fine."

BEN DID NOT remember the doctor appearing at his bedside, declaring him infected with an illness that was, perhaps, the same as Little Ben had. He did not hear the doctor telling Lottie, "Maybe it'll go away as quick as it did with your boy, if it's the same, but sometimes it's easier for little ones to throw off an infection than it is for us older people." He did not know who had undressed him and moved him between the bedsheets. His body demanded sleep and he obeyed, drugged by medicine and by the illness that had probably crawled from Little Ben to him.

He did not know that in the afternoon a powerful storm had hurled out of Missouri and Illinois, battered Nashville with rain and hail, and above Nashville, a tornado had skittered across the land, killing a dozen people who had gathered in a church to plan a week of camp meeting services.

He did not know that, before the storm, Elizabeth O'Connor had helped Lottie move Little Ben from the doctor's office to a bedroom across the hall from where he slept. No charge for the stay, Elizabeth

O'Connor had insisted. It was the neighborly thing to do. Besides, she had been young once with her first child, not knowing what to do, and she had been treated kindly, and one could never do enough to pay back such generosity. And, too, she liked Lottie and Ben, knowing they were friends and that Ben was making good on his promise to her dead husband. A fine man, Ben was, she declared to Lottie in her singsong voice. She'd known many people named Phelps, and she had known many people named Lanier. All fine people. All of them. Some of them regulars when they came to Nashville. It was part of the joy of having a boardinghouse—knowing people, trying to connect them, name by name.

He did not know that in Boston, Milo Wade had had four hits against the New York Highlanders, but had been ejected from the game in the ninth inning for brawling with the Highlanders' second baseman, and that a writer from one of the Boston newspapers would pen a story about Milo Wade striking his wife in a fit of anger. The headline would cry: WADE A WIFE-BEATER.

He did not know that, as he slept into the night, his mother had invited Sally Ledford to supper as a gesture to repair any hurt feelings about the encounter she had had with Sally's father, and that, as they talked, woman to woman, they fashioned a bond that would become more powerful than Sally's bond with her own mother.

He did not know that, after the supper, in her own room, Sally had written another letter to him.

My dearest Ben,

Tonight I had supper with your mother and came away from your home loving her almost as much as I love you. If you are at all worried about what happened between her and my father, you shouldn't be. She did not tell me this, but I know they have talked and all is well. I know my father misses you. I see him looking around the store as though he is looking for you. This morning, he said to

Mr. Jesse Taylor that you knew more about the stock than he did, and that you were a born merchant. I think he said it for me to hear, since Mr. Taylor only wanted to pay a bill for his wife and had no reason at all to be interested in the stock.

It was so wonderful being in your home. Your mother invited me to see your room. I could feel you there, the little-boy you and the you that you are now. (I loved the photograph of you with your father. Why haven't you told me about it?) Your mother told me you were a good housekeeper and seldom had to be asked twice about helping out with the chores. But I knew that. You're the same way in the store.

Oh, one thing about supper tonight: Your mother gave me recipes of all your favorite dishes, including fried okra, and I plan to start practicing on them. I don't think I'll ever be as good at it as your mother, though.

It seems you have been away for so long, although I know it's only been for a few days. The hours seem to crawl by without you in them, and no matter how much I wish it, I cannot make the clock spin faster. Tomorrow will be an eternity, but you will be home the day after (I hope!) and we will be together.

I love you with such joy I think I can feel it lifting me up off the ground, taking me cloud-high with happiness.

Sally

FIFTEEN

ON WEDNESDAY, JULY 20, six days after leaving Jericho, Ben awoke in O'Connor's Inn before sunrise. The dampness of perspiration soaked into the bedsheets. His mouth was dry, his throat raw. His body felt lead-heavy and useless. He dragged his arm from the bed to his chest, letting his fingers rest over his heart. An unsteady flutter drummed in his chest.

The room was dark except for the copper coating of net curtains drawn against an outside streetlight, and in the confusion of first-waking, Ben wondered where he was. He had been on a train — he remembered the train, the rocking, the steel-clicking of wheels — and now he was in a bed. Not his bed, though. Not his room. He rolled his head, licked his lips, and then his mind cleared. He was in O'Connor's Inn. He had taken ill, in all likelihood the same illness that Little Ben had.

He rolled his shoulders, forced his legs over the side of the bed, and pulled himself into a sitting position. He felt woozy. His stomach was queasy. He tilted forward and slowly slid from the bed, carefully balancing himself. Across the room, in the cast of the copper light, he saw a chair and in the chair the curled shape of a person. He stepped cautiously toward the chair. Lottie. It was Lottie. Her head was buried in a pillow and she slept peacefully.

At the chair, he leaned to touch her and she jerked awake, pushing hard against the chairback.

"Ben?" she whispered.

"What—day is it?" Ben asked hoarsely.

Lottie blinked away sleep. "Wednesday," she answered after a moment. "It's not sunup yet, but it's Wednesday."

Ben slumped to one knee and Lottie reached for his hand. He said, "How's Little Ben?"

"He's better," Lottie told him. "Still a little weak, but he's better. What about you?"

Ben shook his head. "Not too good, I guess."

"You need to get back to bed."

"I think I need to stand up some," Ben said. Then: "Wednesday? Did you say it was Wednesday?"

Lottie nodded.

Ben struggled to stand. Wednesday, he thought. One day left. One day to go to Augusta and then back to Jericho. It was impossible. He would be a day late.

"We have to leave this morning," he said.

"No, Ben, you can't," Lottie said patiently. She pulled from the chair. "You're still sick."

Ben shook his head. "I'll be all right." He turned to stumble back to the bed and realized suddenly that he was dressed only in his underwear. He stepped clumsily into the room's shadow, away from the window light. "I'm—sorry," he muttered. "I didn't know—"

"You don't have to be ashamed," Lottie said quietly. "Me and Mrs. O'Connor got you ready for bed."

For a moment Ben did not speak. He stood hidden in the dark of the room, trying not to look at Lottie. He was embarrassed, and he did not know why. Two nights before, Lottie had slept next to him and he had not been embarrassed, or ashamed.

"Are you afraid of me, Ben?" Lottie asked.

"No," Ben said. "I—"

"You know what I don't understand, Ben? I don't understand why it feels so easy being around you, but it does. I feel as good being around you as I ever have with anybody. I think I knew that the first time I ever saw you." She crossed to him, took his hand. "Come on. Go back to bed. I'll get you some water."

"I think I better sit up awhile," Ben said.

"If that's what you want," Lottie said. She guided him to the chair and helped him sit and then she took a blanket folded at the foot of the bed and covered him with it.

He sat without speaking as she helped him take water from a glass, and he watched her moving about the bed, stripping it of the perspiration-soaked sheets. He listened as she talked quietly about the doctor visiting him, about Elizabeth and Ralph O'Connor's kindness, about his need to wait another day before traveling.

"You're a stubborn man, Ben Phelps," she said. "Not as bad as Foster, but bad enough. I couldn't hardly handle Foster. He was wanting to walk on crutches two days after they cut off his leg. Doctor told him he wadn't strong enough to stand up, but he made me get him some crutches so he could see for himself. Fell flat on his face. Made me so mad, I was going to leave, but I said I'd help out, so I couldn't."

Ben had forgotten about Lottie nursing Foster back to health after the amputation of his leg. No wonder she's not uncomfortable or timid being here, he thought. Helping a sick man was natural to her, a gift even. He wondered if she had cared for her father on those nights when her father stumbled home drunk. It was likely. She would have learned patience with her father, learned that men were bewildered by weakness.

"Mrs. O'Connor said to give you some of her soup when you woke up," Lottie told him. "You stay right there and I'll go get some. I'll have to fix a fire to warm it up, so it'll take a little bit. Will you be all right?"

Ben nodded, whispered, "Yes."

"I'll get some more sheets, too. She showed me where they are."

"Lottie?"

"Yes, Ben."

"I'm in your debt. I want you to know that."

"Why did you say that, Ben?"

"I just am."

"No, you're not. It's the other way around."

"I don't see how you can think that," Ben said.

"You're taking me home, Ben. Nobody's ever done that."

———

THE AFTERNOON TRAIN from Nashville to Chattanooga and then to Atlanta left at ten minutes after four. It would not arrive in Atlanta until late in the night, and there would be an hour wait before catching the train to Athens and then to Augusta. By the schedule, the train would pass through Jericho before sunrise, too early for travelers, Ben believed, too early even for Akers Crews, who seemed to live at the depot.

He was still weak, still perspired freely. The doctor had suggested that he stay in bed for another day. Two would be better. "You'll see I'm right when you get on that train," the doctor had said.

Ben had lied, saying he felt stronger after eating, and then he tempered the lie with what he believed was the truth—that being home would be the best medicine for him, the sooner the better.

Ralph O'Connor had taken Ben and Lottie and Little Ben to the train station in his buggy, though the station was only a block's walk away, and when Ben tried to pay him for the stay, he refused it. "There's a difference between running a business and helping out when helping out's needed," Ralph said. "Me and the wife, we talked it over. It's what we want to do. If you ever get back this way, we'll make it a business stay."

"I'll see you again," promised Ben. It was a promise he could not keep, though he would visit the site of O'Connor's Inn in 1915 on a buying trip to Nashville. He would learn that Elizabeth O'Connor had been struck and killed by a motorcar in December of 1911 and that Ralph O'Connor had returned in sadness to Ireland in 1912.

ON THE TRAIN, Lottie made a pillow for Little Ben from a rolled-up towel that Elizabeth O'Connor had given her — "In case you need it" — and she took her seat beside him, across from Ben. She held open in her lap the ivory-handled fan that Foster had given her. The fan was her only medicine against the illnesses lingering in Ben and in Little Ben.

"Are you all right?" she said to Ben.

Ben nodded. The lurch of the train in its pull away from the station vibrated in his body. He braced his hands on the seat. "I sure hope you don't come down with something," he said.

"I won't," Lottie promised. "I don't never get sick, Ben. Not ever. Tired, sometimes, but I never been bad sick." She smiled. "I been thinking about Foster."

Ben nodded again.

"One time he got sick right after he started using his crutches, and he wanted to go out to see a ball game," she said. "I kept telling him not till, but he wouldn't listen, wouldn't listen at all. He got so bad at the game, he passed out, and I had to get a colored man that worked there to help me get him back to where we was staying.

Know what I did, Ben? I hid his crutches, and wouldn't let him have them back, not till I knew he was strong enough."

She smiled warmly, turned the fan in her hand, gazed at the painted flowers, then she looked up at Ben. "Foster got mad at me," she said. "Madder than I ever saw him. Told me it wadn't right for a woman to go against a man like that. Only time he ever treated me like my daddy treated my mama."

"You did what was best," Ben said.

Lottie dipped her head once, but did not take her eyes from Ben. "You get sick, Ben, I'm going to do the same thing to you. I'm going to do what's best, and I hope you don't get mad at me for it."

SALLY SAT, AS always, at the side of the dining-room table, in a position that conveniently separated Arthur Ledford from Alice Ledford. From her childhood, she had been a conduit for the brief messages her parents passed between them from the ends of the table, passed back and forth like the food dishes prepared by Lena, their maid. She knew her birth had become a treaty of civility that her parents honored with vigilant caution, like neighboring nations always armed for war. The narrow dining-table space that Sally occupied—her mother to her left, her father to her right—was a territory of neutrality. Still, to Sally, it was territory as unstable as a festering volcano. Formal. Polite. Orderly. And tense. Always tense. After each of the three suppers that Ben had taken at her home, she had become ill late in the night, knowing he could sense what was invisible, yet as terrifying as chains rattled by ghosts.

The marriage of Arthur and Alice Ledford had been a pretense for years, a secret that everyone in the town knew, but never spoke of, and no one knew it better than Sally, who had accepted it not with bitterness, but with pity.

When she married Ben, there would not be any ghosts. Or territories. Laughter and easy chatter would be at her table. And she would sit close enough to Ben to touch him.

Her father spoke first of Ben: "Does Ben's mother still expect him home tomorrow?"

"I think so," Sally answered. "I haven't seen her since our supper."

Her mother sniffed. "Don't get your hopes up too high."

"What does that mean?" her father said.

"I'm sure Sally knows what I mean."

"No, Mama, I don't," Sally said.

Alice Ledford pushed her plate away, still filled with food. "It means he may not be back tomorrow, or the next day, or the day after that. It means there's no telling when he'll show up again — Mr. World Traveler."

A rush of anger pulsed through Sally. She drank from her tea to control it. Her father did not look up from his eating.

"I think he'll be here," Sally said quietly.

"He'll be here," her father said.

Sally saw her mother's eyes turn in a glare across the table toward her father. "He's never been away from home," she said. "Except for that short time thinking he was a ballplayer, and we all know how that turned out. He's always been right here, tied to his mother's apron strings, and you think he's not going to be carried away by all the goings-on in a big city like Boston?" She sniffed again. "I wouldn't put it past him to fall in with that group of ruffians Milo Wade associates with."

Arthur looked up, matched the glare in his wife's eyes.

"Don't give me that look, Arthur," she said. "You know exactly what I mean. Why, there was a story about it in the Boston paper only yesterday, how Milo Wade was a wife-beater."

"Where did you see a Boston paper?" Arthur asked.

"I didn't. I happened to be talking to Charlotte Crews this afternoon, and she said that one of the train conductors had given Akers a copy of it on a stop at the station — knowing this is Milo's home."

"I haven't heard anything about that," Sally said.

"Me, either," her father mumbled.

"If you don't believe me, go see Akers tomorrow," her mother said. "Call him on the telephone tonight, if you wish."

"It's got nothing to do with Ben," Sally said defensively.

Her mother looked at her and a condescending smile swept over her face. "Of course it doesn't," she said. "What I meant to say was that I hope he didn't get caught up in all of that. Ben's a good boy. I'm just wondering when he's going to ask for your hand, and stop keeping us on pins and needles."

Sally knew the smile was false and the words were false. Her mother had not mentioned Ben since her warning talk about the in-between time of her life. Then she had sounded sad and regretful. Now she sounded shallow.

"In his own time, Mama. If it's what he wants, it'll be in his own time," Sally answered. She quivered at the sound of her own voice.

———

THE FEVER STRUCK Ben again ten minutes after leaving the Athens train station. He was sitting, leaning his body against the seat, his eyes closed, and then he coughed once and collapsed forward, falling into Lottie. A passenger across the aisle, a man who identified himself as a preacher in the faith of the Baptists, helped her lift Ben to the seat, turning him to stretch out with his suit coat rolled into a pillow for his head.

"Father God, reach out your healing hands and through the grace of your son and our Savior, bring comfort to this poor man in his illness," the preacher prayed earnestly. "Give his good wife the strength to care for him, and take away any fear his child may be suffering, for we bring our petition of mercy before you, acknowledging our sins and weakness, yet knowing that, in Jesus, we have the great physician as our caretaker. In his name, we make this prayer. Amen."

Lottie thanked the preacher with her eyes. There was no reason to correct him about Ben being her husband, or Little Ben being his son. The preacher would not have understood, and he had prayed a good prayer. Correcting him might waste it.

"If you need anything, I'll be right across the aisle," the preacher whispered. He added, "You better think about getting off at the next stop and finding a doctor."

"Yes sir," Lottie said. "That's where we're headed. How much longer do you think it'll be?"

The preacher fingered a watch from his vest and looked at it. The watch was attached to a soft leather fob with the imprint of a cross. "Less than an hour, I'd say."

"Thank you," Lottie said.

"I'll give you a hand with him when we get there," the preacher told her.

"I appreciate it," Lottie said.

"Least I can do," the preacher replied. "But don't you go worrying. He's in God's hands. God don't take time off."

"Yes sir," Lottie said. "I guess he don't."

AKERS CREWS STOOD on the platform of the depot, one hand propped against a post. The arthritis in his back throbbed, forcing him into a hunch, yet he could not complain. Not openly. He hated early-morning stops, but the stop on this morning was for his wife. She intended to visit her sister in Augusta and wanted to have a full day of it. Gab time, Akers called it. Damned hen convention. Bad as it was, it was still better that his wife visit her sister than her sister visit his wife. Goda'mighty, they made a racket. Worse than hens.

You could shut hens up by filling them full of corn, but his wife and her sister would cluck their way through a tornado.

He watched the train slowing to a stop. It was not yet dawn, though the coming light of day was on the eastern horizon like a bruise. Not long now, Akers thought. Get her on the train and get back to bed. A little whiskey for the pain, and then sleep.

Akers twisted his body toward the depot and motioned for his wife. "Come on. They running late. They not gone wait long."

"Why, look at that," Charlotte Crews said in a surprised voice.

Akers turned back to the train. He saw a man helping Ben Phelps from the passenger car, half-dragging him. A woman carrying a young boy was behind them, and a conductor followed with a suit-case and a wrapped bundle.

"Looks drunk," Akers mumbled.

"Akers, don't go saying things like that," scolded Charlotte. "That's Ben Phelps. You know he's not been drinking." She paused, craned her face forward. "Wonder who that is with him?" Then: "Go on, Akers, give them a hand."

Akers hobbled forward to the man holding Ben. "What's the trouble?" he asked.

"Got a young man here who's terrible sick," said the man. "My name's Reverend Bolly Curtis of the Baptist persuasion. Just giving him and his family a hand."

"Family?" said Akers.

"I think the boy's a little sick, too," the preacher said. "If you'd catch his other arm, maybe we can get him up the platform there."

Akers glanced at Lottie, then took Ben's arm and helped the Reverend Bolly Curtis drag-walk him up the steps of the depot to a bench. Ben sat weakly. He gazed at Akers and whispered, "Mr. Crews."

"You're home, boy," Akers said. "We'll take care of you."

Bolly Curtis leaned to Ben. "You'll be all right, son. God's with you. God and this good man. I'll be praying for you and your family."

Ben nodded a confused nod. He tried to stand, could not.

"I'd better be going," the preacher said. He looked at Lottie. "You take care of him, young lady. And your boy. Better get them both to the doctor."

"Yes sir," Lottie said. "Thank you."

The preacher tipped his fingers to his hat and turned and quick-stepped back to the train.

Akers pivoted to his wife, who was staring at Lottie in disbelief. "Go on," he snapped. "It's about to leave."

"But—" Charlotte said.

"But, what?" Akers growled. "You going, or not?"

Charlotte stepped back, toward the train.

Damn, Akers thought. That's all she needs: something else to talk about.

"Maybe I better—"

"Get on the train, Charlotte," Akers commanded. "I can take care of things here." He thrust his face toward her. "And before you go off spreading tales, I think you'd better remember that you don't know nothing about what's going on here."

"Akers—"

"Get on the damn train, Charlotte."

Charlotte Crews turned and crossed to the train and took the steps into the passenger car without looking back.

Akers stood for a moment, watching the train struggle to move, then he motioned for Lottie to follow him out of Ben's hearing. He said in a low voice, "You want to tell me what's going on? You Ben's family?"

"No sir," Lottie answered quietly. "The preacher just thought so, and I didn't tell him any different. Me and my boy, we just met him

on the train. My boy got sick coming out of Kentucky and Ben—
Mr. Phelps—helped me with him, and then he got sick from the
same thing, I guess, and I felt obliged to see after him, since he'd
been so good to us."

"What's your name?" asked Akers.

"Lottie Lanier," Lottie told him. "My boy's name is Ben."

Akers frowned in suspicion.

"Just like Mr. Phelps's name," Lottie said quickly. "That's how we
got to talking. He heard me call my Ben, and he thought I was
talking to him."

"Where you headed?" Akers asked.

"Augusta," Lottie answered. "My husband just died a few days ago
and I was going home to where I used to live. But I haven't been
there in a long time."

Akers turned his head to watch the train slide away from the station. "You missed the train," he said.

"Yes sir," Lottie said. "I was afraid my boy was getting sick again,
and, like I said, I thought I owed it to Mr. Phelps to make sure he
got home all right."

Akers studied her with a narrow gaze. It was hard to judge her
age. She could have been sixteen or thirty. She had soft, haunting
eyes the color of honey. She did not wear a hat and her hair, pulled
up in a bun, was blond-gold. A faint blush was on her cheeks, but
not by the making of rouge. It was a blood-blush, the look of a
woman at work, or pleasure.

The story she told sounded good enough, Akers decided, but when
it got out in Jericho that Ben had arrived home from his trip to
Boston in the company of a pretty woman and a boy carrying his
name, there would still be talk. People would make something of it,
more than it deserved.

Still, it couldn't be helped, he reasoned. He would be careful to
set the story straight when the talk reached him. He would say he

was there to help Ben from the train, and that a preacher was there, and that he was the first to talk to the woman, and he believed her. Besides, the boy she held looked frail, and probably did need to see the doctor. Ben did. No doubt about it.

"All right," he said at last. "I got my motorcar here. Let's get everybody up to Ben's house and call for the doctor."

"I don't want to be trouble," Lottie said.

"Trouble's something that nobody can handle," Akers said. "We can handle this. And I know the boy's mama. She'll probably adopt you and your boy before the day's over."

SIXTEEN

LOTTIE SAT ERECT in the chair at the dining-room table, her hands in her lap, her chin level, her gaze given to the three people also at the table. She heard their words, but their words were hollow. She concentrated only on breathing—inhale, hold, exhale, pause. *Inhale, hold, exhale, pause.* It was a trick her sister had taught her. "Don't think about nothing but breathing," her sister had said. "Sooner or later, whatever's going on, it'll be over, and if you still breathing, you know you still alive, and that's the only thing that matters."

It had been a good trick to follow, and Lottie had used it thousands of times, it seemed. Enduring the rooting passion of men pressing against her, their wadded money on a nearby table or cot. Loneliness in a Kentucky cabin on a Kentucky mountain during a Kentucky winter. Caring for Foster and Little Ben. Waking from night dreams of her mother and her father and her sister. She thought of her breathing, counted the evenness of the inhales and exhales, imagined the air being the size of a half-cup, and the breathing calmed her.

She looked only onto the eyes of the people speaking, yet she wanted to let her gaze wander over the room. The room was large and comfortable, and like the rest of the house, furnished with imposing furniture darkly polished, furniture made for men of breeding and substance. Still, it was the touch of Margaret Phelps that gave the house its warmth. Paintings decorated the walls, ornately framed. Embroidered pillows leaned against chairbacks. Delicate, slender flower vases with threads of color stood on tables beside settings of teacups as thin as paper, the handles and rims fired in gold. Everywhere there was something, almost hidden, that announced Margaret Phelps. Glassware of crystal. Porcelain candlesticks holding candles with wax bubbled over the sides, like drippings of frosting on a cake. Lace handkerchiefs. Photographs in silver stands.

Her memory of Ben's home was more pleasant than any memory she had, she believed, and only her breathing prevented Lottie from bolting from the chair to touch all that her eyes had seen.

The doctor, who had been introduced as Oscar Morgan, was speaking: "As I said, I'm only guessing, but I'm going to start off treating them for rheumatic fever. Ben's worse off than the boy, no doubt about it, but it's hard to tell with little ones sometimes, and to be truthful, they may not have the same problem at all. I'm guessing rheumatic fever with Ben because he had that bad throat two or three weeks ago, but that's just a guess. I'll know more about that later. Main thing is to give them lots to drink—water, preferably. I've left some sulfur tablets in Ben's room. Just follow the directions. Now, can I answer any questions?"

"How long until they get better?" asked Margaret Phelps.

"Depends on what it is," the doctor said. "Honestly, Margaret, I don't know. We'll just have to keep watch over them." He looked at Lottie, then took his eyes from her gaze. Her eyes were mesmerizing. "I know you want to get home, but I'd rather you stay in Jericho for a few days to give the boy time to get back some strength, since he's such a little tyke. There's a boardinghouse not far from here, and I —"

"I'll not hear of it," Margaret said firmly. "They'll stay with us, as our guests. We've got plenty of room and I could never pay Lottie back for taking care of my son the way she did."

Lottie saw a cloud sweep over Sally Ledford's face. "I don't want to trouble anybody," she said quietly.

"It's no trouble," Margaret insisted. She turned to Sally. "Sally and I both want to thank you, don't we, Sally?"

A bright smile popped onto Sally's face. "Of course," she said. "Ben said he didn't know what would have happened to him if it wasn't for you." The smile dimmed.

"Thank you," Lottie said in a voice almost too soft to hear. She twisted her hands in her lap.

"Where did you say you came from?" asked Oscar Morgan.

"Kentucky," Lottie told him. "A little town called Beimer."

"You know of anybody being sick up there before you left? Like Ben and your son, I mean."

"No sir. But we lived up in the hills. That's where my husband died."

"Did he have this sickness?"

Lottie did not move her eyes from the doctor. "No sir. Not like — like Mr. Phelps."

"Call him Ben, please," Margaret said. "He told me that he called your son Little Ben."

Lottie nodded slightly. "Yes ma'am. That's what he — what Ben — said to do, so as to keep the names straight."

Margaret smiled at the strange speech pattern. The girl was from the country, yes, but there was also something refined about her. Something in her face, her eyes. She was poorly dressed, but unusually pretty, the kind of woman who caught the attention of men by no greater effort than a look. She wondered if Ben had seen the look, and if that was why he had helped her with her son. No, she thought. Ben would not turn from Sally, not for a woman on a train. Ben had merely offered to help someone who needed help. He was that way. Like his father.

"So, your husband wasn't sick like Ben?" the doctor said.

"No sir. He'd been sick a long time. He just kind of wasted away."

The doctor frowned and rubbed his chin with his fingers. "Well," he said after a moment, "whatever it is, it could be catching, but I don't see how Ben could have come down with rheumatic fever if he'd just been around your boy for a short time. Those kind of things usually take days. More I think about it, the more I'm starting to doubt if they've got the same ailment."

Lottie did not reply. Her eyes stayed on the doctor.

Oscar Morgan pushed himself wearily from his chair. He smiled at the three women watching him. "One thing about it, I won't have to worry about him being looked after — him or the boy, either one. I'd say I'm standing in the middle of enough looking-after power to run a hospital." He dipped his head in a bow toward Margaret and Sally. "Margaret, Sally, it's nice to see you." He turned to Lottie. "Mrs. Lanier, I'm pleased to make your acquaintance. You've got a fine-looking boy."

Lottie smiled. "Thank you," she said quietly. "He favors his daddy."

Margaret stood. "We'll take good care of them, Oscar," she promised. "I feel better now that you've seen them."

"Me, too," Sally said quickly.

"I'll walk you to the door," Margaret said.

"It's all right," the doctor told her, but Margaret was already leaving the room. He shrugged, nodded again to Sally and Lottie, and followed.

Lottie could feel her body tense. Her palms were perspiring in her lap. She was alone with Sally Ledford, and she did not know what to say, or do. It was a moment she had known would happen, yet one she dreaded. Sally Ledford was young and pretty and childlike, her body only beginning to take a woman's shape. Yet she behaved in a woman's way. A town woman's way. Mannerly. Well-dressed. Well-spoken. She was a woman by mimicry, not by instinct or practice.

Still, Sally Ledford made her more uncomfortable than anyone she had ever met.

EARLIER, SHORTLY AFTER sunrise, she had overheard Ben's mother on the telephone, talking quietly to Sally, telling Sally of Ben's return and of his illness: "There's a young woman here, with her little boy. He's sick, too. Ben met them on the train and was helping her with him when he got sick himself. . . . A very nice young lady. Her husband died a few days ago in Kentucky, and she was going back to live with her people in Augusta. . . . I just wanted you to know, just so you wouldn't be surprised."

Sally had arrived at the Phelps home an hour later, anxious and confused.

"Sally, this is Lottie Lanier," Margaret had said graciously. "And Lottie, this is Sally Ledford, Ben's—special lady."

She had felt Sally's eyes explore her, saw shock in them. Sally had stammered a greeting, then had turned to Ben's mother. "May I see him?" she had asked in a small, frightened voice.

"Of course," Margaret had answered. "I'll go with you."

And they had rushed away, leaving Lottie alone.

SALLY FLICKED A smile at Lottie. She moved nervously in her chair and played her hands on the table. Her hands were small, the nails of her fingers manicured perfectly. "It's funny about Ben and your little boy having the same name," she said.

"Mr. Phelps thought so, too," Lottie said.

"No, call him Ben," urged Sally. "Like Mrs. Phelps said."

Lottie dipped her head and let her gaze float to an arrangement of flowers in the middle of the table. Sometimes she had picked wildflowers and put them in a glass in her cabin in Kentucky. She liked flowers in a home. Daisies. Daisies were her favorite. And roses. She liked roses. She thought of rose petals popped against her forehead.

"Ben was in Boston," Sally said. "Did he tell you?"

Lottie thought of breathing. *Inhale. Hold. Exhale. Pause.* "Yes," she said at last.

"I can't wait for him to get well enough to tell me all about it," Sally said enthusiastically. "I'd love to see a place like Boston. Wouldn't you?"

Lottie remembered the cities she had seen with the carnival — Atlanta, Knoxville, Nashville, Lexington, Louisville, Birmingham, Memphis. So many cities. Not Boston. Still, cities. She said, "I guess so. But it's a long way off."

"Someday, I'm going to make Ben take me," Sally cooed. She sounded giddy.

"That'd be nice," Lottie said.

"Well, he really hasn't asked me to marry him yet, but he's going to. He's as much as said so, but I know I shouldn't be making plans before there's a real reason to. I guess I just can't help it. But you know what I mean, don't you? You were married. I'm sure you felt the same way I do."

A flash-memory of Foster's face, his half-grin, made Lottie blink. She had never thought of making plans with Foster. Things happened, and that was all. Things happened. "It's been so long ago since I got married, I can't hardly remember what it was like," she said simply.

Sally leaned forward at the table, made an instinctive gesture toward Lottie, then withdrew her hand. "I'm so sorry," she said gently. "I'm being rude, talking about getting married when you've just lost your husband."

Lottie tilted her head to accept the apology.

"How long were you married?" asked Sally.

"Five years. Almost six," answered Lottie.

"Where did you meet him?"

Lottie was surprised at the wiggle of a smile she felt on her lips. She said, "On a train."

"Oh—"

"I was going to Knoxville with—my uncle," Lottie said. "He knew Foster."

"Foster? That was your husband's name?"

"Yes," Lottie said.

Sally smiled awkwardly, then slipped from her chair and stood. "I know Daddy must wonder why I'm staying so late, when there's so much to do down at the store," she chattered. "I think we've both learned a big lesson about how much work Ben does, but that's the way it is, I suppose. You never know how much you miss somebody—or need them—until they're gone. Anyway, Daddy must be wondering. I told him I'd be there as soon as I could." She paused, glanced toward the front of the house, wondered why Margaret Phelps was so long in returning. "I think I'll just run up and check on Ben before I go."

Lottie moved her hands to the table, made a gesture to stand.

"Oh, no, don't get up," Sally urged. "I know you must be worn out. You need to get some sleep. I'm sure I'll see you this afternoon."

"All right," Lottie said.

"I'm glad to meet you," Sally told her. "And I do thank you for taking care of Ben."

"Least I could do," Lottie said. "He took care of my Ben."

WHEN SHE AWOKE, late in the afternoon, Lottie knew instantly that Little Ben was not in bed with her. The door to the bedroom was closed, yet the room was pleasantly cool. She turned her face to the window and saw that it was open. A breeze fluttered against the net of a curtain that had been slightly parted. She sat up in the bed, then slumped back against the pillow. She had never slept so peacefully, she thought. The bed mattress was cushion-soft, the pillow as puffed as a cloud.

She did not worry about Little Ben. She knew that he was with Margaret Phelps and that he must have trusted her intuitively. Or maybe he thought that Margaret Phelps was his grandmother. She had talked to him about going away to meet his grandmother and his grandfather, and had tried to teach him to say Grandma and Grandpa, but he had chopped the words in his hearing and had repeated, "Gra-Ma" and "Gra-Pa."

She did not know if Little Ben's grandmother and grandfather still lived.

Home was still a place she had not seen in many years.

She arose from the bed and bathed her face in the water basin on the dresser, and then she dressed and stood at the mirror, gazing at herself. The dress she wore was the best she owned, and it was old and faded. She had the money left that she had put away years earlier, money she did not want to spend, but now she would use it to buy a new dress. Two would be better. And some clothes for Little Ben. Her train ticket to Augusta had been purchased by Ben. She had objected, but he had insisted.

"It's my promise," Ben had said. "I owe it to Foster to keep it, and this is part of it. Besides that, it's what I want to do."

He had sounded as proud as some of the boys she had known at the carnival stops before her marriage to Foster—boys with their first woman, boys who fell in love with her and moaned their pledges to show up again and take her away from the carnival and marry her and share their riches. But the boys never returned, and the trains pulling the carnival cars always left with her aboard.

She turned from the mirror, made the bed, and then eased from the room, closing the door behind her. Across the hallway was Ben's room. She moved cautiously to the door, paused to listen. No voices. She tapped lightly at the door. Still no voices. She looked toward the staircase, heard Margaret's laughter from downstairs, and then she slowly turned the knob and slightly opened the door. Ben was in bed, his head elevated on a pillow, his eyes closed. She stepped inside the room and crossed quietly to the bed and stood gazing at him. He looked as young as the first time she saw him. She leaned to him, kissed him gently on the cheek, and then left the room.

Little Ben was sitting at the dining-room table, tiny in the largeness of the chair, and Margaret Phelps was in a chair pulled up close to him. A plate of food was on the table and a glass of milk. Little Ben was smiling shyly, and Margaret was beaming.

"You're awake," Margaret said brightly as Lottie entered the room. "I hope you rested well."

"Yes ma'am," Lottie said. She smiled at Little Ben. He grinned and tucked his head.

"Well, I stole this young fellow right off the bed," Margaret said. "I peeked in to check on you and he was sitting up beside you, looking around."

Lottie moved to Little Ben and knelt beside him and touched his face with her hand. She could not feel fever. "I hope he's been behaving," she said.

"Oh, my goodness, he's the sweetest child I think I've ever seen, and that includes my own," Margaret enthused. "But he's not much of a talker, is he?"

"No. Not much," Lottie replied.

"He's feeling better, I think," Margaret said. "I've managed to get a little food in him." She glanced up at Lottie. "And you've got to get some food in you, so help yourself. It's all in the kitchen. Some chicken and beans and creamed potatoes and biscuits in the warmer oven. And, oh, you'll need tea. You'll find the glasses in the cabinet over the sink, and there's ice in the icebox, already chipped, and the tea's on the counter."

Margaret Phelps continued to talk as Lottie got the food and tea and returned to the table and sat across from Little Ben. Margaret's voice was song-happy, a sound of chirping, like a bird in spring, glad for sun and greenery. She talked of how many people had called concerning Ben, of how Ben seemed to have improved with rest, of fussing with him over taking water and soup broth.

She told Lottie that Ben had asked about her and about Little Ben, and was relieved to know they were still there, and the asking had made her proud. Ben was like his father, she declared. Always caring about other people. It was the strength of his character. Everyone said so, and nothing could please a mother more than having people say that her child was a caring person.

"And you're the same way," Margaret crooned. "You have to be, the way you put aside your own plans, so soon after your husband's death, and helped Ben when he needed help."

"He was the one helping us," Lottie said.

"Maybe so, but you were there when he needed somebody, and I can tell you, not everybody's that way," Margaret said. "Not today. The world's changing, and I don't know if it's for the better." She sighed, urged Little Ben to take another bite of creamed potatoes, then added, "But none of us should complain, not really. Ben's always telling me that, always telling me we're in the twentieth century. Of course, I remember how it was growing up, right after the war. I was born the year that it ended and was just a baby, but I still remember how hard it was for everybody. I wouldn't want to go back to those days for anything. Not at all. Not at all. I'm the most grateful person on earth for all the things we've got now—electricity, running water, the indoor bathroom, the telephone, my electric iron." She laughed easily. "Even motorcars, although I'm scared to death of them." She paused again, reached to smooth back Little Ben's hair. "It just sometimes seems that the more you have of things, the more you lose yourself."

The smile on her face turned sorrowful and she looked at Lottie. "I'm sorry," she said. "I'm chattering on so much I haven't given you a chance to get a word in."

"I'm glad to hear some talking by a woman," Lottie told her. "I didn't get to see many women back where we lived."

"You're at the right place, then," Margaret said. "Since Ben's father died, I don't get out very much. Church. A little shopping. Ben works such long hours, we don't spend much time just sitting around and talking, especially since he's starting courting Sally, and I miss having someone just for that purpose. So I'll probably overdo it while you're here."

"That's all right," Lottie said. She added, "The food's real good. Thank you for it."

Margaret waved away the compliment. "I'm glad to see somebody enjoy it." She paused, then said, "The truth is, Lottie, I'm glad you and Little Ben are here. Sometimes I feel so lost in this rambling old house, I think I'm just wasting away. Having you here brings some life back to it, and I hope you don't mind, but I'm going to enjoy every minute of it, and I'm going to start by taking you shopping when Sally comes over. She called and said her father was letting her leave the store early."

A puzzled look crossed Lottie's face.

"And before you say a word about it, what I'm going to do is what I want to do," Margaret said forcefully. "And I want to say something up front, right now, to get rid of any kind of embarrassment either one of us may have." She paused, inhaled for courage. "You don't have to tell me that you've been on hard times. I know it. And I know you don't have the money for the things I want you to have, so I'm going to do the paying, and all I want out of you is that pretty smile you've got. It's like having the sun roll through the windows and stay awhile, and that's something nobody can ever buy."

"Oh, no ma'am, you can't—"

Margaret raised her hand. "Hush, now. Yes, I can. I've been blessed. My husband was successful and he left me well cared for, but I never get the chance to spend money the way I want to. I don't need anything for myself, and Ben does well, so I'm going to do this, and the way I'm going to look at it is that I never had the daughter I wanted, so I'm going to pretend you're that daughter." She laughed nervously. "I don't really believe in such things, even if I am Presbyterian by marriage, but I have a feeling that I've been waiting all my life for you and Little Ben to show up."

Lottie could feel a blush on her neck, a racing in her heartbeat. She had never known anyone like Margaret Phelps. "I—can't," she whispered.

"It'll make me happy," Margaret said softly. "I'm not talking about much. Just a few things. Will you let me be happy?"

Lottie nodded after a moment.

"Besides, I can't ignore who I guess I must be, but didn't know it," Margaret said.

Lottie looked at her quizzically.

"Listen," Margaret said. She leaned to Little Ben. "What's my name, Little Ben?" she whispered.

Little Ben grinned. He put his hands to his chin.

"What's my name?"

Little Ben looked at his mother, then back to Margaret.

"Who am I?" Margaret said.

"Gra-Ma," Little Ben answered in a giggle.

The laugh that sprang from Margaret Phelps rang like a bell.

THERE WAS NO one in Ledford's Dry Goods when Margaret Phelps and Lottie entered the store, and Lottie felt relieved. On the walk from the Phelps home to the store, she had sensed the eyes of the townspeople on her, judging her, and she guessed that their judgment was one of hostility or pity. Walking beside Margaret Phelps, she must have appeared like a beggar, she believed. Old dress. Hatless. Shoes that were worn to throwaway. Yet, if her appearance bothered Margaret, it was not obvious. Margaret acted indifferent to the curious stares. She talked gaily, like an excited guide conducting a tour of Jericho.

In the store, Margaret moved immediately to the ladies' wear department, calling for Arthur Ledford.

"We're here, Arthur."

Arthur Ledford appeared from the back of the store. He was dressed in a gray suit, neatly pressed. The gray of his suit matched the streaked dark gray of his hair. Margaret smiled broadly as he approached.

"Well, you're sure handsome today," she said. "That's a good color."

Arthur's face tinted rose. He nodded a bow with his head. "Margaret," he said formally.

"I know you've heard about the young woman who was good enough to help Ben out when he got sick on the train," Margaret said. "I want you to meet Lottie Lanier. Lottie, this is Sally's father, Arthur Ledford."

"Hello," Lottie said.

Arthur turned to her. She saw him blink once, and there was a pause, a single, missing stroke of time that she had seen many times from many men.

"Mrs. Lanier," Arthur said. "Welcome to Jericho. Sally told me about you, of course. She's very grateful for your concern about Ben." He paused again, his eyes locked on her face. "And so am I. He's a fine young man, very valuable to this store."

Margaret laughed easily. "I'll tell him you said that."

The rose blush in Arthur's face turned red.

"All right, Arthur, we're here to buy," Margaret announced in a voice that was a command. "And we don't want to be too long about it. Sally's sweet to watch over Ben and Lottie's little boy, but I don't want her to feel like we've left her for good. We'll need some outfits for Lottie, and for her son." She smiled. "Little Ben. Isn't that ironic, Arthur? Lottie's son is also named Ben, so we have two Bens. Little Ben and Big Ben."

"Yes," Arthur said awkwardly. "Sally told me. She said he was a fine young boy."

"He's an angel," Margaret enthused. "An angel. Now, let's get busy."

They shopped for an hour, twenty minutes past closing time for Ledford's, and in that hour, Lottie was provided with more clothes than she had ever owned. Dresses, skirts, blouses, undergarments, sleeping gowns, hats, shoes, stockings, a purse. And three outfits for Little Ben, including shoes and a small derby hat.

Lottie had tried to stop the buying, had protested each item, but her words were ignored. It was as though Margaret Phelps had decided to refurbish her home and Lottie and Little Ben were the new furnishings. Money did not matter, only the glee of finally spending it, and she did not care if Arthur Ledford's looks of surprise, his guarded words of caution, warned that she was being foolish. She was ecstatic, and money was a cheap price for that long-dead feeling.

"Now, Arthur, I saw that new Model T motorcar of yours outside. Could you drive us home?" Margaret asked pleasantly. "If not, I'm afraid we'll have to make a couple of trips. And you can speak to Ben while you're there."

"Of course I will," Arthur said in a defeated voice.

———

THERE WAS A look of confusion on Sally's face as she watched the unloading of her father's car, a confusion she attempted to cover with a forced smile and with compliments for Margaret's selections of the gifts to Lottie. She knew each item purchased, knew where they were found in the store, knew them by size and color and price, and she gushed again and again, "That's perfect, just perfect. I can't wait to see you wearing everything." Still, her eyes betrayed her. Her eyes said, "*So much, so much. Why so much?*"

Having Lottie model was a grand idea, Margaret decided. She selected an ensemble and begged Lottie to put it on. "And these shoes," she said, lifting a pair of shoes from the display that had been spread about in the living room. "And this hat." She glanced at Little Ben, who sat watching with puzzled interest, not understanding what had happened. "And Little Ben, too. We have to see Little Ben all dressed up in his new knickerbockers." She took an outfit from a chair and handed it to Lottie.

"He'll be so handsome in that," Sally cooed. "Like a little man."

"It's a sin for a boy to be that beautiful," Margaret said softly. She bent to him. "Did you have a good time with Sally?"

Little Ben blinked a timid yes.

"Oh, he's been wonderful," Sally said quickly. "We were drawing some animals. He's such a little gentleman. So quiet."

Margaret lifted Little Ben from the chair. "Come on," she said. "We're going to show everyone what a really handsome man looks like." She glanced at Lottie. "I'll take him upstairs for you."

Lottie smiled weakly and followed. She could not remember being so uncomfortable, yet she knew she could not object. She and Little Ben were on exhibit, but it was not for meanness; it was for joy. And she also knew that deep within her, a small girl squealed with delight.

At the stairs, Margaret called over her shoulder, "Sally, bring your father up to speak to Ben."

"If he's sleeping, I'll come—" Arthur began.

"Arthur, quit being so stiff-necked in my home," Margaret said lightly.

The rose-red blush flowed again over Arthur Ledford's face.

BEN HEARD THE tapping at the door and from behind the tapping, Sally's voice, small and hesitant: "Ben? Ben?"

He pulled the bedcovers up over his chest, though they were heavy and hot and the pajamas that he wore were damp and sticky. He called, "Come in." His voice was still hoarse and weak.

The door opened and Sally stepped inside. She checked Ben quickly with a look, saw that he was presentable, then said, "You've got a visitor."

Ben raised his head on the pillow to look at her. His body jerked involuntarily when he saw Arthur Ledford standing in the doorway.

"Mr.—Ledford," Ben whispered.

Sally caught her father's arm and pulled him to the bed.

"How are you, Ben?" Arthur asked gravely.

"A little better," Ben said, attempting to pull up in the bed. He could feel the band of perspiration thicken on his neck.

"Stay just where you are," scolded Sally. "Daddy just drove your mother and Lottie home in his car from shopping at the store, and he wanted to say hello to you. You don't have to get up."

"Sally's right," Arthur said. "You need to keep still, preserve your energy. You still look under the weather to me."

"Yes sir," Ben murmured. "I guess I am." He licked his lips. "How are things at the store?"

Arthur nodded authoritatively. "Good enough. Good enough." He paused, let a furrow fold over his brow. "We're a little behind with stocking some reorders, but we'll manage."

"Wish I could be there to help," Ben said.

"Don't even start thinking that way," Sally told him. "You'll take the time to get well, no matter how long it is, and that's all there is to it." She turned to her father. "Isn't that right?" It was not a question; it was a directive.

"Yes, of course," Arthur said.

"If we need to, we can hire somebody else temporarily," Sally added.

Her father cut his eyes to her. The look was a warning. "We'll be fine until Ben gets back," he said.

Sally ignored her father. She said, "I was thinking that maybe Lottie would like to work a few days, while she's here, waiting for Little Ben to get better. I mean, she wouldn't have to sell or anything like that. Just restock, and I could show her how to do that."

Arthur shifted his weight, set his jaw in argument. "We don't need anyone," he said stubbornly.

"Why, of course we do, Daddy," Sally protested. "What you mean is, we could get by without somebody helping, but that doesn't mean we don't need them, and I just thought it'd give Lottie something to do, other than just having to sit around here all day. Mrs. Phelps is right here with Ben, and I know she'd love to watch over Little Ben. Besides—and I don't mean this in a belittling way—but I imagine that Lottie could use the money."

Arthur began to gnaw on his lower lip. He touched the knot of his tie and coughed lightly, a useless signal to his daughter to stop her suggestions. He did not want Lottie Lanier working in his store. Lottie Lanier's eyes bothered him.

"What do you think, Ben?" Sally asked.

"I—don't know," Ben answered feebly.

"Well, I do," Sally said. She turned to her father. "Let's ask her. Please. She's so nice, and I think it'd be fun working with another woman. Besides, you know that every lady in town would drop in, just to see her. Everybody's talking about how she took the time to help Ben."

Arthur felt trapped. He knew his daughter did not want Lottie Lanier in the same house with Ben, not day-long at least. And he also knew that his daughter was right: Lottie's presence in Jericho was news. More than news. It was gossip. He was in a corner, with no escape. Again, his daughter was manipulating him with the kind of bright charm that he was helpless against.

From the bedroom door, Margaret Phelps called in a happy voice, "All right, everybody, close your eyes."

Sally looked at Ben, smiled pleasantly. They closed their eyes.

"Arthur, you, too," commanded Margaret.

Arthur bowed his head, closed his eyes. He could hear the rustling of movement.

"All right," Margaret chirped. "Open them."

Lottie stood inside the room, near the doorway, with Little Ben beside her. They were dressed as Margaret had instructed.

"Oh—" Sally said in a whisper of awe. She glanced quickly at

Ben, saw his amazed stare, and then looked back at Lottie. She had never seen anyone as beautiful. The skirt Lottie wore was maroon. The white, ruffled shirtwaist billowed over her arms, rode gracefully across her breasts. The high, stiff collar circled her neck sensuously, and her hair, wheat-blond, pulled up in a bun, was shining under a broad, feathered hat that matched the maroon of the dress. A pale touch of rouge and lipstick colored her face. Her eyes were as startling as rare gems.

"Didn't I tell you?" Margaret cried to Lottie. "They're speechless. And look at my Little Ben. Isn't he handsome? So handsome." She knelt to embrace Little Ben. "So much more handsome than any man I know."

Arthur could feel heat in his face. He moved his eyes from Lottie to Little Ben. "Very nice," he mumbled. He looked back at Lottie. "Both of you." Then: "You did a fine job, Margaret. A fine job."

————

IT WAS LATE night, quite as late night becomes, and the silence rested gently on Ben. He had been awake for hours, alert to the sounds of the house beyond his closed door — voices muted, his mother's laughter, the movement of footsteps, a surprising summer wind that pushed the limp tip of an elm against the boarding of the house — and now there was nothing but the singing of cicadas from beyond the opened window, and even that seemed distant.

He had been home for less than a day by the clock, yet it seemed longer. The fever had subsided and then refired, and he had slept, confusing minutes for hours. He remembered faces bending to him. His mother. The doctor. Sally. And he remembered their voices, asking questions, and his confused answers. They had talked of Lottie and of Little Ben, telling him that it was Lottie who had cared for him on the train, and he had dreamed that Lottie was also there, in the room, not speaking. And in his dream, she had leaned to him and brushed her lips against his forehead, and then she had vanished into the sleep that bridged his dreams.

In late afternoon, he had awakened, his mind clear, and Sally was there with her father, and they had talked of his mother shopping with Lottie and of the work needing to be done at the store and of offering Lottie work while he and Little Ben recuperated. And then his mother was at the door, and Lottie and Little Ben, dressed in new clothes. Lottie. So beautiful, the image of her caught him by surprise, burned into him.

The arrangement had been made in a spilling of words. Lottie would work at Ledford's, helping restock, and his mother would care for Little Ben. Ben could not remember seeing his mother as happy. "Listen, Ben, listen," she had cooed. "Listen to Little Ben. He calls me Gra-Ma."

Lottie had not spoken to him. She had stayed near the door, her face blushed with discomfort and embarrassment, poorly covered with flickering smiles. Still, she had looked at him once, a holding look, and Ben knew that she was telling him she would never reveal the truth of knowing him.

He pushed the covers from his body and opened the shirt of his pajamas to feel the night air drift over his chest. He wondered what time it was. Well past midnight, he guessed. But he had slept for long hours and now he was awake. His body still ached, his breathing was still shallow, and he knew that whatever sickness had invaded him would linger. The doctor had predicted a week of bed rest, maybe longer. "We won't push it," the doctor had advised. "I'm not even sure what we're dealing with, but it's not going away overnight."

No one had asked him about Boston, but they would, he believed. When he recovered, they would ask simply to make conversation. And he would tell them it was a good trip, that he had tried to see Milo, but had failed. He did not know about the games, but there would be time to read of the results, and he would talk of the games with sufficient authority not to be doubted. It would be enough said.

He knew that Sally had doubts about Lottie staying in the house, even with the news that Lottie's husband had recently died. He had seen the look of astonishment on Sally's face when his mother presented Lottie and Little Ben in their new outfits. It was not jealousy. It was awe and fear. He was certain that Arthur Ledford had also seen it. The offer of work at the store had come immediately. "It's going to be wonderful, having another woman at the store," Sally had gushed. She had urged Lottie into a full turn to show off the dress, and she had added, "Every lady in Jericho will want that outfit once they see you in it. I'm sure we'll have to order a dozen more by closing time tomorrow."

Before leaving for her home, Sally had visited privately with Ben for a few minutes, and she had teased, "I don't have competition, do I?" And Ben had frowned quizzically. The frown said he did not understand, though he did. "Lottie," Sally had whispered. "Why did you say that?" Ben had asked. "She's so pretty," Sally had said. Ben had replied, "I only see one pretty girl here." What he said had pleased her. She had touched her fingers to her lips and then eased them across Ben's lips.

He closed his eyes, thinking that he would sleep and dream of Sally, and it would not be hard to do so. He had always been able to fix his mind on something, or someone, and then dream of it, or of them. He thought consciously of Sally, imagined her close to him, and, slowly, against the purple coating of his closed-eye seeing — deep as dawn — her face materialized and floated in the center of his seeing, gracefully revolving. The face smiled, then turned up, like a child enthralled with the sky, and the smile became a sound-less squeal and light glittered in her eyes. And then the squeal and the smile faded and her face rolled to gaze at him. Clouds washed through her hair, pulled a veil of shadows across her forehead, and she turned once more, dipping her chin in the pose of the cameo.

A hand touched his face and his eyes flashed open.

Lottie.

She stood beside his bed, dressed in a long silk nightgown the color of pearls. She did not speak. She took his hand and kneeled at the side of his bed and placed her face in his opened palm. After a moment, she stood and looked down on him, and she whispered, "Ben, I won't talk to nobody about you coming to see Foster. I just wanted you to know." Then she turned and moved silently out of the room, her nightgown shimmering in the dark like an apparition.

LOTTIE LANIER, AS Sally predicted, was an immediate attraction for both women and men at Ledford's Dry Goods, and after they had had their look at her and had purchased their excuse items, they went away with her name spilling from their lips.

In Jericho, Lottie was either a saint or a harlot, depending on the teller of the gossip about her involvement with Ben Phelps. To some, she was a Lady Samaritan, sacrificing her time and dignity to help someone deathly ill; to others, she was too beautiful not to have bent Ben's attention away from Sally, and there she was in his home, sleeping in a room across the hall from him. Two doors and a few feet of separation meant nothing to a woman ripe for taking.

"I think about half the town's been in for one thing or another," Sally said to Ben, "and I don't know who's the most curious, the women or the men. The dress Lottie was wearing yesterday, we sold three of them—one to old Miss Mayhall. She's going to look ridiculous in it, but she thinks she's going to look like Lottie."

There was an edge to Sally's voice, the sound of nervous energy. "Do you see her a lot?" she asked Ben hesitantly.

"No," Ben answered. "She comes in with Mama and Little Ben maybe once a day, just to see how I'm feeling, but that's about all."

It was not a lie. Ben had reversed his sleeping habits, night to day. At night, when he was awake, Lottie was asleep.

"I just wondered," Sally said. "I ask her about you and all she says is that you look like you're getting better. It's like she doesn't want to talk about you, and that seems a little strange to me."

"Maybe she thinks it'll make you feel funny about her being here," Ben said. "And, like I said, I don't see her at all hardly."

Sally smiled to hide her doubts. "It's all I want to do—talk about you. I sometimes think I do it too much around her, but she doesn't say anything. Just nods and smiles and keeps on working. She's a good worker, though I can tell she's never been around really nice clothes—the way she looks at them and the way she's always touching the material—but she's not lazy."

"She won't be there much longer," Ben said. "It won't be long before I'm back."

"You're not coming back until you're well," Sally insisted. She laughed. "Besides, I don't think everybody in town's been in yet. It's like a Christmas sale around there."

ONE OF THE visitors to Ledford's, and later to Ben's home, was Keebler Colquitt, editor of the weekly *Jericho Journal*. He had heard of Lottie and wanted to do a story about her and about Ben. The story read:

WIDOW PUTS ASIDE GRIEF
TO ASSIST MR. BEN PHELPS

Nobody wants to get sick, especially on his own, away from his home and the tender care of loved ones concerned about his health. But sometimes things don't work out the way people would like them to, and that was the case this last week with local businessman Mr. Ben Phelps.

Mr. Phelps, renowned in these parts as a swatter of baseballs off one-armed carnival giants and then living to tell about it, was returning by train last week from that northern-most city of Boston, Massachusetts, when he became unexpectedly ill after doing a good deed for a fellow passenger and her son.

On that same train was a Mrs. Lottie Lanier, who, two days earlier, had buried her husband in Kentucky and was returning to her home-town of Augusta, Georgia. She was traveling in the company of her three-year-old son, also named Ben, and it was that coincidence of two people named Ben that caused Mr. Phelps and Mrs. Lanier to strike up a polite conversation.

As fate would have it, the young Ben became sick on the trip, and Mr. Phelps volunteered to help care for him, being of good Christian character and from one of Jericho's finest families. After a stop in Nash-ville, Tennessee, to have young Ben observed and treated by a physi-cian, Mr. Phelps himself fell ill, in all likelihood to the same uncertain ailment suffered by young Ben Lanier. However, determined to return home to Jericho as soon as possible, Mr. Phelps insisted on departing Nashville. As it turns out, it was a hasty decision. Not long out of Athens, headed east, Mr. Phelps collapsed in the passenger car and was immediately assisted by Mrs. Lanier and a gentleman of the cloth from the Baptist religion, who was also a passenger on the train.

Delivered to the home of his mother, Mrs. Elton Phelps, by Mrs. Lanier and train station manager Akers Crews, Mr. Phelps and young Ben Lanier were immediately attended by Dr. Oscar Morgan, who pronounced Mr. Phelps ill with a suspected case of rheumatic fever.

Dr. Morgan reports that young Ben Lanier may or may not have the same ailment, but, if so, it is not as severe as that suffered by Mr. Phelps. Young master Lanier, in point of fact, has been observed lately in the company of Margaret Phelps, and seems to be recovering nicely under her care.

Word of Mr. Phelps's illness soon reached the ear of his employer, Mr. Arthur Ledford of Ledford's Dry Goods, and Mr. Ledford has done his part in expressing the community's appreciation to Mrs. Lanier for her brave attention to Mr. Phelps. He has afforded her a temporary position in his store until Mr. Phelps is well enough to return to work. Many citizens of Jericho have found time and reason to visit Ledford's since Mrs. Lanier's employment, and they have come away highly praising the good nature of our visitor. Reports of her beauty and kind smile are being spread throughout the area, and all marvel over her composure after suffering the loss of her husband only days ago.

In a brief meeting with Mr. Phelps at his home, this scribe learned that his trip to Boston was made to enjoy watching his boyhood friend and former Jericho resident, Milo Wade, take the diamond for the Red Sox baseball team. Mr. Phelps said he was unaware of any reports regarding the recent accusation that Mr. Wade was cited as a wife-beater, laying the blame for such slanderous allegations squarely at the feet of the Boston newspapers. Mr. Phelps also stated that he was unable to visit with Mr. Wade due to the failure of the Red Sox office staff to relay messages to Mr. Wade. However, he brings back the news that all of Boston continues to be amazed by Mr. Wade's magnificence at bat and in the field.

For laggards who have yet to pay their respects to Mrs. Lanier for her Christian-like concern in regard to Mr. Phelps's hour of need, Mr. Ledford assures us that she will likely remain in his employ for at least another week.

Coleman Maxey read the story that Keebler Colquitt had written and decided to see for himself if Lottie Lanier was as pretty as everyone said, and as Keebler had suggested in his newspaper. Thirty minutes after entering the store, Coleman emerged with a new straw hat too dandy for his wearing, and with a smile waffling his face that very much resembled his slack-jawed drinking smile.

"Lord bless Ben Phelps," Coleman crowed to Bill Simpson, who was waiting in Coleman's shop to retrieve a pair of restitched dress shoes. "He gets dog-sick and shows up with the prettiest damn woman I ever laid eyes on. It's like that time he got that hit off that old one-armed boy at the carnival. Every man we had on the team tried, and couldn't come close, and then old Ben steps up and slaps it out of sight. But that's nothing compared to this woman. I swear, Bill, Ben could fall in a tub of cow turds and come out smelling like a barber shop."

"I hear that Sally Ledford's a little touchy about that woman," Bill suggested.

"If she is, she don't look it," Coleman said. "She was dragging her all over the store, introducing her to people."

"Well, you can't believe everything you hear," Bill allowed, thinking of the tight-lipped opinion his wife had delivered after meeting Lottie Lanier. His wife was more than a little suspicious of Ben's illness. "Probably caught it from that woman," his wife had guessed.

"The way Keebler wrote about it, Ben sounds pretty sick," Coleman said. "Maybe she'll be around longer than another week."

"You got that look, Coleman," Bill said. "I know that look."

Coleman grinned, smacked his lips. "Won't get past dreaming," he said. "That woman's too pretty for me. I wouldn't know what to do."

"I wouldn't go saying that out loud," advised Bill.

"Why not?"

"People that know you might think you getting old."

"I guess I am," Coleman said. His body rocked in a nod, in the way of a man preoccupied with a thought, and then he added, "You been by to see her yet?"

"Not yet," Bill told him. He thought again of his wife. "The wife went by. Said she didn't look plain, but she wadn't all that pretty."

"You got a jealous woman," Coleman said. He added, "Tell you what, though, the first time I saw her, I could swear I'd seen her somewheres before. I just can't place where."

"Well," Bill drawled, "you did say something about dreaming."

"I never had no dreams like that," Coleman said. He shook his head in admiration. "Maybe I'm just wishing I'd seen her before."

"Lord, Coleman, I'm yet to lay eyes on the woman, but everything I heard about her, I wish the same thing."

Coleman sighed. "All I know is, Ben Phelps is in hog heaven and he probably don't even know it."

––––––––

BEN REALLY KNEW only one thing: he felt caged. He was regaining strength daily, but slowly, from his mother's pampering attention and from the doctor's assortment of medicines. Still, he was confined to his bedroom, except for bathroom visits, and everything that was happening around him seemed vague and fragmented. Sally was there early each morning and often late into the night, and the way she occupied his time was territorial and numbing in its intensity. When Lottie appeared, always with his mother or with Little Ben, she was as distant as a shadow. Her silence, Ben thought, was Lottie's signal that she understood her place in his life. She was a patient but uneasy guest, waiting for him to take her home.

At least, Keebler Colquitt's story of his misfortunes had provided one reprieve for Ben: he would not have to sidestep the questions about being in Boston, and he knew that Lottie had kept her word about holding secret his time in Kentucky.

There was still a chance that his mother would question him about Boston, Ben reasoned. Later. When Lottie and Little Ben were gone and she needed the words to fill the silence, she might ask him about it one day. Idly. An afterthought. And he knew it would be hard to keep the truth from her. Or maybe she would not think about it. Maybe she would think only about the emptiness of Little Ben's absence. Because of Little Ben, the instinct of mothering — or of grandmothering — had erupted in her, filling her with a joy that seemed inexhaustible. From his bed, Ben could hear her laughter, her cheerful chattering, the lullabies she sang to Little Ben at nap time, and he knew that she was clinging desperately to the awakening of a maternal passion long contained.

One afternoon, alone with him as Little Ben slept, his mother asked, "When they leave us, do you think they'll be all right?"

And Ben answered, "I hope so. They're good people."

"He's so small for his age," his mother whispered.

"He's bigger since he's been here," Ben suggested.

His mother smiled warmly. "He is, I think. And he talks more, too. He asked me this morning where his daddy was."

"What did you tell him?"

"I told him his daddy was in heaven with Jesus and the angels. He said his daddy was in a box."

"He's just a baby, Mama," Ben said.

For a long moment, tender in its lingering, Margaret Phelps did not speak, and then she said, "I wish they lived here."

"They've got their own lives, Mama."

"Maybe Arthur will give Lottie a full-time job," his mother said hopefully. "Sally tells me she's a good worker and that a lot of people have started coming by since she's been there."

"Mama, that's just from being curious about her," Ben warned. "That won't last. Anyway, Mr. Ledford wouldn't have her around with Sally there. What he's doing now is charity he got pushed into doing. He won't do it long."

———

BEN WAS WRONG about Arthur Ledford.

Each day that Lottie appeared at his store, a spell that could have been witchcraft worked its way out of her eyes and wrapped Arthur in a vapor as lethal as poison. And it was that—exactly. He inhaled her, felt her coating his lungs and then flooding through his bloodstream. He also knew it was not something that she worked on purpose. It was simply a part of her, as her hair was a part of her, or her fingers. He was sure that no one could see it, or sense it, but him. It was not obvious. It was even hidden by her off-looks and her bowed head and her whispered talk in his presence.

He would not speak to her of his feelings, he vowed to himself, even though the impulse to do so seemed stationed in his throat. He was her employer, a married man, a family man, a citizen of standing in the community. He had lived long enough to know it was not uncommon for a man in his late forties to be distracted by the beauty of a younger woman, and in his case, there was probably more danger of it than for a normal man in a normal situation. Since before the birth of Sally, his wife had turned cold and unresponsive and somehow competitive in the way that people are when they set themselves like a post, refusing to be moved. He did not know why. He had discussed it privately with the doctor, Oscar Morgan, and Oscar Morgan had no answers, only guesses. A physical change, perhaps. A chemical disorder that affected her mentally and emotionally. And Oscar Morgan had added, "Could be, Arthur, that she's just now catching up to her family traits." Her family traits included a mood of meanness that left welts on the souls of victims. For seventeen years, she had denied him her body, but more damaging, she had denied him any show of tenderness, and tenderness was like oxygen for Arthur Ledford.

And Lottie Lanier had been blessed with tenderness. Anyone who looked into her eyes would know that. A weak man would crumble before her. A strong man would know to keep his distance.

Arthur believed he was strong.

He was not.

One week from the day he first saw Lottie Lanier, Arthur opened the door to his storeroom and found her standing beside Ben's rolltop desk. It was late afternoon, after closing, and he believed he was alone in the store. Seeing her startled him.

"Lottie," he said. It was the first time he had called her by her familiar name. "I thought you were gone."

"No sir," Lottie said nervously. "Sally left."

"Why—are you here?" Arthur asked.

"I had some things to do," she said, "but more than anything I just wanted to thank you for all you been doing for me, knowing Ben will be coming back soon."

"No need for that. You're a good worker. You've been an asset."

Lottie touched the desk as though she needed to lean against it. She said, "I never worked in a store before."

"Well, you have a talent for it," Arthur told her. "I have some friends in the business in Augusta. If you'd like, I could—"

"No, sir," Lottie said quickly. "You already done more than enough."

Arthur nodded his understanding: she would not be a user.

And then she asked the question she had stayed to ask: "You don't hold it against Ben, do you? Me being here."

Arthur glanced at the opened storeroom door. From across the store, through the front window, he could see the withered figure of Lucille Bellflower peering in at the displays. He closed the door. "Of course I don't," he replied. "What you did was an honorable thing."

"Ben, he helped me out. I couldn't just leave him at the train station."

"I understand," Arthur said. "Everything's worked out for the best."

Lottie did not reply. She dipped her head, then looked up again, and a faint, uncertain smile tipped across her lips, then quickly vanished. She began to move to the door. As she approached him, Arthur put out his hand and touched her shoulder. She stopped, turned her face to him, and the power of her eyes drove into him. He whispered painfully, "God help me. God help me." And then he caught her gently and pulled her to him. She wedged her arms stiffly between his chest and her breasts and twisted her face away from him, hard over her shoulder. She could feel him trembling, could hear him sob-gasping to breathe, and she slowly pulled down her arms and moved obediently to fit against him.

———

BEN HAD DRESSED for supper, had even walked outside for a few minutes, taking in the late sun and the still-thick summer air. He tired quickly, but the walk invigorated his spirits. He had lost weight and strength and there was a tenderness in his chest, like a bruise, yet Oscar Morgan had proclaimed him fit enough to be out of bed, and that was enough for the time being.

"You'll have to go easy, Ben," the doctor had said. "If it's rheumatic fever you've had, you're going to have to pay attention to it the rest of your life. We don't know as much as we need to, but we know it can cause you heart troubles down the road."

It was a judgment that would sentence Ben to caution and worry until the day the warning became true, like a debt collected, in his early seventies.

Sally arrived to find him sitting in the porch swing, with his mother seated nearby in a rocker, cuddling Little Ben, who was looking at pictures in a children's book.

"You're up," she said in delight. And then she saw the pale coloring of his face. "Are you all right?" she asked. "Are you sure you're ready to be out of bed?"

"Just a little winded," he told her. "I took a short walk."

"It's too hot," Sally protested.

"I didn't let him go far," Margaret said. "Just to the corner and back. Little Ben walked with him." She paused, peered down the street. "Where's Lottie?"

Sally sat in the swing next to Ben. "She stayed to put away some things that came in today. I told her it could wait, but she wanted to do it." She laughed lightly. "If Ben doesn't come back to work soon, I'm afraid Daddy's going to dismiss me and hire Lottie. She's really a good worker."

"A few more days," Ben said. "Maybe by Monday or Tuesday."

"Not until you're ready," cautioned Margaret. She wiggled Little Ben from her lap. "You two visit," she said. "Little Ben and I are going over to Betty Render's house to get some tomatoes she picked from her garden this morning. She told me they were almost as big as the ones Ben's father used to grow, but I doubt it. Nobody could grow tomatoes like Elton. You remember them, don't you, Ben?"

"Yes, Mama, I do," Ben said.

"We won't be gone too long," Margaret said. Then, to Sally: "Don't let him stay out here but a few minutes. The heat cooks the energy right out of a person."

"I won't," promised Sally.

Ben and Sally watched Margaret and Little Ben leave the yard and cross the street. Little Ben ran ahead of her, then back, ahead and back, like a happy puppy, playing his child-game.

"She sure loves that boy," Sally said quietly.

"She does," Ben agreed.

"It's going to seem awfully lonesome for her when they leave," Sally added.

"I guess," Ben said.

"She'll need to keep herself busy," Sally suggested. "Find something else to occupy her time, something that'll take her mind off what Little Ben might be doing."

Ben rocked the swing gently. He knew the hints, had listened to them for a week. The something else that Sally wanted for his mother was the preparation for a wedding.

"I think you'd better go inside," Sally said. "It'll be cooler."

"In a minute," Ben told her.

"I promised your mother—"

"I know. Just another minute."

"All right," Sally said in surrender. She reached for his hand, stroked it with her fingers. "Coleman Maxey came back in the store today," she said in a cheerful, racing voice. "That's three days this week he's been in, and I don't think I ever remember him even opening the door before. You should see him around Lottie, Ben. He's just plain silly. Bought a shirt today. Yesterday, it was a pair of work pants. And I told you about the straw hat, didn't I? It's the most ridiculous thing I've ever seen on a man. You could wear it, and it'd look wonderful, but not Coleman. But it's Lottie he's coming to see. Every time he looks at her, he gets red-faced. He even asked me if she'd ever been here before. He swears he's seen her."

Ben thought of the carnival. It had been years, and Lottie had only worked a food tent, but Coleman could have seen her and remembered. Coleman had an eye for beautiful women.

"I don't know where he could have," he said.

"I told him it must be somebody who looks like her," Sally said. "Everybody's supposed to have somebody who looks like them. I saw a man on the street one day that looked enough like my daddy to be his twin brother, but he was just somebody who was doing business with the quarry. He was from Italy, Daddy told me."

"I think I remember him," Ben lied.

"You can pretty much predict when Coleman will take to his bottle again," Sally said. "When Lottie leaves."

"Maybe so," Ben said nonchalantly.

Sally laughed easily. "But he may not be the only one that mopes around when she's gone." She squeezed his hand, stopped the motion of the swing with her foot. "I'm just glad you don't drink."

For a moment, Ben did not speak. Then he said, "I think I'm just going to be glad when she's on her way home, after all she's done for me." He paused. "Anyway, I'm going to be too busy to think about it."

"Too busy," Sally said hopefully.

"At the store, getting back to work."

"Oh," Sally said.

"And I've got that other thing to do," Ben said.

"What other thing?"

"I've got a wedding to get ready for."

Sally could feel a quivering in her chest. She whispered, "Whose wedding?"

Ben turned to look at her. "Mine," he answered. A grin broke on his face. "Or did I forget to talk to you about that?"

"Ben —"

Ben furrowed his brow. "I could swear we talked about this. I did ask you to marry me, didn't I? Or did I dream it when I had the fever and my mind was wandering all over the place?"

"Ben, don't tease —"

Ben touched her lips with his finger. "Well, if you don't remember, I must have dreamed it and it wouldn't count, of course, but I'll tell you about it if you want me to."

Sally could hear the echo of her heartstroke. She inhaled, held the breath.

"We were sitting here in the swing — just like we are now," Ben said casually. "And you were saying to me, 'Marry me, Ben Phelps. Marry me.' And you sounded so desperate about it, I thought the only kind thing to do was to ask you, so I did. I said, 'Sally Ledford, will you marry me?' "

"Ben—"

"I don't remember your answer in my dream," Ben said.

Sally began to cry. She leaned her face against his shoulder. "Ask me again, Ben."

And Ben whispered, "Will you marry me, Sally Ledford?"

"Yes, Ben, yes," Sally said. And a cry of exultation flew up from her throat.

Across the street, standing in front of Betty Render's home, Margaret Phelps heard the cry, knew what it was, and she smiled relief. Soon she would have the daughter she wanted.

TO TELL THE story of his marriage proposal to Sally Ledford would be one of the pleasures of Ben's late life, for his memory of it was exaggerated humorously and he would develop an old man's habit of pausing to think over what he had just said before continuing with his story, and the pausing somehow made it all seem more interesting.

In Ben's telling, the news squealed from the porch of his mother's home, paused for a gasp in Betty Render's yard, and then was shot with electric quickness throughout Jericho, going house to house, shop to shop, in a relay of words that every woman in town seemed to be waiting to hear. No one used the telephone, Ben vowed. There was no reason for it. The telephone was not as quick as the tongues of women.

"And once it gets told, you might as well forget taking it back," Ben always added philosophically, and with a wink. "Men don't know it, but women do. When the word's out, you're already married. You just haven't had the ceremony, or anything else that comes with it."

It was a tale containing foolishness and a great deal of truth.

By the time Sally reached her home, less than an hour after accepting Ben's proposal, her mother had heard the news and had retired to her bed, leaving instructions with Lena, the maid, that she felt particularly exhausted, but held good thoughts about the proposal and looked forward to speaking with her daughter about it at breakfast.

"Miss Alice ought to be ashamed of herself," Lena fumed boldly.

"She can't help having bad health, Lena," Sally said in a weak defense of her mother.

Lena shook her head vigorously. "Honey, you just been asked the biggest question you ever gone be asked, other than are you ready to pass through the Golden Gates, and your mama takes to her bed without so much as a hug. That's not right." She motioned for Sally. "You come here, let Lena hug you."

The embrace from Lena was powerful and warm. Sally could feel trembling from inside the huge woman, and she wondered if it was for joy or pity. Or both.

"You got you a good man, honey," Lena said, nodding her head against Sally's shoulder. "I been knowing his mama a long time. His daddy, too, when his daddy was alive. They good people."

She released Sally and looked at her for a long, gazing moment. Then she said, "You go off and be Miss Sally. Don't you try to be like your mama or your daddy. Now, they good people, too. Always treated me fine. But they don't talk to each other enough, honey. Don't you let that happen to you and that fine Mr. Ben Phelps. You keep talking to him. Ask him every day how he feels. Make out like you just can't wait to hear the next word that come falling out his mouth."

Sally could feel tears rinsing the corners of her eyes. Her mother had never given her such advice.

"Lord, honey, having a husband's a lot like having a puppy," Lena said softly, touching a tear from Sally's face. "You just got to talk mush-talk and keep him fed and watered and scratch his belly once in a while, and when he starts to wagging his tail, it'll be you he's wagging it at."

Sally pushed herself close to Lena again, felt Lena's arms circle her. "I love you," she whispered.

"And I love you, too, child," Lena said.

SALLY DID NOT ask her father who informed him of Ben's proposal. He had worked late at the books, and when he arrived home, he knew—from someone, he knew; someone on the street or someone lingering at a front-yard fence on the walk across town—and he embraced her warmly, telling her he was glad. It was expected news, of course, he said, but it was still good to have something firm in place.

"Have you set a date?" he asked at the dining-room table, during their supper.

"November," Sally told him.

"Very good," her father said, forcing an accommodating smile.

"Are you all right?" asked Sally.

"Of course I am. What makes you ask that?"

"You just seem like you're somewhere else."

Her father turned his face to the food before him. "Just a couple of things in the books," he said. "I'm thinking about having a sale."

"If you do, can we wait until Ben gets back?" Sally asked.

"I'm sure we can," her father said. "I expect he'll be on his feet, good as ever, in a few more days."

"He looks a lot better," Sally said.

Her father nodded, chewed his food, gazed out the window at the gathering night.

"Did you put out some more women's cologne after I left?" asked Sally.

Arthur turned to her, frowned darkly.

"I just smell it," Sally said. "I thought you might have gotten some on you."

Arthur lifted his hand to his face and sniffed. He could smell the perfumed scent of Lottie Lanier, and a stroke of panic and guilt washed through him. He wiped his hand over the napkin, fought to keep the redness out of his face. He said in a serious voice, "I don't remember putting any out, but I must have moved a bottle, or something." He touched the napkin to his lips and then to his forehead, as though in thought. "Now that I think of it, there was a bottle that somebody had left the cap off of," he added. "Probably one of Carla Dupree's girls. I put it back on just before I left. I didn't notice that any had spilled, but I guess that was it."

"You're blushing, Daddy," Sally said lightly.

Arthur put down the napkin and picked up his glass of tea. "It's a little embarrassing to be going around with women's cologne on you," he said. "I suppose I'm so used to it, I don't smell it anymore." He drank from the tea, then added, "I'm sorry your mother's not feeling well. She'd like to be sharing this time with you, I'm sure."

Sally smiled, but did not reply. Her father was merely playing his role. He had apologized for her mother for so many years he did not know when he did it, or to whom.

"Maybe having a wedding to plan will be good for her," Arthur suggested. "Give her a responsibility to enjoy."

"I hope so," Sally replied.

"You will have to be aware of one thing," her father added, "and that's to not let Margaret Phelps take over things."

"She won't do that, Daddy."

"She's a strong-willed woman, Sally. Don't ever forget that. I've known her since childhood, and she's always been — well, forceful."

"I'll get Mama and Mrs. Phelps together, and we'll work things out," Sally said.

Her father glanced at her. A frown wormed over his eyebrows. It was not a meeting he would want to attend. His wife had never cared for Margaret Phelps — not even enough for polite pretension — and he knew how such a meeting would end: his wife's face hard-set, her lips sealed, her eyes cold. And Margaret Phelps would not notice anything unusual. His wife had been a near-recluse for so many years, people had long given up hope of seeing happiness in her. Margaret Phelps would ring bells of laughter; his wife would sit in silence and resentment.

"Take my advice," her said after a moment. "Don't get them together until you have to."

Sally turned to her father. An expression of amusement was on her face. "Daddy," she said, "you make it sound like a war instead of a wedding."

"I don't mean it that way," he replied. "I just want you to be aware of what you could be facing, that's all, and to let you know if you ever want to talk about it, I'll listen. Right now, I suspect you've got stars in your eyes, and sometimes that makes a person blind." He paused. "Happens to everybody," he added quietly.

Sally reached across the table and touched her father's hand. She said, "I'll watch out for them. I just hope Mama feels up to everything. Sometimes I think she gets tired around me, and I'm not really sure she thinks my marriage to Ben is a good thing."

"Why do you say that?"

"I don't know. She never said anything, but sometimes I can feel it. Maybe it's because he's older."

"May I ask you something?" her father said gently.

"Yes."

"Are you happy?"

"Of course I am."

"And it's because of Ben Phelps?"

Sally nodded.

"Then hold to that," her father said. "No matter what happens, hold to it. No matter what people say, hold to it. If you don't, you'll always wonder, always regret." He paused again, gazed into his daughter's large, bright eyes. She was a child. A child. "Believe me," he whispered, "you don't want that."

Sally did not speak. She slipped from her chair and moved to her father and embraced him awkwardly as he sat.

"Go see Ben," Arthur told her. "I would imagine he wonders where you are."

"Maybe I shouldn't," Sally said hesitantly. "Maybe I should sit with Mama."

Arthur shook his head. "No, you go see Ben. I'll take care of your mother."

"I won't be long," Sally promised.

"It's all right," her father said. He smiled faintly, and she saw moisture in his eyes. "I might as well start getting used to you being somewhere else."

———

IT WAS AFTER sunfall—not light, not dark—and Ben sat in the swing on the front porch of his mother's home, waiting for Sally to return from sharing the news of her engagement with her parents. He had expected her earlier and now wondered if something had happened. An argument, perhaps. He had been around Alice Ledford enough to know that argument thrived in her bitter look, that it could erupt suddenly, unexpectedly.

His mother had guessed his worry. She had said, "I'm sure they're

as excited as I am, and they're just spending some time with her."
It was meant to comfort him. His mother also knew Alice Ledford.

The mood at his home had been festive. After their supper, his
mother had found the ice cream churn and made ice cream with
fresh peaches, taking turns with Lottie for the cranking. He had
volunteered to help, but was refused. He was not strong enough for
such labor, his mother had declared. Besides, the night was in his
honor—and Sally's.

"She'll be here soon enough," his mother had said, leaving him
on the porch. "I'm going to help Lottie get Little Ben ready for bed,
but be sure and get some ice cream for Sally, and tell her I'll see
her in the morning, if not tonight."

Ben had stopped her. "Mama, do you think Lottie's all right?"

"Seems fine to me. Why?" his mother had replied.

"I don't know," Ben had answered. "She was real quiet when you
told her about me asking Sally to marry me."

"Well, son, maybe it took her by surprise," his mother had said
quietly. "And maybe she's had a little crush on you herself, the way
you helped her out so soon after her husband died. Women never
forget that sort of kindness from a man, and, who knows, maybe her
husband was as sorry as a carpetbagger." She had glanced at the door
of the house and then moved close to Ben. "I haven't said anything
about it, but I have noticed how shy she seems around you. That's
usually a pretty good sign that a woman has an interest, and I think
you should know that Sally sees it, too. Oh, she hasn't said anything
about it to me, but she doesn't have to. I can tell."

"I think you're wrong, Mama," Ben had protested.

"And I think you're still a little boy sometimes," his mother had
replied.

If his mother could see that Lottie might have affection for him,
could she see anything else? Ben wondered. Something he could

not see. Something about Lottie that he seemed to sense, but did not understand.

Lottie had arrived from work an hour later than usual, her face blushed from the heat. She had heard the news of the engagement from his mother, and had turned to him, offering a smile. Her only words had been "That's good." And then she had excused herself to change clothes and to play with Little Ben. Throughout their supper, and the making and eating of the ice cream, she had seemed remote and preoccupied. It was not in her behavior, or what she said—or didn't say—but in a mood that seemed to wrap around her like an invisible shroud.

And perhaps, Ben thought, she was merely tired from the work in Ledford's, or she had grown weary of the role-playing to protect him. There were times when he caught her gazing out of a window, and the cast of her eyes went far beyond their seeing. In those times, Ben believed she was unbearably lonely, and that she missed the traveling of the carnival and the places she had visited. Missed the pitched tents with quilt flooring, the smell of earth and lantern oil. Missed the trickery of silk-scarf magic and the calling of drumbeat and calliope whistle, like an anthem for wanderers. Missed the hope of dreams promised by slicksters selling chances at winning cheap prizes.

Curiously, at such times Ben did not think that Lottie missed Foster as much as she did the carnival. If she did, she did not show it. She had spoken to him only once of Foster since arriving in Jericho, and that was the first night, in her promise not to talk of his visit to Kentucky.

Yet, at other times, he watched her huddled with Little Ben, her face tucked against Little Ben's face, and he knew that she was once again in Kentucky, sitting before the embers of a fire from the fireplace, listening for the rattle of Foster's breathing, waiting for the breathing to stop.

In a few days, when he was again at full strength, he would accompany her to Augusta, as he had promised Foster. He would explain to Sally and to his mother that he felt an obligation to Lottie, and that his duty to her would be done when he led her, and Little Ben, to the front door of her parents' home. He would also say he wanted a day to find a suitable engagement ring in an Augusta jewelry store.

He pushed his toe against the porch floor, swaying the swing. It would be strange not having Lottie around, he thought. And Little Ben. Little Ben seemed born to the home. Without Little Ben, the home would be tomb-quiet.

The moving chain of the swing had the sound of cicadas.

He wondered if he would ever see Lottie Lanier after taking her home.

Maybe for the wedding. His mother would want to invite her, because she would want to see Little Ben.

But she would not come to the wedding, Ben reasoned.

When she left Jericho, she would disappear from their lives.

He heard his name being called and twisted his body to the street to watch Sally rushing toward him, lifting the hem of her skirt. She slipped onto the swing and folded her arms around his chest.

"Did you miss me?" she asked.

"Yes," he admitted.

Sally stayed only long enough for ice cream and to sit again in the swing with her head nestled against Ben's shoulder. She did not say anything about her mother's sudden illness or her father's advice to her. She was, Ben thought, more relaxed than he had ever known her.

Before she left for home, she asked, "Do you love me, Ben?"

"If I don't, I think I've let myself in for a lot of trouble," Ben told her.

"Just say yes, Ben."

"Yes," Ben said quietly.

"You're going to make a wonderful husband."

"And you're going to make a wonderful wife," Ben replied.

"Do you think of me as a little girl, or a woman?" Sally asked.

"Some of both," Ben answered after a moment. "It's hard to forget when you used to aggravate me to death, running around all over the place, keeping things messed up just to make me straighten up after you."

"Did I do that?"

"Yes, you did."

Sally leaned to him, kissed him. "I'm sorry. I'll make up for it. I promise you."

"You already have," Ben said.

"How?"

"By growing up to be who you are."

————

AFTER MIDNIGHT, LOTTIE again opened the door to Ben's room and slipped quietly inside. Again, she was wearing the pearl-silk nightgown. Again, she knelt at his bed, took his hand and opened it and gently rested her face in his palm, like someone giving alms to a beggar.

"I'm glad for you," she whispered.

"Thank you," Ben said.

She looked up. Ben could see that her eyes were damp with crying.

"What's wrong?" he asked.

"I just had a dream," she told him.

"What dream?"

"I dreamed it was me you married."

Ben said nothing.

"I was dressed in a dress that was white as a cloud, Ben, and we were out in a field like the ones in Kentucky, and you were there, and so was Foster, and he was standing up by a tree watching us, a grin all over his face. The preacher was there, too—him and his wife, and Mr. Quick and some of the others, and so was your mama and Little Ben and Mr. Ledford and even Sally. And I was standing close to you and the preacher was saying we'd been married."

She paused, sucked in a quick breath, rolled her face in his hand, leaving it damp.

"It's all right, Lottie," Ben said softly. "It was just a dream. Me and you, we're friends. We always will be. I'd say you were dreaming that our friendship got married. I've had that same dream myself. Almost exactly the same."

For a long moment, Lottie did not speak or move her face. Then she said, "I need to leave, Ben. I need to go on home."

"I understand," Ben told her. "Two or three more days, and I'll be up to it."

"You don't need to go with me. I can go by myself."

"No," Ben said. "I promised Foster."

Lottie nodded against his palm.

"A lot of people here wish you'd just stay," Ben said. "Including me."

Lottie stood. "I can't," she said.

"I could talk to Mr. Ledford about work," Ben said. "I know he thinks you're a good worker, and Mama would keep Little Ben. In fact, she'd probably steal him from you if she could."

Lottie shook her head. She turned away from the bed. "I got to go, Ben. I can't stay. If I stayed, nothing would be right." She moved quickly to the door and out of the room.

Ben lifted his hand to his mouth and let his tongue tip the palm. He could taste the salt of Lottie.

COLEMAN MAXEY DID not understand why he awoke suddenly, fully alert, from a black, dreamless sleep, knowing where he had seen Lottie Lanier. The mind must keep working when the body shuts down, was Coleman's theory. Like a pocket watch tucked inside a pocket. You couldn't see it at work and you probably couldn't hear it ticking, but still it worked, still unwound minutes and hours off the spring inside its steel casing. The mind had to be made up of things like watch springs, Coleman decided. And thinking hard and constant about something was like twisting a watch stem tight; it worked even when you were busy with other matters, or when you slept so hard you were only a breath or two away from death.

He sat up in his bed when the memory came to him, and he thought: Well, by God. That's it.

Lottie Lanier was the same woman who had bought a quart of moonshine whiskey from him all those years ago when Ben Phelps had made the baseball hit against the one-armed giant and was later beaten up and the giant found murdered.

Coleman was sure of it. She was dressed better now, and she was older, and she seemed to possess a quiet nature that could easily be mistaken for haughtiness, except for the gentleness of her eyes. Yet, in Coleman's thinking, it was her eyes that gave her away. A man could not look into such eyes without being haunted by them.

The memory was immediately clear to him. A town boy hired for helping to set up the tents came to him late in the afternoon, saying one of the men in the baseball show wanted to buy a quart of good makings, and he told the boy—Farley Roberts was his name, now moved away—that he would have the order ready at first dark and to have the man meet him at the rail yard where the cars for the carnival had been routed and uncoupled.

He was startled when the girl appeared.

"You Mr. Maxey?" she asked.

"That's me, little lady," Coleman answered. "Who's asking?"

"I come for the jar," the girl replied.

"Well, by damn," Coleman muttered. "I was expecting some fellow."

"He sent me."

A broad smile crawled over Coleman's face. "You got money, or you planning on a trade?"

The girl thrust two dollars toward him.

"I'm up to trading, if you want to keep that for yourself," Coleman told her.

The girl did not speak or move.

"Damned if you not the prettiest thing ever been in this town," Coleman said eagerly. "You work the girlie tent when they got it up, don't you?"

Still, the girl did not speak.

"Why don't I throw in the jar and five extra dollars," Coleman suggested. "And me and you crawl up in one of them train cars and get this deal done."

The girl turned and started to walk away.

"Wait a minute," Coleman called. "Where you going?"

The girl stopped and turned back. "To tell him what you said."

Coleman laughed nervously. He had seen enough carnival gangs to know they stood together, and he knew he had pushed too hard in his bargaining. "Aw, I was just fooling around," he said. He stepped to her. "Here's the jar."

The girl handed him the two dollars and took the jar and lifted her face to him and fixed him in her gaze. It was then that he put her eyes away in memory.

"Hope he likes it," Coleman said weakly.

The girl walked away.

Coleman laughed softly, a cackle from his throat, and then he fell back on his pillow heavily, causing his bedsprings to squeak. He stared at a wash of moonlight in the corner of his room, a quaint light spill that had the appearance of a dangling triangle. He thought: I knew I'd seen her. He whispered in amazement, "Well, by God."

ARTHUR LEDFORD SAW Coleman step from his shoe shop and wave, and he frowned wearily. It was twenty minutes before eight o'clock and the morning sun already baked the concrete of the sidewalk. Too early and too humid for Coleman Maxey, he thought. Besides, he had seen enough of Coleman over the past week, Coleman showing up to buy items he would never wear and for no other reason than to steal glimpses of Lottie Lanier. It was embarrassingly childlike behavior, making each visit a deplorable charade to be suffered. If possible, Arthur avoided Coleman and all men like him. He did not like the rough style such men adopted. They were barely civilized, and nothing seemed to matter to any of them — nothing beyond their lust and the pleasure of that lust. None of them knew the souls of women they pawed over. They knew only the heat of flesh and the swelling of their loins. Love, to them, was won in brawls of taking, not giving. None of them understood the conquering power of a gentle embrace, or the surrender offered in touches so light they seemed like water running warm over the body.

A weakness gathered in his chest. With Lottie, he had been like those men. Or, if people knew what he had done with her, they would think of him in such a way. Yet it wasn't the same. To him, the tenderness had mattered. More than passion, more than taking.

Still, there was shame. Great shame.

He stopped at the sidewalk opposite Coleman's store. He saw Coleman quick-striding toward him. He thought: Lottie. The memory of her body, slender and firm, pressed against him, and a surge of sorrow filled his chest.

"Arthur, wait up a minute," Coleman called.

"Good morning, Coleman," Arthur said in the voice he used in his store. "Warm enough for you?"

"It keeps this up, we better think about renaming this place Hell," Coleman replied with a grin. He stepped onto the sidewalk to stand beside Arthur.

"I'll bring that up at the next council meeting," Arthur said.

Coleman's grin turned into a laugh. He glanced down at the sidewalk. "Say, Arthur, you remember me telling you I thought I'd seen that girl you got working for you down at the store?"

"Mrs. Lanier?"

"Yeah, her," Coleman said. "Lottie. That's her first name, right?"

"Yes," Arthur replied. "Why?"

"Well, I remembered," Coleman said proudly.

Arthur could feel the muscles across his chest tighten. He tilted his head to look at Coleman. "You did?"

Coleman's head wagged vigorously. "Sure did. Woke up in the middle of the night, bolt up in bed, and it come to me. She was working that carnival that come through here six or seven years ago, the one when Ben got beat up and that one-armed fellow got his head split open. I met her."

A chill rippled over Arthur's shoulders. He could feel his eyes blinking in surprise. "You must be mistaken," he said firmly.

"Well, could be, I guess," Coleman said, "but there's some faces a man don't never forget, and that's one of them. I'm telling you, Arthur, that's her, and it makes me wonder about her showing back up here with Ben. You ask me, there's more to it than meets the eye."

Arthur crossed his arms at his chest to calm the trembling. He said, "Have you mentioned this to anyone else?"

"You the first one," Coleman told him. "Since she's working for you, I thought you ought to be the one to know."

"I appreciate that," Arthur said quietly. "Personally, I think you're wrong. I think she may look like somebody you've seen, but Mrs. Lanier couldn't have been that same girl. She's been living in Kentucky for several years now."

"Like I said, it's been six or seven years," Coleman reminded him.

"That's true enough," Arthur said, "but we don't want to harm the reputation of a good woman by making statements that could be wrong, do we?"

Coleman shrugged. "Never said I wanted to do that. I just thought you'd like to know, that's all." He paused, flicked a smile toward Arthur. "But if it is her, I'd say her reputation was in question a long time ago."

"How's that?"

"I told you: I met her. She was working the girlie tent as far as I could tell, even if they had that tent packed away when they stopped off here."

For a moment, Arthur did not speak. He lowered his head and nibbled on his lower lip. Coleman Maxey was a despicable man who could not be trusted, yet he had no choice but to trust. "I'll inquire into it," he said at last. "But I'm going to ask you to do the gentleman's thing, Coleman. I'm going to ask you to keep this between us. There's more at stake here than the possibility that you may be right, and it's personal with me. Maybe you don't know, but Ben asked Sally to be his wife last night, and this is the sort of thing that could cast suspicion on him and bring great grief to my daughter. I don't want that, and I don't think you do either. Am I right?"

Coleman nodded again. He had never had a man of Arthur Ledford's standing confide in him with such sincerity. "Lord, no, Arthur. I hadn't heard about Ben and your girl getting promised, but I sure don't want to be part of anything that could come between them. They're fine young people."

"Good. Let's have it stay between us," Arthur said. "At the appropriate time, I'll find an opportunity to ask Mrs. Lanier about it — in a roundabout way, of course. I think I'll know if she's covering the truth. And then I'll let you know what I've learned."

"Fine with me," Coleman told him. "And don't you worry. You say so and I'll take it to my grave."

Arthur licked his lips. He stood stiffly and extended his hand to Coleman. "I'm in your debt," he said. Then he inhaled and added, "I'm grateful for your friendship."

Coleman grinned. He squeezed Arthur's hand deliberately hard. "I'll stand with you, Arthur, but I know I'm right," he said. "I don't never forget a pretty face, and me and you both know she's got the prettiest face this town ever saw."

ARTHUR WATCHED COLEMAN cross the street, lifted a hand of acknowledgment — of comradeship — when Coleman turned to flick a wave before stepping into his shop, and then he walked away, continuing toward his store, his pace slow, his legs lead-heavy, his mind aching.

He had not slept the entire night. Could not. What had passed from his thoughts, and from his lips, as prayer had seemed little more than hollow begging. He had wanted to say to God, and to Lottie, "Forgive me." Yet he had not felt the condemnation of sin. Sadness, yes. Great sadness. And confusion. It had been impossible to hide under the covering of his bed from the presence of God, or of Lottie, and he had lain awake through the night, not moving, waiting for the voice of God, or of Lottie, to grant him pardon for his weakness. In the seeing of his mind, the eyes of God were murderous with anger. The eyes of Lottie were soft and merciful.

He could sense her face against his shoulders, the moisture of her breathing coating his chest, and he swept his hand over his throat to ward off the feeling.

She had submitted to his clumsiness quietly and gently, letting her body unfold in his hands like the cloth of silk, and he had been stunned at the ease and grace of her giving. He had whispered stupidly of her beauty, had apologized shamefully for his behavior — behavior he could not stop — but she had not seemed to hear him.

"What I've done is wrong," he had said painfully as he walked her to the door of the store. "I can only ask you to forgive me. It won't happen again. You have my promise."

She had looked at him warmly, as though she did not understand why he was suddenly sad, had reached to touch his face, and then she had said, "I'm glad you don't hold it against Ben, me being here."

And that, too, was something that had lingered in his sleeplessness. Her concern for Ben seemed to be more than appreciation; it seemed deeply personal. And perhaps neither she nor Ben had told the whole story. Perhaps her husband was not dead, and she was only fleeing from him and had confided in Ben, and Ben had taken it upon himself to protect her. It would be like Ben to do so. He had his father's compassion for people who needed help, and since he had stopped boasting of his skills in baseball, he had become almost invisible when attention was turned on him. How would he explain being the protector of a woman on the run to Sally — or to anyone?

And maybe it meant nothing, what Lottie had said. Maybe it was the only thing she could think to say. He did not believe she had given herself so freely simply to shield Ben. There was too much in the giving, too much.

He stood inside his store, at the window, and searched the street for her, watching the early-morning shoppers arriving in their motorcars and buggies. He wondered if she would return to work, and if she did, what he would say to her.

She would leave Jericho soon, and it would be best. In time, he would remember her only with joy, not fear and regret.

He thought of Coleman Maxey.

Coleman was not right about Lottie. Believing he had seen her with the carnival was only the wildness of his imagination, the kind of trick that magicians used when they locked someone in a box and twirled it and then keyed open the locks to show it empty, and moments later called the disappeared person to materialize in the back of the auditorium.

Coleman wanted Lottie to be the girl of the carnival. It would make his fantasies of her worth the gossip he was bound to spread after she left.

He would not question her about the carnival, Arthur decided, but he would tell Coleman different. He would say he had asked her directly about it and she had provided him with certain proof that she was in Kentucky at the time. And then he would propose that no one else in Jericho had remembered her from the carnival, and she had been seen by most of the townspeople since coming to work in his store. Not just seen, but stared at, examined. He would say that he, too, remembered a girl — pretty like Lottie — but the girl he remembered was much shorter and had a dull, used look hidden in her soft eyes. With persuasion, Coleman might change his story.

He might say that Lottie had a look-alike. Pretty, but shorter, a dull, used look in her eyes. Almost a dead ringer, though. Almost.

He saw Lucille Bellflower crossing the street in her curious wad-dle, her protruding chin bobbling with her steps. She had found her buy in the window on the day before and had pondered over it and now was returning to take it away with her. She would prattle end-lessly over its size and color, and she would solicit praises from him for the wisdom of her selection. And he would gift-wrap the item, knowing her secret of sitting alone in her living room, pretending there were onlookers as she carefully unwrapped the surprise present from her addled husband. Before she left the store, Lucille would also remind him that it was her husband who had campaigned for him to sit on the city council. A tender illusion, Arthur thought. Her husband had not been out of his home in ten years. Those who knew him knew he still believed the Civil War raged outside the windows of his home.

He glanced past Lucille and saw Lottie, and he stepped back from the window. A single, hard blow struck in his chest and he inhaled quickly to calm himself.

———

IF IT WAS false energy, as his mother cautioned, Ben was glad to have it. He had slept well after Lottie's visit, and when he awoke, he was eager to be out of bed and to move about. His muscles were tender from bed rest, but his lungs did not ache and his vision was clear. He ate a hearty breakfast in the dining room with Sally and Little Ben keeping him company, and then he announced that he felt fit enough to walk with Sally to the store.

"I wish you wouldn't," his mother fretted. "It's already hot and you're not used to it. You'll tire out."

"It's not that far," Ben said. "And I won't rush things. If I get tired, I'll stop and rest."

Margaret Phelps sighed defeat. "You talk to him, Sally. He won't listen to me, but he'd better start listening to you."

The assignment pleased Sally. It was Margaret Phelps's first act of surrendering Ben to her care, a small but significant gesture of understanding that went unrecognized by Ben, yet established territory between the two women. "Maybe he needs to learn for himself," she said. "I'll watch him. If he pushes too hard, I'll make him come home."

A glance was exchanged between Margaret and Sally. Nods that were not nods. Eyeblinks. A rite of passage exercised in the kind of secrecy that only women could share.

"All right," Margaret said, and she sounded pleased.

To Sally, the moment was important enough to write about in the journal she had begun keeping, beginning with a line that read: *Today, Ben's mother began to let me become part of his life in the way it will be when I am finally his wife. . . .*

The walk with Sally from his home to Ledford's Dry Goods — only a few blocks away — was more taxing that Ben had predicted, but it was not from the summer heat or from his disappearing illness; it was from chattering good wishes flung toward them as they passed neighboring homes and, eventually, the stores and shops of Jericho. To Sally, the voices were like bright strips of confetti rained over a parade — something to reach for and keep as souvenirs — and she seemed to dance around Ben, pirouetting to touch hands or to be embraced by women who were celebrating romance remembered, or wished for. To Ben, it was a feeling of awkwardness, of being looked upon as a trophy from a hunt. He had no defense for the giddy spiels of prattle other than a grin that felt lopsided and foolish on his face. It was not a walk of leisure for Ben, but a sentence of the gauntlet, and realizing his discomfort amused Sally.

"It won't be so bad after today," she whispered to him.

"It was easier playing baseball, having people hooting at you," he confided.

Sally laughed. The sun was on her face, the music of voices surrounded her. She had never felt as grand.

At Brady's Cafe, Vernon Brady stepped from the door and intercepted them. Vernon was a small, smiling man, generous and likable. The apron he wore seemed a permanent part of his dress, like a costume on an actor. His wife vowed that he slept in it.

"Well, by heavens," Vernon boomed, "he's up and about." He extended his hand to Ben, shook heartily. "We've missed you, boy. You feeling better?"

"Sure am," Ben told him.

Vernon turned to Sally. "And I think I know why this pretty young lady looks so happy, but I want to hear it firsthand. It is true that you finally got him hog-tied?"

"Well, we're engaged," Sally said, "but I think I like your way of saying it better."

Vernon's laugh rolled down the street. "Come on in for a minute," he insisted. "I want to hear all about Boston and how Milo's doing, and I've got a peach pie just out of the oven. My treat." He laughed again. "And probably my wedding gift, too."

"Maybe we better take up that offer another time," Ben said. "Sally's already late for work."

"Good Lord, Ben, you don't think her daddy's going to fire her, do you?" Vernon teased. "Arthur can wait, but that pie can't." He opened the door to the cafe and motioned them in with a sweep of his arm. "He gets uppity about it, tell him I'll hire both of you away from him. Besides, it's too early for him to be doing anything but raising the prices on everything."

TWENTY-ONE

LOTTIE HAD HELD the door open for Lucille Bellflower, had nodded pleasantly to the high-pitched wail of Lucille's complaint about the morning heat, and then she had turned her eyes to Arthur, held them for a moment, and, without speaking, she had walked past him to the storeroom.

"That's a sweet little woman," Lucille had said in a purr. "Looks so pretty in that dress she's got on."

And Arthur had replied, "Yes, she does." He had wondered if Lottie heard him.

It took thirty minutes to please Lucille and send her on her way, proudly carrying a lace shawl, gift-wrapped, and when he turned back from the door, Arthur saw Lottie watching him from the front of the storeroom.

"Are you all right?" he asked.

The expression on her face was the same as it had been each day she had worked for him—a simple, girlish look of wonder, a look of surprise and fascination, and then of melancholy. Often the expression made it seem as though she did not hear when someone spoke to her.

Arthur asked again, "Are you all right?"

She blinked. A smile, barely visible, played on her mouth. "I'm fine," she answered. "I was just wondering what you wanted me to be doing."

Arthur crossed to her, uncertain of what to say.

"Sally said something about setting up a table for some men's shirts," she added.

"Yes," Arthur mumbled. "That—would be fine."

"I don't know which ones she was talking about," Lottie said.

"The new boxes that came in yesterday," he replied.

She dipped her head in a nod and then turned to go into the storeroom.

"Lottie, wait," Arthur said.

She looked back at him.

"I—have to say it again," he whispered. "How sorry I am about yesterday. I've never done anything like that."

She did not speak. The expression on her face did not change.

"I thought about it all night, and I don't know what to do," Arthur said, rushing his words. "I've behaved in a way that I would never believe I could, and I've violated every trust I would expect of myself, or of anyone else. And I don't know why I did it."

"I thought you were lonesome," Lottie said softly. "When you put your arms around me, you felt that way. You felt like you were lonesome."

Arthur shook his head in regret. "That's no reason. No reason at all."

"It seems like a reason to me," Lottie said. "It seems like the best reason to me."

"But I took a vow."

"Are you lonesome?" Lottie asked.

For a moment, Arthur did not reply. Then: "I suppose so. Sometimes. Everybody is."

"Did you take a vow for that?"

"The vow covers everything," he said weakly. He moved his eyes from her, opened his mouth to speak, but did not. He shook his head again, touched his forehead with his fingers as though he wanted to hold back pain. He could feel the damp coating of perspiration.

"I remember my mama waiting up all night for my daddy when I was little, not knowing if he was coming home or not," Lottie said in a voice that seemed far away. "Sometimes I'd sit up with her and she'd pull me up in her lap, and she'd say to me, 'Come here and let your mama hold you so she won't be so lonesome.' And I'd ask her why she looked so sad, and she'd say, 'Don't ever let yourself get so lonesome there's nothing left but wondering.' And then she'd laugh quiet-like and she'd rock me and say, 'You going to be an angel that watches over lonesome people, Lottie. Angel of the lonesome, that's what you'll be. Making people's frowns turn up to smiles, just like some fairy godmother out of a picture book.' " She paused. "I guess I always believed there was something special in being that."

My God, Arthur thought. He had never heard anyone describe himself, or herself, so perfectly, and yet with such condemnation. He reached to touch Lottie's arm, without realizing he had touched her. She bowed her head to look at his hand.

"You are that, Lottie," he said gently. "Yes, you are. But that's not all you are. You're special in a lot of ways."

"No," Lottie whispered. She touched his hand.

"Yes, you are," Arthur insisted. "Look at how many people have come in here this week, and I know why. It's not because of the store, or me, or Sally; it's because of you. And every one of them that I've talked to think you've brought life to this store, and you have, Lottie. You have. That's special. Nothing is as special as that. Don't you know? You can be anything you want to be."

Lottie pulled from his touch. "No," she said. "No, I can't be. Not like you, or Ben. You know about things I don't. I just know how to be what I am, and what I am is somebody from Augusta." A muscle twitched over her lips. "Do you know that's what my name was? Augusta. Lottie Augusta Barton. My mama said if she put where I was born in my name, I'd always know where I belonged."

"That's just where you're from, not where you belong," Arthur said. "Maybe your mother meant for you to remember where you came from, after you found where you needed to be."

Lottie shook her head firmly.

Arthur paused, inhaled slowly, fought the impulse to reach for her. He said, "Is that why you like Ben so much? You think he's a lot more special than you are?"

She looked up quickly, a shine of tears in her eyes. "Ben's nice." She sounded protective.

And then Arthur knew. In an epiphany of understanding, sudden and absolute, he knew that Coleman was right: Lottie had been to Jericho with the carnival, and, somehow, she had met Ben and that meeting had led to her being with him again. A thought flashed: Was Little Ben the son of Ben and Lottie? No, he reasoned. It couldn't be. Ben had not left Jericho in years, and it would have been impossible for Lottie to be in the town without someone knowing it. That was not the answer. He knew also why Lottie felt a closeness to Ben, why she defended him, and it was a reason he was certain Lottie did not recognize: Ben was the angel of her loneliness. And that made sense. For whatever purpose, Ben had made himself available to her, and that had given her comfort.

"Yes, he is nice," Arthur said. "Not long ago, I almost lost him, out of my own fault. But I don't know anybody I'd rather have around me — as somebody who works for me, or somebody to be my son-in-law. His father and I were close friends."

"He was a lot better this morning," Lottie said. "I expect he'll be back to work in a day or so, and then I'll go on home."

"You don't have to go," Arthur said gently. "I've got a place here for you."

Lottie shook her head slowly. "I told Foster I'd go home. He always wanted me to, since I'd been gone so long."

"Foster? Was that your husband?"

She nodded.

"Maybe you could go home to visit and then come back and stay here," Arthur suggested. "Make this your home."

She did not reply for a moment, and then she said wistfully, "That'd be nice. I feel more at home here than any place I ever been." She paused. Her eyes floated to his face, still shining. She turned and went into the storeroom.

———

BEN DID NOT remain long at the store. His presence caused shoppers to stop their browsing to greet him and inquire about his health, and to remark on the turn of events that had introduced him to Lottie Lanier, remarks ending always with a compliment for her.

Also, he felt restless in the store. He had never considered how fully his work had become his life, and how he belonged to every inch of space that incorporated Ledford's Dry Goods. The scent of new clothes, of leather, of cologne, made him eager to take up the routine he had followed diligently for so many years — a comfortable, easy routine, one that had purpose and dignity. He had never before understood his destiny so clearly. He was a merchant, not a baseball player, even if his failure in the game still affected him. Milo Wade was in Boston, washed in fame, and that was Milo's destiny. Yet, in so many ways, it seemed that Milo had gotten the worse of it. From all the stories, Milo was tormented. He consorted with demons, and one day the demons would devour him.

In his last years, Ben would remember the day of first visiting Ledford's after his illness as one of the profound moments of his living. He would say, "It's when I quit wanting something I never could have and started being glad for what I'd had all along."

He spoke briefly to Lottie while in the store, saying to her, "You look like you've always been here."

She smiled, deferred to Sally's presence, and continued her work of arranging a table of men's shirts.

Arthur told Ben of the sale he was planning. "Sort of a welcome-back-Ben sale," he said. "But I don't plan to do anything until you feel up to coming back to work."

They were standing alone at the pay counter as Sally displayed a dress for Katherine Spearman, the wife of the mayor.

"Yes sir," Ben said. Then, in a low voice, "I was thinking something and wanted to have your advice on it."

"All right," Arthur replied.

"I was thinking that I ought to offer to see Lottie and Little Ben on to Augusta," Ben said. "And while I was there, I want to look for a ring for Sally."

Arthur frowned in thought. He looked across the store to Lottie and then turned his face to Sally. After a moment, he said, "I think that's—that's a good plan." He paused. "Sally may feel a little uneasy about it, but that's to be expected."

"She could go with us," Ben suggested.

Arthur shook his head. "I don't think that's appropriate. People like to talk, and that's something neither one of you want, especially from her mother."

Ben blushed. He had never heard Arthur Ledford speak critically of his wife. Still, it was the truth. Alice Ledford would find fault in anything he did, now that his engagement to Sally was official.

"Let me bring it up," Arthur suggested. "Maybe if it comes from me — if I say that I've asked you to do the gentlemanly thing — it'll be more reasonable."

"Yes sir," Ben said in relief.

Arthur swallowed. He looked again at Lottie. "When — would you be prepared to leave?"

"Day after tomorrow, I think," Ben answered.

Arthur nodded 'solemnly. "I'll talk to Sally this afternoon."

———

KNOWING WHAT HE knew about Lottie Lanier, what he had shared only with Arthur Ledford, had made Coleman anxious and jittery. Keeping such news sealed behind his jaws was the same as holding his breath underwater. He had to say it, or drown. Or he had to calm his nerves.

He took his first drink at ten o'clock. At noon, he locked the door to his shoe repair business and tilted a Closed sign against the window, and went into his back room to continue drinking and to work on the repair of a saddle for Simon Greer. By four-thirty, he could feel the corn-made whiskey crawling on his skin, like ants, yet he did not feel drunk. He felt free, exhilarated. He could taste Lottie Lanier with each swallow of the whiskey, could feel her close against him, her naked breasts pressed into his naked chest.

He washed his face to clear his eyes and then he rubbed lilac water into his neck and cheeks to hide the smell of the whiskey. He put on a clean white shirt and a new pair of trousers he had purchased at Ledford's, balanced the new straw hat on his head, and left by the back door.

He avoided the main street of Jericho, knowing the street would likely be crowded with last-minute shoppers. They were the worse kind, he thought. Rushing in, making demands, expecting people to put aside a day's worth of work to do their bidding. In his shop, he had sent many of them on their way red-faced with anger or shock. Anybody who knew him knew he would invite the president of the United States to kiss his ass if the president got too pushy.

He laughed aloud at the thought.

Kiss my ass, Mr. President.

He passed the back of the pharmacy, where Dewey Capes, the pharmacist, stood packing trash into a trash can. Dewey was smoking his pipe. When he saw Coleman he nodded and called, "You looking all spiffed up there, Coleman. Looks like you're going to revival."

Coleman tipped his finger to his hat, knocking it from his head, but he caught it before it hit the ground.

Dewey laughed.

"Kiss my ass, Dewey," Coleman growled. He replaced his hat on his head and walked away. He could hear Dewey's laugh following him.

At Confederate Street, he turned right and continued to Main Street. He stopped under the shade of an elm tree that grew in the corner of Merriweather's Furniture and Appliance. Across the street was Ledford's Dry Goods. He pulled his handkerchief from his pocket and wiped the whiskey perspiration from his neck, and he fanned his face with his hat.

All he wanted was a look. He wanted to get close enough to smell her perfume. Maybe speak to her. If she spoke back, he would know for sure she was the carnival girl who had bought the jar of whiskey from him. He grinned, felt a shiver along the back of his arms. Maybe she would say to him, "You don't tell on me, I'll give you what you want."

The door to Ledford's opened and Sally Ledford rushed out of the store, turned right, and walked briskly down the street.

Going to see Ben, Coleman thought. Ben was a lucky son of a bitch. Had one woman hightailing to him and another one sleeping across the hall from him. Two best-looking women in Jericho.

Wouldn't mind a go with that Sally myself, he mused. Got to be hot and tight and high-strung as a colt.

He licked his lips and let the grin sink deep into his body. He wished he had brought along a drink.

He crossed the street to the store, paused for a moment at the door, letting his eyes sweep the street. He saw two boys running up the sidewalk, away from the store. No one else. He opened the door only enough to slip quickly and silently inside. He stood, scanning the store, listening. He did not see anyone, but from the back, in the storeroom, he heard the quiet voice of Arthur Ledford. Not the words. Only the voice. He moved noiselessly across the marble floor to the menswear department and found a rack of suits to hide behind. Giggled softly. He felt like a boy playing a prank. So what if Arthur Ledford came out of the storeroom and found him? He could say he was thinking of buying a suit, but didn't see anybody when he came in, and was looking for one himself. What would Arthur do, anyway? There was a bond between them. Arthur was as trapped as a fox in a den surrounded by hounds.

He removed his hat and peeked through the suits to the door leading to the storeroom, and he saw the door open and Arthur step through it, followed by Lottie.

He heard Arthur say, "Don't be long. They'll be expecting you."

"I won't," Lottie said.

He saw Arthur glance around the store, then saw him reach to touch Lottie's face, saw Lottie smile.

"Give the key to Sally," Arthur said. "She'll bring it to me. But if you forget it, I've got another one."

"I won't forget," Lottie told him.

Coleman fought not to laugh. The old bastard, he thought. No damn wonder he wants it kept quiet about Lottie being with the carnival. He's getting his fill of her, there in the storeroom. Probably holding it over her. Probably told her it was known about her being in Jericho, and if she wanted to keep it quiet, she'd better do what he wanted done. The old bastard.

He watched Arthur leave the store and lock the door. Through the window, he could see Arthur hurry down the street, toward his home. He thought of Alice Ledford, and thinking of her, he could understand why Arthur would take to Lottie. Alice Ledford was a bitch. Cold as an icehouse. Meanness in her eyes.

Coleman stepped from behind the rack of suits. He could see Lottie in the storeroom, holding a broom, sweeping. He moved quickly across the store, staying close to the wall and the displays of clothing. When he reached the storeroom, he saw that Lottie had her back to the door, and he stepped inside the room and closed the door with a hard push. Lottie whirled to the sound.

"Hello, miss," Coleman said. He smiled.

Lottie held the broom in both hands. She said, "Mr. Ledford's gone."

"I know it," Coleman told her. "Saw him leave. Saw that sweet little touch he put on your face. Saw him lock the door. I was trying to find me a suit, but wadn't nobody out there to wait on me."

"I—don't sell," Lottie said.

Coleman stepped toward her. "I know you don't, honey. I know what you do. Been knowing it from the first time I laid eyes on you. Maybe you don't sell, but you buy." He rolled his hat in his hands.

Lottie looked nervously at the closed door.

"Don't go worrying about it. They's nobody here but me and you," Coleman said easily. "Just me and you, and I thought we'd take up where we left off about six years ago."

A look of surprise flickered in Lottie's eyes.

"You don't remember me?" Coleman asked. He laughed.

Lottie moved back, toward Ben's rolltop desk.

"I was the one you bought the jar of corn from," Coleman said. The look of surprise faded from Lottie. She remembered.

"I made you a offer. You recall that?" Coleman continued. "A little trade? Well, I got another little offer. Why don't we get on with what we could of done six years ago, and I won't tell nobody about you and Mr. Arthur Ledford, or about you being here before with that carnival and knowing Mr. Ben Phelps, which is the only way you would of showed up with him. What'd you and Ben do? Have you a little time together?" He stepped closer to Lottie. "You show him what it's about? Does his mama know? What about Sally? You tell her yet?"

"What do you want?" Lottie asked in a whisper.

Coleman could feel the whiskey streaming through him, cheering him. His mouth filled with saliva, his tongue burned against his teeth.

"First thing, I want you to take off every stitch of clothes you got on," he said in a low, threatening voice. "Then we gone go from there."

Lottie leaned the broom against the rolltop desk. She began unbuttoning her dress.

"Slowlike," ordered Coleman. "I want to see it kind of peel off." He dropped his hat and stroked the front of his pants, touching the erection rising against his leg.

Lottie thought of her sister, of Lila. Could hear Lila's voice telling her that all she had to do was think about breathing, and everything would go away. Sooner or later, everything would go away. *Inhale. Hold. Exhale. Pause.* Her fingers worked in the rhythm of her breathing.

And then she was nude.

"Great Goda'mighty," Coleman whispered in disbelief. He did not believe it was possible for anyone to be as beautiful, and he had seen many naked women, from rough-skinned farm girls in hay barns to creamy-skin whores in mansions turned into whorehouses. The nipples of her breasts were honey-gold, matching the color of her eyes.

The V-patch of hair gathered at her legs was luxuriously dark, oil-coated, fluffed.

Coleman shook his head, blinked rapidly. A cackling little laugh raced from his throat. She did not move, but the whiskey in him believed she did, believed the shadow of a smile flew to her lips, perched on them birdlike. And then he believed he saw her legs part slightly, her hips turn, her breasts rise up to lick at the light that fell over her.

"You goddamn whore," Coleman sneered. Blood roared through him, his erection was hot against his skin. He ripped at his belt, fingered his trousers open, yanked them down with his underwear. He stood, exposing himself, glaring at her. His face was flushed and damp. He was breathing in slow, hard swallows of air. "I been waiting six years for this," he said. He touched the tip of his erection. "Six years." He moved toward her.

Lottie closed her eyes. She inhaled, held the breath, exhaled.

The door flew open before Coleman could reach her, and Arthur Ledford stepped inside the storeroom. A look of shock was on his face. He opened his mouth to speak, but did not. Coleman stumbled back, tripping on his trousers, and suddenly Arthur was in front of him, grabbing him by the shirt, flinging him against the desk.

"You son of a bitch," Arthur growled.

Coleman struggled to stand. He said, "Goddamn it, Arthur, get your hands off me."

Arthur did not move. His face flamed with rage. "You son of a bitch, I ought to kill you," he hissed.

Coleman raised his hands in defense. "What the hell's wrong with you?" he whimpered. "She's a whore. I saw you with her."

A cry erupted in Arthur's chest and his fist flashed through the air, hitting Coleman in the mouth, breaking teeth. Blood spurted from Coleman's lips. He slumped to the floor. Arthur leaned over him, spitting words into his face. "You've got a choice, damn you. Either you get out of here and forget you ever saw this woman anywhere, or I'll call the sheriff and have your sorry ass arrested for attempted rape, and I'll make certain everybody in Caulder County knows what happened here if I have to go house to house to do it. Do you understand me?"

Coleman nodded. He held his hand over his mouth, and the blood seeped through his fingers. He glanced past Arthur to Lottie. She was holding her dress in front of her. "It was her," he said hoarsely. "I was right."

"No, you weren't," Arthur snapped. "What you saw was a woman who looked like her, but not as tall. The woman you saw had a hard look. I saw her myself." He paused, leaned over Coleman. "Do you doubt me?"

Coleman did not answer.

"You're lucky Dewey Capes told me he saw you headed toward the store," Arthur said. "If you had touched her, I promise you one thing: you would have died one way or the other."

"Jesus, Arthur," Coleman whined. "You want her, you can have her."

Arthur did not move from Coleman. "You are talking about a lady, you bastard. Someone who just lost her husband, someone who took it on herself to help somebody from our town, and that's how you will think of her, and how you will treat her. Now get up and get out of here, and don't ever show yourself in this store again, and don't ever speak to me again. Have I made myself clear?"

Coleman nodded. He pulled himself away from Arthur and worked his pants back over his waist.

"You leave through the back door," Arthur told him. "I don't want anybody to even know you've been here."

Coleman's face dripped with blood as he dressed. He picked up his hat, took one look at Lottie, still holding her dress in front of her, and then he staggered to the back door of the storeroom and left.

Arthur turned to Lottie. "Are you all right?" he asked gently.

She nodded. "Yes," she said.

"Did he touch you?"

She shook her head, pulled the dress closer to her body. Her eyes were moist.

"He won't say anything," Arthur told her. "I know him. He won't go against me." He paused, looked at the back door, then back to Lottie. She seemed as helpless as a child, yet she was not a child. She was a woman, as beautiful as a woman could be. "Why don't you dress," he said softly. "I'll wait up front."

Lottie nodded.

TWENTY-TWO

MARGARET PHELPS HAD met her late husband during the year of her eighth grade when a cotton broker named Jonathan Phelps moved to Jericho from Greensboro, North Carolina, bringing with him a wife named Louise and a lanky, freckle-faced, forever-grinning ninth-grader named Elton. It took exactly one second of looking into Elton's eyes during their introduction for Margaret Grace Lowell to know she had met her future husband.

It was the nature of Margaret to believe that life was not complicated if you did not make it complicated. She took the good, nurtured it, and refused to let the bad linger. The only exception—and it was still painful—was the death of her husband. Because it was sudden and unexpected, she had never fully accepted it, and there were moments when the thought of him caused her to feel faint, and she would have to sit and take short, gulping swallows of air to keep the thought from suffocating her.

Now, there was another sadness, one that had caused her to weep into her pillow late at night and to make her claw at the bedcovering, pulling it to her chest, as though holding on to something that was being ripped from her.

The something was Little Ben.

After supper, sitting with his mother on the porch, Ben had announced he would accompany Lottie and Little Ben to Augusta in two days.

"Mr. Ledford and I talked about it," Ben had said, "and it's time. Mr. Ledford thought it would be the right thing to do if I went with them."

"Sally won't like that," his mother had warned.

"Mr. Ledford explained it to her," Ben had replied. "And then she talked to me when she came over after work. I think she's all right with it. She might even be a little relieved. No matter how much she says she likes Lottie, I can see a little bit of jealousy in her once in a while."

His mother had sighed with grief. "Ben, I don't know if I can stand having that little boy going away."

"It's going to happen sometime, Mama."

"I know, son, but he's so happy here."

Ben had smiled and reached to pat his mother's arm. "I think he is, too. About as happy as somebody else I know."

She had begun to cry, and could not stop crying.

It was early, before sunrise, and Margaret moved as quietly as possible in the kitchen, building the stove fire, preparing for breakfast. She would cook pancakes for Little Ben, she thought. Pancakes were his favorite. Pancakes drenched in maple syrup. And she would cook the sausage that he liked. And after breakfast, when the stores of Jericho opened, she would take him to buy some toys and books that she would send with him to Augusta, and she would stop by Tolliver Barkley's home and pay Tolliver to set up his camera and take a photograph of Little Ben for her to keep.

She sat at the kitchen table, taking the one cup of coffee she allotted herself each morning, though today, she thought, she would cheat on her habit. She needed the coffee after a sleepless night. The burning wood in the stove had a sweet smoke odor, and somehow it reminded her of the pipe that her husband had enjoyed after his evening meal. Even now, years after his death, she would take the pipe from a drawer and sniff it, and the still-sweet scent of tobacco would bring her to tears.

She wondered if she would cook pancakes simply to remember Little Ben, and if she would weep.

It was inevitable that Lottie and Little Ben would leave. She had known so from the beginning, and yet she had wanted to believe the leaving would not be so soon. Their presence had filled the house with energy, and she had reveled in her role as hostess and caretaker, as mother-figure and grandmother-figure. It had been like living in the highly charged gaiety of a festival that did not rest or stop, and as she sat, drinking from her coffee, she believed she could hear the rollicking laughter of it caught in the kitchen curtains like sunlight.

She closed her eyes and lowered her head at the table and thought of Ben.

It had not been easy for Ben, having Lottie and Little Ben in the house, knowing, as he must, that Lottie had feeling for him, though it did not seem a feeling of want as much as gratitude. It would have to be that. Lottie was a widow, her husband recently buried. Women—even young women such as Lottie—did not turn immediately to other men. There was a time of mourning. Yet, Lottie did not speak of her marriage, which meant that her husband could have been a difficult man whose death was a blessing. Not like Elton. Men such as Elton were mourned for a lifetime, and when her friends gently suggested that at her age—not yet fifty—she should think again of marriage, for companionship if for no other reason, she hushed them with a look.

Lottie was young. Ben's age, perhaps younger. She would marry again. There would be many willing and eager men vying for her attention and for the privilege of sharing her bed. If not for Sally, Ben likely would have been one of them, Margaret suspected. Still, Sally was the right woman for Ben. No one, including Lottie, would care for him as completely, or as passionately, as Sally.

And in time, there would be another Little Ben, she reasoned.

But not the Little Ben who had nuzzled so quickly, so completely, into her soul.

She heard a movement near her and looked up. Lottie was standing at the kitchen door, dressed in her silk nightdress and a green cotton robe.

"Oh, goodness," Margaret said in relief. She stood. "I didn't hear you."

"I could smell the coffee," Lottie told her quietly. "I guessed you were up."

Margaret moved away from the table to the stove. "Well, come on in and I'll get you a cup."

Lottie crossed to the table and sat and watched Margaret pour the coffee.

"I just couldn't sleep," Margaret said, trying to sound cheerful. "Sometimes I go for days like that. Can't sleep a wink, so I get up and make myself busy, thinking I'll get sleepy, but I never do, and then I have to take an afternoon nap to make up for it." She carried the coffee to the table. "But maybe it's the coffee. Keeps me awake."

"Does the same to me," Lottie said. She put two teaspoons of sugar in the coffee and stirred it. She, too, had slept fitfully, remembering the attack of Coleman Maxey, knowing Coleman Maxey had recognized her from the carnival and knowing Arthur Ledford also harbored that secret. Arthur Ledford had rescued her from submitting to Coleman Maxey. And she would have submitted. Submission had always been safer than resisting, and she would have done it to stop the stories Coleman Maxey would tell. In the wondering of her sleepless night, she had thought warmly of Arthur. She could not remember anyone risking so much for her—not even Foster, or Ben. Her feeling for Arthur was surprisingly tender and good. Not a child's feeling for a father, as she wanted to believe, but a woman's feeling for a man.

"I like that robe on you," Margaret said. "It's a good color for you."

Lottie looked at the robe, touched its lapel, then she looked up at Margaret. "We'll be leaving tomorrow," she said simply.

"Yes, I know," Margaret replied after a moment. "Ben told me last night." She sat across from Lottie. "It makes me sad, thinking about it."

"I am, too," Lottie admitted. "You've been better to us than anybody ever could be, but we stayed long enough. It's time we went on home."

Margaret rubbed her eyes with her fingers. She tried to laugh, could not. "I swear it's going to be so quiet around here without that baby. I'll probably go crazy."

"He'll miss you, too."

"You've got your own life and I know it's wrong of me to say it, but I do so wish you lived here," Margaret blurted.

"Thank you," Lottie whispered.

"I just don't want you to forget us," Margaret said desperately. "And I want you to come back to visit. Stay as long as you want to. You'll always have a place here you can call home."

Lottie smiled and let her eyes slowly scan the kitchen. "You've got the prettiest home I ever saw."

"It's just a place, Lottie," Margaret said. "It becomes a home when there's people like you and Little Ben in it."

Lottie tasted from the coffee with her spoon. "It's good," she said.

"I like the way you make coffee. My mama never could do it. She always made it so weak it was like colored water. Foster — my husband — taught me how to make it stronger."

It was the first time Margaret had heard Lottie speak of Foster. "He must have been a good man," she suggested tentatively.

Lottie gazed at the coffee. Her eyes smiled. "Yes, ma'am, he was," she said. "He was older than me, and he didn't have much, but he took good enough care of us."

"Did you always live in Kentucky?" Margaret asked.

Lottie shook her head in a slight movement. "We used to move about, but when Little Ben come along, we went to Kentucky." The smile in her eyes moved to her lips. "I liked it there good enough, even when it got so cold in the wintertime. I told Foster that when he died, we'd stay there, me and Little Ben, but he wouldn't hear of it. He said I hadn't been home since he'd met me, and he always promised that he'd get me back there. He always said the only place a person ought to go to when he wants to start over, or to die, was at the home he'd been born to." She paused, kept her gaze on the coffee cup. Then she added, "I didn't know it, but that's what he was doing when we went to Kentucky."

Margaret looked away from Lottie. She could sense the salt burning of tears covering her eyes. Across the table from her was a woman who was the age of her son, yet older and, in her way, wiser than anyone Margaret knew. In her life, Margaret Phelps had never traveled more than a hundred miles from Jericho, and the domain of her existence had been the house they were sitting in. Lottie seemed to have seen the world, like some high, warm wind swirling over oceans and continents, dipping down on a whim to rub against places and people, leaving the places and people jittery with her presence.

"I think I'll check on Little Ben," Margaret said, standing. "I'm going to do pancakes for him and then we're going to dress up and go into town and I'm going to spend my last day with him spoiling him, and if you or Ben or anybody else tells me I can't do that, well, I may just pack him up and take him down to the train station and buy the two of us tickets to some place like California."

For a moment the two women looked at one another, and then Lottie stood and moved to Margaret and embraced her, and both wept.

———

ON THE LAST day that Lottie would be employed at Ledford's Dry Goods, Sally Ledford awoke determined to be as gracious and as ebullient as possible. She wanted to leave Lottie with the impression that she was regretful over Lottie's leaving, yet also happy for her. And both emotions were real. She would miss Lottie, especially at the store. Even with the time required to be a public attraction, Lottie had worked feverishly at changing the displays of goods and, to Sally, the store had never looked as appealing. Still, secretly, Sally knew she would not be as tense around Ben with Lottie gone. She would have Ben to herself, and she would not have to wonder what happened in the dark rooms of the Phelps home during the deep hours of night.

On the night before, in her journal, Sally had written:

Tonight, Ben and I talked about him going with Lottie to Augusta, which is something that Daddy thinks is the right thing to do. At first, I was upset about it, but after talking to Ben, I'm all right. He wants to do the honorable thing and I know in my heart that he feels he owes Lottie for taking care of him. I will miss her. She has seemed like a sister to me, but I think it is best for her to leave and find her life away from Jericho. She will not have trouble finding a good husband. Every man I know seems taken with her, and that includes Ben and my own father. They try not to show it, but they do. Lottie's special that way, I think. It's not just because she's pretty, but because she has a way about her that makes people want to look at her. I do want her to remember me as a friend, and as someone who is grateful to her for bringing my Ben home to me.

Oh, Ben said nothing about it, but I think he's going to look for a ring for me while he's in Augusta. I heard my father say something to my mother about it, when he didn't know I was listening. I hope so.

I want to make tomorrow special for Lottie.

The art of forced celebration was an art Sally had learned from customers of Ledford's, where gifts were often purchased not out of joy, but out of obligation. The difference between joy and obligation was seldom obvious, yet Sally could see it in the aura of the shoppers. It was in the shape of their smiles, in the tittering of their voices. For Lottie, Sally would strive mightily to pull an aura of joy around her, brightly coloring it with her smile and with her energy. She would not allow silence. Silence was the sound of remorse.

The first act in Sally's plan for the day was to walk with Lottie from the Phelps home to Ledford's, stopping for early-morning coffee and peach pie at Brady's Cafe. "It's something I've always wanted to do, but never have, except when Ben and I stopped in yesterday," Sally explained cheerfully. "So I told Daddy this morning that we'd be a few minutes late. You've got to have a piece of Mr. Brady's peach pie. It's the best in the world."

To the customers of Brady's Cafe, the appearance of Sally and Lottie was a welcomed interruption of their snickering talk about Coleman Maxey getting drunk and falling into a tree and knocking his front teeth out, the story Coleman had told when Dewey Capes sold him cotton to pack his gums. Coleman was a topic of discussion as common as predictions about the weather. Lottie Lanier was fresh as a rain shower on a spring day, as pretty as the rumors said she was, and as quiet and as polite. She seemed at ease with Sally's happy chatter, replied pleasantly to introductions, but said nothing about leaving Jericho when Sally announced it was Lottie's last day at Ledford's.

"It's a loss to the town," Vernon Brady said kindly. He added, "But if it's a job that'll keep you, and Arthur's too blind to see a good worker when he's got one, why, you can come to work here any time you want to."

The people who heard Vernon cheered the offer.

THE DAY PASSED quickly at Ledford's, a day of motion and noise from Sally, a day during which Arthur Ledford busied himself with paperwork in his office, occasionally going to the window that looked out over the store and gazing at his daughter, with Lottie in tow, enlisting Lottie to help with questions about fabric and style. He had a sad, vacant expression on his face, like someone on a deathwatch, and even the coming and going of customers — heavy from the word that went out of Brady's Cafe about Lottie's leaving — could not bring him to the floor.

AT CLOSING, ARTHUR sent his daughter away to Ben's home to help Margaret Phelps prepare a farewell supper for Lottie and Little Ben.

"I need to settle up with Lottie," he said privately to Sally, "and to see if I can offer her some help with getting work in Augusta."

"Don't keep her late," Sally said.

"I won't," her father promised.

HE HAD SPENT the day thinking of the right thing to say to Lottie, yet nothing seemed adequate or appropriate. He had resolved to be gentlemanly and professional, to keep a space between them that would say as much as he would say in words, or more. He would tell her again that his earlier behavior had been boorish and for that he apologized and hoped she would not hold it against him when she turned her thoughts to the days she had spent in Jericho, and he would thank her for understanding him in his weakness. He would assure her that Coleman Maxey would keep his tongue about her, or he would make good his threat to Coleman. He would offer again to contact merchant friends in Augusta and to provide her with a persuasive recommendation for employment. He would give her the envelope of money that he had for her—a sum considerably greater than the agreed-upon wage.

Arthur's resolve was wasted. What he said when he saw her was "You are the most beautiful person I've ever seen, and I will never forget you. When I'm an old man I will believe that for a few days of my life I was blessed because of you. Last night, all I could think about was what could have happened to you yesterday." He could feel a single tear roll from his eye, down his cheek. He reached into the inside pocket of his suit coat and withdrew the envelope of money. "This is for you," he whispered, holding it toward her.

Lottie did not look at the envelope. She moved to him and brushed away the tear with her fingertip, and then she slipped her arms around his waist and turned her face against his chest. She could hear the racing of his heart.

"My God, you are remarkable," he said in a voice barely heard.

————

IN HER JOURNAL, Sally wrote:

Tomorrow morning Ben will go with Lottie and Little Ben to Augusta, leaving on the 7:10 train, and things will be different. Tonight, Mrs. Phelps (I already think of her as Mother Phelps) had a supper for Lottie and Little Ben, and I was happy to help her with it. My parents were invited, but my mother is still suffering from the summer heat, and so both declined. It was more than a meal. It was more like a banquet, and we ended it with having ice cream again. The ice cream was for Little Ben, who said to Lottie that he wanted to stay with his Gra-Ma. It made Mrs. Phelps misty-eyed.

My father has volunteered to drive Ben and Lottie and Little Ben to the train station, but I'm sure Mrs. Phelps will go also. With all the new outfits and other gifts that Lottie and Little Ben have, and all the people, it will probably take two trips. If all works well, Ben should be able to return tomorrow night, and if he's not too tired, he will be at work day after tomorrow. Tonight he seemed like his old self.

It was a good night, but a little sad. Everybody talked to Lottie about coming back for the wedding, but I don't think she will. I don't know why, but I don't think any of us will ever see Lottie again. I don't think any of us will ever forget her, either.

Sally put her journal away in a desk drawer, then dressed for bed, but she was not sleepy and she slipped from her room and moved quietly past her parents' bedroom to the kitchen. She was surprised to find her father sitting at the kitchen table in the dark.

"Daddy?" she said, worried. "What are you doing awake?"

"Couldn't sleep," her father answered.

"Are you feeling all right?"

"I'm fine."

"Mama? Is Mama all right?"

"I'm sure she is," her father said. "She was asleep when I went up to bed."

Sally sat at the table beside him. "Are you bothered by something?"

Her father shook his head.

Sally did not know why the question filled her mouth. It was simply there, and she asked it: "Is it Lottie?"

Arthur did not answer for a long moment. He seemed to be staring at something across the room, hidden in the shadows of night. Then he said, "A little, I suppose. She was a good worker and a good person. I think I treated her poorly."

"What makes you say that?" Sally said. "I don't know anybody who would've given a person they didn't know a job, but you did."

"Against my judgment," her father said heavily. "And that's what bothers me. I was thinking about myself and the store, not what somebody else needed. I'm glad you pushed me to do it."

"I liked having her there," Sally said.

"I know," her father whispered. He pulled himself out of the chair. "We'd better get some sleep," he added. "We've got a busy morning."

"All right," Sally told him.

In her room, Sally took her journal from the desk drawer and added a line:

I couldn't help the feeling that Ben was in love with Lottie. I was wrong. It wasn't Ben. It was my father.

TWENTY-THREE

AKERS CREWS WAS not surprised by the gathering on the platform
of the train depot, not after selling Ben tickets for the trip to Augusta
on the day before. He knew Margaret Phelps and Sally would be
there, and he guessed that Arthur Ledford would provide the trans-
portation. He had heard the back-and-forth talk about Lottie Lanier,
had even defused some of the gossip, yet he knew that her leaving
would cause an outbreak of tongue-wagging from busybodies who
seemed to find delight in declaring the right and wrong, the good
and bad, of everything from gnats to elephants. None was worse than
his wife, Charlotte. Charlotte was certain that Ben Phelps had more
to do with Lottie than anyone would ever know. Akers's only com-
ment to her had been "You make me want to throw up sometimes."

The leaving was tearful for Margaret. She surrendered Little Ben
only when she had to, telling him that his Gra-Ma would miss him.
Little Ben reached for her as Lottie stepped onto the train, holding
him. He said, "Gra-Ma. I want Gra-Ma." And Margaret did some-

thing she would later think of as an embarrassment: she turned into Arthur's chest, weeping, forcing him to embrace her.

Sally stood close to the train window, where Ben and Lottie and Little Ben were seated. She tried to smile, but she, too, had tears. She called out to Ben, "I'll see you tomorrow." The way she said it was almost a prayer.

And then the train began to move away in its laboring crawl, yowling with the hiss of steam and the squealing of steel pistons and the pealing cry of the whistle.

"I miss that baby," Margaret wailed over the noise, and Arthur held her tight in his arms and watched the face of Lottie fade away through the light-splashed window of the train, and he shuddered involuntarily against an aching of sorrow that he believed was permanent.

———

THEY DID NOT speak for several miles. Lottie leaned her head against the backrest of the seat and gazed out of the window. Little Ben was huddled close to her, holding a rag rabbit that Margaret had given him. Ben sat across from them, watching.

Finally: "We've been on a lot of trains together," Ben said.

Lottie smiled, blinked a yes.

"Are you all right?" Ben asked.

Lottie moved her head in answer. The answer was vague.

"It's not going to seem right, you and Little Ben not being at the house," Ben said.

Again, the smile moved softly over Lottie's lips.

"I wish you'd think about coming back to live in Jericho," Ben added.

"I can't do that, Ben," she said.

"Why not?"

Lottie turned her gaze from the window to Ben. She said, "There's lots of reasons. No matter how much I'd like to do it, I can't."

"What reasons?"

"Maybe I love you, Ben. Maybe I have since that first night I saw you on the train."

"Lottie, I—"

"It's not like the way I loved Foster," Lottie said. "It's more like I feel safe with you, and sometimes I just want to touch you." She looked at Little Ben. "Maybe it's like the way Little Ben was with your mama. Maybe it's just wanting to know somebody's there, somebody who has a good feeling for you."

"And you think that's wrong?" Ben said.

She shook her head. "I don't want it to be." She closed her eyes for a moment, then opened them to look again at Ben. "But that can't be, Ben. Not when you're about to be married, and Sally's right for you. She is. I'm glad you have her. She'll make you happy."

Ben leaned forward in his seat, bent at the waist as if in pain. He was holding his hat and he turned it nervously in his hands. He saw Little Ben staring at him curiously, the rag rabbit tucked in his arms, and he wondered if Little Ben would remember his mother's words.

"Lottie," he said, "I'm just a clerk in a store. That's what I'll be all my life. I used to think I'd be somebody else, somebody who was famous like Foster or Milo, but I won't be. And that's all right with me now. You—you're different. There's something about you that's—I don't know. Eternal, I think. It's more than being famous. Everywhere you go, you leave part of yourself, like—I don't know. Like something a person sees that he can't forget, because he never thought he'd see anything like it. You're like somebody I read about in a book one time. It was about the Greeks, thousands of years ago, when they had all kinds of gods and goddesses. My father had some of those books. He liked the stories and he used to read them to me, but made me promise I wouldn't talk about them in church." He paused and smiled at the memory of his father's admonition, then he added, "You're like one of those—those goddesses."

Lottie reached for him with her hand, touched his face, then pulled her hand away. "I don't know about them, Ben. I just know about me. And I know some about you." She paused. "You love me too, don't you? I don't mean like needing to have me, but like caring what happens to me."

For a moment, Ben did not move. Then he bobbed his head. "Yes," he whispered.

"That's all I want to know, Ben. That's all. Just knowing it, that's enough."

———

THE AUGUSTA TRAIN station was crowded with travelers and cargo workers, and a sense of panic seemed to hang suspended in the hot late-morning air. Ben remembered the feeling from years earlier, being awed by it, wondering how anyone could ever work in such a frenzied place. Now the frenzy—a commotion, his mother would call it—had about it the same mood as a baseball game. Tense. Energetic. No different from players standing in the shadow of a covered shelter, their bodies tilted toward the playing field like flowers tilted toward the sun, waiting for a thrill to explode in front of them.

It took a half hour to find a motorcar taxi service and to load the gift packages that Margaret Phelps had provided for Lottie and Little Ben. Among the packages was the bundle that Lottie had taken from Kentucky, still wrapped with the cord she had found in the barn, and Ben remembered that it was the one item that Lottie had carried personally to the train in Jericho. He believed it held her collection of memories.

The address that Lottie gave the driver was on River Road, and the driver frowned irritably. He said, "You got the money for going out there?"

"I have the money," Ben told him.

"Well, you got more than anybody that lives out there's got," the driver said sarcastically. He looked at Lottie. "There's lots better places to stay."

"That's where we want to go," Ben said firmly.

THE DRIVE THROUGH Augusta stirred memories for Ben. It had been, for him, a magical place, a place of dreams, and even the hurt of seeing those dreams end with the finality of a death could not dim the exuberance of the one grand moment of his life. In the catch of a baseball — impossible even to those who witnessed it — Ben had been as much a god as those gods from the stories of the Greeks. Hercules. He had been Hercules.

The route taken by the driver did not pass Hornet Field, yet Ben knew he would not leave Augusta without going there. For a few minutes only. A walk around the field. Or maybe there would be a game, and he would watch young boys with dreams, sucking dust and hope into their lungs with each play. He wondered if Arnold Toeman was still the manager. Likely so. Men such as Arnold Toeman liked the killing of dreams.

The driver turned onto a narrow, washboard-rut side road that mimicked the flow of the Savannah River, and a row of shanty homes — small, unpainted, with patched roofs and sidings, the yards eroded, cluttered in trash and covered with wilting weeds — began to appear on the down side of the road, overlooking the river. Ben watched Lottie. She pushed deeper into her seat, the look on her face becoming pale, a look of resignation.

"You show me which one," the driver said curtly. "They all look alike to me. Looks like Niggertown."

"Around the next curve," Lottie said in a weak voice. "Number seventy-two. First one."

The home of Lottie's childhood was no different from any of the houses on the road. They had been built for workers of nearby textile mills on land useless for anything but the shanty homes that were there. A sense of dread welled up in Ben. He was glad his mother was not with them.

Lottie and Little Ben got out of the car and stood near the walkway leading to the house. She seemed to be waiting for someone to open the door and speak to her.

"Could you wait for me?" Ben asked the driver.

"How long?" the driver said.

"A few minutes," Ben told him. "I just need to make sure her people still live here, and then we can unload everything."

The driver shrugged. "You wouldn't catch me staying out here, neither," he mumbled. He cast a glance toward Lottie. "That your woman?"

"She's a friend," Ben said. "Her husband died not long ago. I'm just making sure she gets home."

"Damn, she's a looker," the driver said. He grinned. "Maybe I better remember where this place is." He wiped the perspiration from his face. "All right. Take your time. Gone cost you a little more, but I'll wait."

Ben crossed to Lottie and touched her arm. He said, "Are you ready?"

"Stay here with Little Ben," she said.

"Why?" asked Ben.

"I need to go back by myself," she said.

"All right," Ben replied. He took Little Ben's hand and watched Lottie move down the walkway to the house. At the door, she hesitated, took a step back, and waited. After a moment, the door opened and a frail woman with graying hair stood in the doorway. Ben could see her mouth move, but he could not hear the words. He saw the woman push her face forward to hear something Lottie was saying, and then the woman craned to look toward him. He saw her frown and look again at Lottie. She said something, then lifted a thin arm to push her hair from her forehead. She seemed to nod, then stepped back into the house. Lottie turned and crossed back to him.

"Was that your mother?" Ben asked.

"Yes," Lottie answered.

"Is your father home?"

"He's dead. Somebody killed him."

"I'm sorry," Ben said.

"It's all right," Lottie told him. "It don't surprise me."

"Your sister? Lila. Is she here?"

Lottie nodded.

Ben knelt to Little Ben. He tucked the shirt Little Ben was wearing into his trousers. Then he said, "Go back with me, Lottie. Please."

"I can't," Lottie said simply.

"You can't stay here."

"It's my home, Ben."

"No, it's not. It's the place you used to live," Ben said.

"I got to try."

"Is this what you want for Little Ben?" Ben asked.

"Don't say that to me, Ben," Lottie whispered. "You know better."

Ben stood. He glanced toward the house. "All right," he said in resignation. "Let's get your things in the house."

"Just put them out here," Lottie told him.

"I'll help you get them in," Ben said.

"No, Ben. This is as far as you go," she said.

"What do you mean?"

"You did what you promised Foster you'd do," Lottie said. "You brought me home."

"I want to make sure you're all right before I leave," Ben protested.

"I'm all right, Ben," she said evenly.

Ben looked away beyond the house. He could see the steel gray of the river through the trees, its water showing sunspots in its roll. On the river, he saw a small boat with two men in it. Fishing, he thought.

He had brought Lottie home, as far as she would allow. She did not want him to see behind the door of the house, and he would not argue. He could not intrude on her pride.

"I'll get your things," he said. He turned and crossed to the car and began to unload the packages, helped by the driver.

"Just give me another minute," he said to the driver. "In private, if you would."

The driver cocked his head and grinned and walked back to his car.

"Will you remember something?" Ben said to Lottie. "Will you remember that you can come back anytime you want to. You got a home with us."

Lottie looked at Little Ben. "Yes," she said.

Ben knelt again to Little Ben. "Come here," he said. "Give Big Ben a hug."

Little Ben moved cautiously to him, put his arms around Ben's neck.

"Someday we'll go fishing again," Ben said softly. "I'd like that."

"Fishing," Little Ben said.

"You watch after your mama," Ben added. He kissed Little Ben on the forehead, released him, and stood, facing Lottie. "There's a thousand things I'll think about saying to you after I'm gone, but the only thing I can think of right now is that I'll miss you."

Lottie stepped to him, took his face in her hands, pulled him to her, kissed him gently. "I love you, Ben Phelps."

"I love you, too, Lottie Lanier," Ben said, his voice quaking.

NO ONE WAS at Hornet Field. Ben sat on the empty bench of the home team shelter and looked out over the field. It had been six years since he played there, played his last game, yet it seemed as though he had closed his eyes, slept the night, and was late for a workout. Nothing, he thought, was as silent as an empty ballpark. Empty, there was no magic in it. It was a place, nothing more.

He realized he was tired, and that the illness he had suffered was still tender in his chest.

He wanted to be home, to be with his mother and with Sally, but he could not put Lottie and Little Ben from his mind. He had left them in a house of shame on a road of shame, left them to take up an inheritance of poverty that would paralyze them with its never-ending numbness.

A flock of gray birds, with wings in glide, floated out of the sky over the shelter and landed in the outfield grass behind second base and began to peck at the ground.

Ben stood and swiped at the dust on his pants legs. He said aloud, "I did all I could do, Foster. I did all I could."

He ducked out of the shelter and walked toward the gate. Behind him, he heard the birds fluttering up from the ground, their wing beats curling through the air. Ben stopped. The wing beats had voices.

"You got it, Ben! You got it!"

"Goda'mighty, Ben! I never see nothing like that!"

"You done it, Ben! You done it!"

LILA SAT IN her rocker on the back porch. Lottie sat close in a chair she had pulled from the front room. The porch, with its lipped roof, was dark. On the river, the moon, two days from being full, rode the water like a pale yellow ribbon. Off in the distance, the lights of Augusta were as dim as fireflies. The air and the heat were almost liquid.

It was late. Little Ben had been coaxed to sleep. Lottie did not know where her mother was. She had left the house after supper and had not returned.

For a long time, the sisters did not speak. They sat and watched the flow of the river and the tricky change of moonlight on the glassy surface of the water. And then Lila said, "You been gone a long time."

"I guess," Lottie replied.

"I used to think you was dead," Lila told her.

"Times, I wished I was."

"When I was gone, that's about all I wished," Lila sighed.

"I thought about you a lot in Kentucky," Lottie said. "I wrote you a letter."

"I remember. It was the only letter I ever got. I read it lots of times. I could say it by heart, I read it so many times."

"Nobody wrote me back."

"I started to one time," Lila said. "Just wadn't nothing to say."

They sat in silence for a moment. Cicadas sang from the trees. Bullfrogs bellowed. The rocker from Lila's chair squeaked rhythmically.

"That boy that brought you home," Lila said. "He was your man?"

"No," Lottie answered. "He was a friend."

"Somebody killed Daddy," Lila said absently.

"I know," Lottie whispered.

"They never said who done it," Lila said. "Maybe it was Mama. He got worse with all his drinking. Maybe Mama hit him with a hammer and drug him off to the river and rolled him in it. Somebody done it. They found him way downstream."

Lottie moved from her chair and walked to the edge of the porch and gazed down at the river. A firefly flew near her face, its blinking light reflecting in her eyes.

"Somebody done it," Lila said again.

"I killed a man, too," Lottie said simply.

"What man?" asked Lila.

"He was somebody my husband worked a carnival with," Lottie answered softly. "He hurt my friend, Ben, and I saw him do it — him and a midget."

"Midget? What midget?"

"He was with the carnival," Lottie said.

"Oh," Lila said, as though understanding the full life of the midget.

"After he hurt Ben, he was trying to have his way with me, saying he'd go back and kill Ben if I didn't," Lottie said. "He was drunk, bad drunk, and he had a baseball bat to kill Ben with. The midget got scared and run off." She paused again. She was breathing hard. "I hit him on the leg and he fell down and then I hit him in the head and killed him."

"Like somebody killed Daddy," Lila said. "Maybe Mama."

"I guess," Lottie said. "He had Ben's wallet. I took the money out of it, but I never spent a penny of it. It was Ben's money."

"What'd you do with it?" Lila asked eagerly.

"He'll find it," Lottie said.

"We could use some money," Lila replied. "The mill don't pay much."

"I got some," Lottie told her.

"Can you buy me something?" her sister asked in a begging voice. "I don't care what."

"All right," Lottie said.

Lila stopped rocking. "I like that dress you got on."

"I've got one for you," Lottie said.

"Maybe if I get me a new dress, I'll go off again," Lila said languidly. "Maybe go to Savannah. I liked Savannah. That's where I was when I was gone before. I got married there, but he left me one day. Maybe he's come back and he's been looking for me."

"Maybe so," Lottie whispered.

Lila stopped rocking. "Sometimes I miss having a man on me," she confessed with a sigh. "The right man makes me feel like I was special. I like it when they pulling on my nipples and grabbing at me with they hands and licking me all over like I was a piece of candy. I like it when they sound like they can't breathe no more, they working so hard. I like it when they say I'm pretty."

Lottie thought of Arthur Ledford. He had called her beautiful when he made love to her, his breathing hard and deep, yet his touches were gentle, like the touches of someone who wanted to warm his hands from the silk of her skin. Arthur Ledford had put his life in jeopardy for her. He had given her money, yes, but it was not a whore's pay; it was because he had nothing else he could offer.

"You gone stay here?" Lila asked.

Lottie did not answer.

TWENTY-FOUR

THE NEWSPAPER-WRAPPED bundle, tied with a string, was in an armoire where Ben kept his clothes, though he did not find it until he dressed for work the morning following his late-night return to Jericho from Augusta. He opened it on his bed. Folded inside was the baseball uniform that Foster had worn in his tryout with the Augusta Hornets, and tucked inside the uniform was an envelope. Ben opened the envelope and found twenty-four dollars. For a moment, it puzzled him. Then he remembered: twenty-four dollars was the amount of money stolen from his wallet by Baby Cotwell and the midget Joseph Callahan. He fanned the bills, found one with a faded X marked in the corner — Coleman's mark from the day of the carnival.

He searched the uniform for a letter from Lottie, but did not find one.

He sat heavily on the bed. There was no reason for a letter, he thought. The money said all he needed to know. Foster had denied killing Baby, but it must have been a lie, and the money taken had never been spent because it was blood money. Lottie knew the truth, of course. Lottie had left the money for him.

He wondered if Lottie had been involved in the killing, if the killing had been a terrible truth that bound them together.

No, he thought. Not Lottie. Not Lottie.

He placed the uniform back inside the newspaper, wrapped and retied it, and then he took it to the attic and placed it in the trunk with his glove. He hesitated before closing the trunk. He could feel the envelope with the money in his pocket, and, after a moment, he removed it and placed it on top of the uniform. Blood money, he thought. If he used it, it would bring tragedy to all who touched it.

It was over. All of it. Foster. Lottie. Baby Cotwell. The midget. He had been inexplicably tied to all of them, and now it was over.

He closed the trunk, locked it, left the attic, and went downstairs to the kitchen, where his mother sat sad-faced, gazing out of the window at the backyard grass as though she expected Little Ben to suddenly roll up from a somersault and wave to her.

"Mama," Ben said, "I need a smile this morning."

His mother turned to face him. "Are you all right?"

"I suppose so," Ben answered. He placed the ring he had purchased for Sally from an Augusta jeweler named Adolph Bergman in front of his mother. "I'm getting married, remember?"

His mother's face blossomed. She picked up the ring, turned it in the light, watched the light splinter into its rainbow of colors in the cut surfaces of the diamond. "It's beautiful," she whispered. She looked up at Ben. "It's time we got to work."

———

THE WEDDING OF Ben Phelps and Sally Ledford would be held on Sunday, November 19, in the Jericho Methodist Church, though Sally had agreed to become a Presbyterian by transfer of faith and letter the following week. The ceremony would be presided over by

the Reverends Harry Alewine for the Methodists and Conley Clarke
for the Presbyterians, two friends of the cloth who were known to
have humorous quarrels over the subject of predestination. For Reverend Alewine, the wedding was proof positive that God did not set
destiny from his workroom of clouds, like some architect pondering
the roof lines of a house; no Methodist was ever destined to be a
Presbyterian. It was a choice, plain and simple, and one usually
made under duress or the questionable influence of man's ignorance.

For Ben, the final days leading to the wedding were fear-filled and
solemn. He had begun the experience with eagerness and pride, with
grins and winks, with a puffed-chest feeling that he was shucking
childhood and, at the age of twenty-four, becoming the man that
customers of Ledford's Dry Goods thought him to be. Yet, as October
funneled into November, he was seized with the sensation of a man
at the bottom of a mountain, looking up at an avalanche of snow
hurling toward him with stunning speed and with a force so great it
snapped giant trees like dry twigs. It was not fear of facing the wedding; it was fear of surviving the preparation and the daily, cackling
warnings of forever-and-ever doom offered to him by carefree men
who had sidestepped the avalanche—often in the nick of time—or
by head-wagging men who had been caught in it.

Getting married, Ben confessed to his mother, was not for the
weak-hearted.

For Sally, the preparation was the most glorious ride of joy she
had taken since her first squealing spin on a carnival merry-go-round.
She was as jovial and as bright as a spirit and seemed to be in as
many places as a spirit could travel by dividing itself into tiny shards
of light. Even the sour, defensive behavior of her mother—more and
more absent due to real or imagined frailties, as well as her blatant
disregard for Margaret Phelps—did not discourage Sally. She simply
ignored her mother, made her own plans, confirmed them with Margaret, and explained them to her father, who nodded approval and,

Sally supposed, relayed them to the sickbed of her mother. She would never say aloud that she did not care if her mother attended the wedding or not, but she did hint of it in her journal:

> *I am at the end of my patience with my mother. She has disagreed with everything I want to do, but has not yet made a suggestion about anything. I wouldn't be surprised if she is too sick to even be at the wedding. If she isn't, I won't cry.*

For Margaret Phelps, the wedding was therapy, a needed distraction from the loss of Little Ben. Her loneliness had not subsided; it was merely pushed aside for a few hours of each day. At night, alone in her bed, she imagined him, listened for the sound of his voice calling "Gra-Ma," remembered the curl of his arms around her neck, the way he fit in the cradle of her arms and against her bosom. It many ways, the loss of Little Ben was greater than the loss of her husband, and she thought of it as transferring grief for grief, as some cosmic sign that life renewed itself, even if there was considerable risk in the perfection of the process. She had written letters to Little Ben, addressing them to:

LITTLE BEN LANIER
72 RIVER ROAD
AUGUSTA, GEORGIA

She was never certain the letters had been delivered, for she had never received a reply from Lottie, not even a response to the wedding invitation she had mailed. In the envelope containing the invitation, she had written, *Please plan to come to the wedding and stay a few days. If you need train fare, let me know.*

Beside her, in a silver frame, was the photograph that Tolliver Barkley had taken of Little Ben on the last day of his stay with her.

The smile was shy, a head-tucked smile, the kind of smile he would have just before his arms stretched to her. Each night, she touched the glass covering the face with her fingertips, as though her touch could leap space and find him as he slept on River Road beside the Savannah River.

Yet, Margaret said nothing of Little Ben. The smile that was fitted on her face was as radiant as the smile that Sally wore, and her voice was as high-pitched and excited. There were times when Ben looked at both of them with confusion and horror. Once he said, "Mama, are the two of you planning a wedding or a reception for the governor?" And she answered, "Son, we're planning a world."

And so it was. A world.

Through August and September and October, the twosome of Sally Ledford and Margaret Phelps worked with fury—selecting, eliminating, altering, creating the world that would become Mr. and Mrs. Ben Phelps.

Ben made down payment on a home on Reed's Gin Road, walking distance from the store. The home had belonged to Esther and Luther Proffitt, but after Luther's death in early spring, Esther had accepted an invitation from her younger sister, Seba, to move to Gainesville, two widows fending for themselves. The home was small, but well-kept, shaded by a pecan grove. One day, Ben would inherit the Phelps home, but until then, the Proffitt place was ideal, Margaret declared, and Sally concurred. To Margaret, it was a matter of economics. To Sally, it was because small meant cozy, and she was eager for cozy.

No one seemed to notice the changes in Arthur Ledford's life. He isolated himself, surrendered more responsibility of the store's operation to Ben, often left work early to drive out of Jericho in his motorcar, explaining that he was investigating property for possible investment purposes. There were nights when he took long, late walks, mornings when he arose early, refusing breakfast, to retire to his office at the store to work on correspondence. All these things were regarded as one of Arthur's periods of contemplation before making a business decision that would likely turn to gold.

His behavior, his mood, had nothing to do with business. He was in mourning.

The only thing Arthur did to cause the people of Jericho to know things were different—and Ben to nearly faint—was to change the name of his store from Ledford's Dry Goods to Ledford-Phelps Clothiers, and to make Ben a minority partner with one-third interest. It was his wedding present, he announced to Sally, adding, "Of course, one day it'll all belong to you and Ben."

For many days after the new sign had been hoisted above the entrance to the store, and the windows had been repainted in gleaming black with white shadowing, Ben would arrive early and stand outside and read the sign with amazement.

In one of his letters to Milo Wade, he had enclosed a clipping from the *Jericho Journal*, which carried a photograph of the new storefront, and he had wondered how Milo would react. He had written of his engagement to Sally, trying to keep the news light and casual, and he had imagined Milo smiling over his comparison of marriage to baseball. He was reaching the ninth inning of his life, Ben had suggested, and it was time to get in the game and do something. He only hoped that he didn't strike out as often as he had in Augusta.

After mailing the letter with the news clipping, Ben had dreamed that he was sitting at the ballpark in Boston with Milo sitting beside him, and Milo was laughing wildly, accusing Ben of finding his way in the world by detouring through the bedroom of his employer's daughter.

Ironically, years later, Ledford-Phelps Clothiers would become one of the largest department store operations in the Southeast under Ben's leadership, and in 1934, he would refuse Milo's offer, made through attorneys, to purchase six of the stores as an investment. It would not be a personal decision. Business only. Personally, Ben would be flattered. Professionally, he would find the offer almost amusing.

———

FOR A WEEK preceding the wedding, the preamble of a hard winter had howled through the South, skimmed off early snow blizzards in Canada and the Dakotas, yet on the morning of November 19, the clouds split and peeled back like the opening of a curtain, and the sun poured warmth over the city of Jericho and the county of Caulder, causing Margaret Phelps to declare it an omen.

At seven-thirty, Akers Crews delivered a package to Ben that had arrived on the early train from Athens.

"Thought it might be something you'd be needing," Akers said to Margaret. "I don't normally take it on myself to make deliveries— especially on Sunday—but this being your boy's big day, I reckoned he'd be busy enough."

"Right now, he just looks dumbstruck," Margaret said, laughing. "But it's kind of you to bring this by, Akers. We'll see you at the wedding, I hope."

"If the Augusta train gets in on time, I'll be there," Akers replied. "I never been one to go to weddings, but I like that boy of yours. He's as good as they come."

Akers's mention of the Augusta train made the smile fade from Margaret's face. She thought of Lottie and of Little Ben.

"Well, I better be going," Akers said. "You be careful handling that box. It's heavy."

"I will," Margaret said.

THE GIFT WAS an expensive silver service from Martin and Christine Wade, with a note of apology for being unable to attend the wedding. The explanation given had to do with pressing government business in Atlanta for the senator. The final line in the note was *Milo also sends his very best wishes to you.*

After reading the note, Ben went to his room and took stationery and wrote to Milo:

Dear Milo,

I received this morning, via a message from your mother, your good wishes for my marriage to Sally Ledford, which is to take place in a few hours at the Jericho Methodist Church. I want to thank you for your expression. I hope this finds you well. As always, I am looking forward to the next baseball season and your continued success. All of Jericho is proud of you.

Ben signed the letter as usual: *Your friend, Ben Phelps.* He addressed it in care of the Boston Red Sox, Boston, Massachusetts, not knowing Milo's off-season residence.

And though he would continue to monitor the progress of Milo Wade in the years to come, it was the last time Ben would ever write a letter to his boyhood friend. He would be surprised when, in 1957, at the age of seventy-two and in ill health, Milo would tell a reporter for *Look* magazine that the best friend he had ever had was a man named Ben Phelps, a boyhood playmate. He would also add that Ben had been one of the few men ever to stand up to him in a business deal and still hold Milo's respect. He did not reveal to the reporter that it had been fifty-three years since he had communicated personally with Ben. The story would cause Ben to laugh. Yet, when Milo died in December of 1960, all of the letters that Ben had written to him were discovered among his personal effects.

———

AT TWENTY MINUTES before two o'clock, the selected hour for the wedding of Ben Phelps and Sally Ledford, Arthur went, as instructed, to the choir room of the Methodist church, where his daughter waited in the wedding dress she had ordered months earlier from the New York tailors Brickmeyer and Colson. When he saw her, he became weak with awe. The little-girl daughter he had heard spilling laughter at breakfast was now a woman so spectacularly beautiful it caused him to flick his head in shock. He turned his eyes to his wife, who stood beside Sally, and for the first time in months, he saw his wife smile.

"Daddy, are you all right?" Sally asked.

"You're—beautiful," her father stammered.

"I thought I was always beautiful to you," Sally teased.

"You are," Arthur said. "You are."

Sally glided to her father, embraced him. "I love you," she said softly.

"And I love you," Arthur mumbled. He blinked away the moisture filling his eyes.

"All right, both of you, leave me alone," Sally commanded. "I need to have the last few minutes of being Sally Ledford to myself." She motioned them toward the door with a sweeping of her hands. "And behave, both of you," she warned lightly. "Remember, this is my day."

THROUGH THE WEDDING, Sally was right. It was her day. From the rippling sighs of astonishment at her appearance in the church, through the glowing smile at Ben's nervous surrender to the questions of the Reverends Alewine and Clarke, the ceremony of Sally Ledford becoming Sally Ledford Phelps belonged gloriously to her. Even her whisper after Reverend Clarke's pronouncement of being man and wife—a whisper loud enough to be heard in the front rows and repeated like a song performed in rounds to the back rows—would be remembered as Sally's Saying: "Now I'm alive."

It was after the wedding, in the basement of the church's recreation-dining room where the reception was held, that Sally's day was surprisingly interrupted.

Akers Crews appeared holding the hand of Little Ben. He stood for a moment at the door, amazed at the merriment of young girls and women dressed in their finest and of men preening in suits that Akers had only seen in magazine advertising. It was a gathering trembling with gaiety, one that had the Reverend Harry Alewine pale with concern over imagined violations of conduct on church property.

"Good God," Akers muttered. He waded through the revelers, guiding Little Ben before him, until he saw Margaret Phelps at the table displaying the three-layer wedding cake. Margaret was talking in a rush of words to Rachel Alewine, the wife of Harry.

Akers called, "Margaret, you got a visitor."

When Margaret turned to Akers's voice, she saw Little Ben, and a shudder of gladness thundered in her. Her hands flew to her face and tears sprang to her eyes. She cried, "My baby."

She rushed to Little Ben, scooping him in her arms, squeezing him, and Little Ben wrapped his small arms around her neck, clinging to her. He whispered timidly: "Gra-Ma."

"What are you doing here?" Margaret squealed. "Where's your mommy?"

A puzzled look crawled over Akers's face. He said, "Wadn't you expecting him?"

"Expecting him?" Margaret answered. "Why, no. I haven't heard from them since they left."

Akers moved close to Margaret. "We better step outside," he said in a low voice.

"Why?" asked Margaret.

"We just better," Akers mumbled.

Margaret glanced around the room. She could see Ben and Sally, surrounded by well-wishers and the music of laughter. Alice Ledford stood in one corner with Oscar Morgan, the doctor. Oscar appeared impatient. She turned toward the door and saw Arthur. He was staring at her and at Little Ben in disbelief, and she pushed her way to him, with Akers following.

"The boy's here?" Arthur said.

"We better talk about this outside," Akers suggested.

"All right," Margaret said.

Outside, Akers led them to an oak tree near the cemetery. He stopped and looked back at the church, and then he said to Margaret, "The train was late coming in, like I thought it might be, which is why I missed the wedding. The boy and his mama were on it. She said you were expecting him to stay a few days while she went on to Athens to help get her sister in a hospital, and she asked me to bring him to you, since the train was about to leave. I put his belongings at the station."

Margaret let Little Ben slip from her arms. He caught her dress and held to it.

"I don't know anything about this at all," she said. "Maybe she wrote to me and I didn't get it."

"His mother was on the train?" Arthur asked anxiously.

"That's what I said, wadn't it?" Akers replied. He sounded irritated.

"Has it left?" Arthur said.

"Hadn't when I left, but it probably has now," Akers told him. "They were taking on some water."

Arthur turned and began to stride away.

"Where are you going?" Margaret called.

"To the station," Arthur answered.

"Wait," Margaret said. "We're going with you." She lifted Little Ben and followed Arthur to his car.

Akers stood, watching them. He had no idea what was happening. He shook his head and started walking back to the church. He had missed the wedding, but he was not going to miss the reception. The only decent thing about any wedding was the reception, as far as Akers was concerned.

IT WOULD BE remembered by Margaret as one of the lasting moments of her life. From the car, she could see the train beginning its slow pull away from the station. Arthur stopped the car and jumped from it and ran toward the platform, taking the steps in one leap before stopping near the door leading into the station. Margaret watched him stand helplessly, his body heaving in hard breathing, as the train took the first long curve leading to Athens. She heard him cry out, "Lottie! Lottie!" The cry sounded desperate.

"Gra-Ma?" Little Ben said.

Margaret pulled him close to her. "What, baby?"

"Where's my mama?"

Margaret did not answer. She brushed her face against Little Ben's face. The bellow of the train began to fade. Arthur's voice sounded like an echo swallowed by a whistling wind.

"Lottie! Lottie!"

And without understanding why, Margaret knew she would never again see Lottie Lanier.

I HAVE LEARNED that few people achieve their dreams. They try, fall short, and settle for what happens to them. Oddly, some become famous, more famous than they would have been if their dream had been realized. Some vanish, taking the easy road out, without realizing — or perhaps caring — that the easy road may be trouble for the people around them.

Still, the dream is always with them, like a birthmark hidden from sight. It is, I suppose, both the blessing and the curse God implanted in the human species when he set all of matter in motion.

If we did not have dreams, we would have no reason to wonder, or hope, or believe.

We would have no reason to care about who we are, rather than who we might have been.

THE PEOPLE WHO knew Lottie Lanier have said that as a child, I resembled her, but there is no photograph of her for me to see and I do not know if there is any truth in what I have been told.

I know only that she was my grandmother and that on November 19, 1910, she left her son — my father, Little Ben Lanier — with the stationmaster, Akers Crews, at the Jericho train station, and, supposedly, she was never again seen by anyone who had known her.

My father was reared by Margaret Phelps, his Gra-Ma, and mine also.

I have never found any evidence that my father ever searched for his mother, yet it does not surprise me. I think he had an understanding with her, even at the age of four. Not a said thing, but something that he carried in his genes as definable as blood type. His mother had given him the best life she could afford to give him, and then she had put him in hands that would lift him up at every stumble. It was those hands, the hands of his Gra-Ma, that he would remember and celebrate.

My father would attend the University of Georgia in the study of law, and in 1927, he would marry JoBeth Kingsley, the daughter of Spurgeon and Katherine Kingsley. I was born in 1929 and was named Foster Arthur Lanier. In 1951, my father succeeded Ben Phelps as president of Ledford-Phelps Clothiers, Incorporated. "He is not my son, but I have always believed he was as much a part of me as my soul," Ben said of my father at the party given to make the announcement of my father's new position. There was poignancy in the remarks. Ben and Sally Phelps had not been able to have children.

My father remained president of Ledford-Phelps Clothiers until 1973, when he sold the firm to a conglomerate from Chicago. It was a wise move by a wise man. He knew the small towns of America were withering, being replaced by malls the size of cities, and by strip shopping centers popping up like mushrooms in damp woods dirt. In 1974, he made a present of the original Ledford's Dry Goods store to the city of Jericho for use as a library named in memory of Margaret Lowell Phelps, and he funded it with two million dollars.

When he was young my father did not search for his mother, but he had his mother's nature. He was a caring person. He would die in 1986 at the age of eighty, only six months after the death of my mother. In the last week of his life, I asked him a question I had never asked: "Do you have any memory of your parents?" He looked at me curiously, waved his hand weakly in front of his face, as though brushing away a harmless insect. After a moment, he whispered, "No." I knew that what he said was not the truth. I also knew he did not have enough words left in him to tell me what he knew, or felt, and that his answer was gently given.

And I think he understood I had already been told the stories.

It was Ben—Big Ben—who began to talk to me, after his retirement, of my grandmother. His Sally had died in 1953 of cancer, leaving him with the kind of loneliness healed only by talked-about memories.

He sold the estate he and Sally had built a few miles outside of Jericho and moved again into the home of his childhood, left vacant in 1952 by the death of his mother. For Ben, it was more home to him than any of the homes he and Sally had owned, and it was there that he began to think often of Lottie Lanier. When I would visit him—not from obligation, but because I liked him—he would sit on the porch swing and tell me stories of my grandmother he had never told anyone, always remarking how, as a baby, I had looked enough like her to make him step back in shock when he saw me.

Same eyes, Ben said. Same gold-honey color. Same look of sorrow, yet bright enough to take in things with wonder, and having the same way of gazing off as though something from another world seemed to be calling.

Ben said, "She did what she had to do, and so will you."

And because of the stories Ben told me when I was young, I began to believe my grandmother was the something calling to me, and I had a need to find her.

WHEN HE FIRST began the stories of my grandmother, Ben told me he had tried to find her after his honeymoon with Sally. He traveled to Augusta, to River Road, and discovered an empty house. None of the neighbors knew what had happened to the three women and small boy who had lived there. One day, in November of 1910, they simply disappeared without a word. Maybe they had thrown themselves into the Savannah River, like trash from barrels, and the river had swallowed them, Ben was told. It was not an uncommon occurrence. The river was used as often as a preacher's baptism to wash away pain.

Ben even returned to Beimer, Kentucky, in 1915. Henry Quick remembered him and went with him to the cabin where Foster and Lottie had lived. The cabin was empty, and the gravesite for my grandfather was overgrown. Ben and Henry Quick cleared it of the briars and weeds. Five years later, in 1920, Ben purchased the property and had the cabin expanded and modernized, and occasionally he and Sally would go there on vacation with Gra-Ma and my father, Little Ben, and, later, with me. I have always thought of it as a place of peace, and there are times when I have an inexplicable urge to go to my grandfather's gravesite and sit in the grass and look at the tombstone Ben had erected. The tombstone reads:

FOSTER LANIER
1875–1910
BASEBALL PLAYER

He did not say it to me, but I believe Ben bought the cabin and kept my grandfather's gravesite cleared because he thought my grandmother would eventually return there and find the place to her liking, and that one day he would drive up to the cabin and she would be standing on the porch, a smile in her honey-gold eyes.

Ben died of complications from a recurrence of rheumatic fever in 1958. He was seventy-two years old. I lived at the time in New York, working as a travel writer for a magazine called *Places*, a publication for people with wanderlust and money, taking excursions to romantic islands and cities, most of them making up for lost dreams. I was often among them, using my profession as an excuse. I had dreamed of being an attorney, as was my father, someone engaged in the noble combat of right and wrong. I learned the combat was not so noble and that right and wrong usually wore the same face. I did not have a tolerance for compromise. Words about far-off places were easier to handle than argument.

Yet, I think I had always been waiting for the call about Ben. It came from my mother: "Come home," she said simply. "Ben's dying."

The last time I saw him, Ben said to me in his death-whisper, "My Sally's with me." He smiled at the thought, then added, "And Lottie." He wiggled his head on the pillow and a small, glad laugh applauded in his chest. "Did I tell you about the catch I made when I was a boy?" he wheezed. He blinked tears, then closed his eyes. Two hours later, he stopped breathing.

IN 1992, AFTER retiring and returning to live in the Phelps home, which Ben had willed to me, I discovered the journals of Sally Ledford Phelps in the archives of the Margaret Lowell Phelps Library during a renovation. In reading the journals, I found the first real evidence that would lead me to my grandmother. It was in an entry written by Sally two weeks after her wedding.

Today, I talked with Mother Phelps about the depression my father is in. She told me she thought it had something to do with Lottie's disappearance. . . .

I began to look into the life of Arthur Ledford.

AFTER HIS WIFE, Alice, died of pneumonia in 1912, Arthur began to travel extensively as Ledford-Phelps Clothiers expanded — first into the city of Commerce and then into Gainesville and then, with surprising rapidity, into dozens of small towns in the Southeast, from Louisiana to Virginia. He was often gone for weeks, immersed in his work, and when he returned, he always seemed exhausted and reclusive, as recorded by Sally in her journal. Her words were words of worry.

Then, in 1914, Sally wrote a note of relief:

> *Today my father returned unexpected from Charleston, South Carolina, and I have never seen him so flush with happiness and energy. I don't know what happened, and I won't ask. Maybe he found a good place for a new store, or maybe the city of Charleston agrees with him, with his old dream of being a sailor and with all of the ships to watch from the harbor. I just hope it continues.*

I do not believe Arthur Ledford found ships to watch in Charleston. I believe he found Lottie Lanier.

By accident, I think.

I think that one day he was on a Charleston street, perhaps near the waterfront, walking with his gaze downcast to the pavement, as was his habit according to Ben, and a woman stepped out of a shop and paused, and he politely tipped his hand to his hat as he stepped around her, and when he glanced up he was looking into a face he could not forget.

I think he stood paralyzed, unable to say her name. And I think that my grandmother smiled with sudden joy and that she embraced him without regard for the curious stares of onlookers. And I think that night, in the elegant suite of the finest hotel in Charleston, they made love that was not hampered by conditions. And for almost twenty years, they were together.

I have no proof of any of this, other than the records that Arthur Ledford maintained a residence in Charleston and in Jericho until 1934. All I have written of the relationship between Arthur Ledford and Lottie Lanier is from my wishes for them.

Yet, I believe Arthur Ledford did love her, and that she loved him, and that they remained secretive about their relationship because they did not want to cause ripples across serene waters.

I do know this as a fact, as recorded in Sally's journal:

In 1933, Arthur Ledford had the body of a woman shipped from Charleston to Jericho for burial in the Ledford family plot, beside the spot reserved for his own body. The coffin was not opened. The gravesite ceremony was brief, attended only by Arthur and Ben and Sally and, at Arthur's request, by Gra-Ma and by my father and mother. I, too, was there, according to the entry in Sally's journal, though I have no memory of it. I was four years old, the same age as my father when my grandmother left him with Akers Crews.

The woman entombed was identified as an unmarried cousin Arthur Ledford had supported for many years, a gracious, dignified lady, and he had thought it only proper that her interment have a few witnesses. I do not believe that anyone asked questions. To do so would have been inconsiderate. Besides, the philanthropy of Arthur Ledford was well known. He had provided for numerous members of his extended family since the death of his wife. There were begging letters and canceled checks in his files to prove it.

Still, only one rested beside him after his death in 1947.

Chiseled into her tombstone was:

AUGUSTA LEDFORD

1887–1933

ANGEL OF THE LONESOME

HOME AT LAST

I do not know why Ben, or my father, or Sally, or Gra-Ma, never told me about Augusta Ledford, for I believe that all of them knew, without asking, who she was.

Perhaps it was because they were Southerners, conditioned to silence about such matters of tender subterfuge.

Or perhaps it was their way of honoring Arthur Ledford.

And my grandmother.

And perhaps they believed that because I resembled her—had the far-off look—I would have to search for her in order to find myself.

I think that is true. Two of my prized possessions are Ben's baseball glove and the baseball uniform my grandfather last wore in Augusta. They are displayed in a large glass case in the Margaret Lowell Phelps Library, and when I look at them, I know I belong to both joy and despair.

We all learn the most remarkable lessons in the strangest ways.

Once, in a small bookstore in Greenwich Village, I read these words on one of those greeting cards intended as a light-strobe of wisdom:

> *Some people wander the world*
> *Only to discover*
> *They have always been*
> *In walking distance*
> *Of themselves.*

I am one of those people.